MW00772516

Books by Elisa Braden

MIDNIGHT IN SCOTLAND SERIES

The Making of a Highlander (Book One)
The Taming of a Highlander (Book Two)
The Temptation of a Highlander (Book Three)—Coming soon!

RESCUED FROM RUIN SERIES

Ever Yours, Annabelle (Prequel)
The Madness of Viscount Atherbourne (Book One)
The Truth About Cads and Dukes (Book Two)
Desperately Seeking a Scoundrel (Book Three)
The Devil Is a Marquess (Book Four)
When a Girl Loves an Earl (Book Five)
Twelve Nights as His Mistress (Novella – Book Six)
Confessions of a Dangerous Lord (Book Seven)
Anything but a Gentleman (Book Eight)
A Marriage Made in Scandal (Book Nine)
A Kiss from a Rogue (Book Ten)

Want to know what's next? Connect with Elisa through Facebook
and Twitter, and sign up for her free email newsletter at
www.elisabraden.com, so you don't miss a single new release!

A Kiss from a Rogue

ELISA BRADEN

This is a work of fiction. Names, characters, places, and incidents are products of the author's imagination or are used fictitiously and are not to be construed as real. Any resemblance to actual events, locales, organizations, or persons, living or dead, is entirely coincidental.

Copyright © 2019 Elisa Braden

Cover design by Dar Albert at Wicked Smart Designs

All rights reserved. No part of this book may be used or reproduced in any form by any means—except in the case of brief quotations embodied in critical articles or reviews—without express written permission of the author.

For more information about the author, visit www.elisabraden.com.

ISBN-13: 978-1-950805-03-7
ISBN-10: 1-950805-03-4

Dedication

For all those who fell in love with vengeful viscounts and ruined angels, willful wallflowers and starchy dukes, wicked scoundrels and resilient pixies, wickeder devils and redheaded disasters, surly giants and starlight fairies, a dragon's son and a certain widow, dangerous lords and domestic bliss experts, lowborn ruffians and steel-spined spinsters, eerie-eyed griffins and thorny briars, valiant knights and determined bumblebees ...
And one tart-tongued dragon.

This one's for you.

Prologue

"Be warned, sir: You have invoked an inexhaustible fire quenched only by the defeat of its enemies. I await your surrender with the greatest of anticipation."

—LADY DOROTHEA PENWORTH to Malcolm Charles Bainbridge, Earl Bainbridge, in a letter of scathing rebuke.

September 11, 1814
Wiltshire, England

SHE WAS FLOATING. HERE, IN A BEDCHAMBER SWATHED IN RED. A room with a single window, two velvet chairs flanking a chess table, and low firelight flickering orange fingers across dim walls.

Hannah floated above the girl on the bed. Pitiful creature. Frozen as though stillness made a difference. Never had before.

Outside, rain poured, slithering gray on glass. Water's chatter upon stone and grass didn't muffle the sound.

Clack, tap. Clack, tap. Clack, tap.

Echoing across the terrace.

Clack, tap. Clack, tap. Clack, tap.

Down the steps.

Clack, tap.

A pause.

She sank down toward the girl, every inch deepening dread.

His voice sounded below the window. Placid. Pleased.

Clack, tap. Clack, tap. Clack, tap.

Receding. Retreating. Fainter. And gone.

Blessedly gone.

She floated again, on the ceiling now. Gray light offered cooling comfort.

"Here you are, miss." The round woman with the Irish lilt waddled near the girl on the bed, placing a tray on the side table. She started to turn then stopped. Fingered the small bottle beside the teapot. "Laudanum should help."

Wrong. Laudanum only dulled the senses. Nothing helped.

"You should not have tried to take his horse, miss. He hurts you worst when you run. Heavens, you never learnt to ride. How far did you imagine you would get, hmm?"

The girl did not move so much as an eyelash.

"If I—if I help you, he'll kill me." The woman's voice thinned until it had no substance, only breath. "You matter. I don't."

True enough. Killing was his answer to many problems— rebellious servants, inconvenient neighbors. Her mother.

In a vaguely maternal gesture, the woman brushed a black, damp curl from the girl's shoulder.

The girl didn't flinch. But, then, she wasn't present. Hannah floated away, curled into the corner of the ceiling where shadows gathered, gray and dark.

"I should like to take that bloody walking stick of his and ..." The woman's vicious utterance trailed away, unspoken. Her plump fingers formed a fist before shoving into her apron's pocket. She plucked a green blanket from the foot of the bed and spread it gently over the girl's body. "There, now," she whispered. "Let old Mrs. Finney care for you." Another brush at the girl's hair, wet from the rain. "Bide awhile, sweet miss. He has enemies. Dangerous folk. One day, they'll find him." The woman's hand shook. A flush streaked her plump cheeks. "One day, he'll be gone, and you'll be free."

Hannah wished the woman would leave. Mrs. Finney was a fine housekeeper, but the girl on the bed did not wish to be touched. Not by anyone for any reason.

"No more bravery," the housekeeper admonished while pouring tea and adding laudanum. "No more of this nonsense. Look at you. Tiny, fragile thing. Mustn't continue inviting his punishments. And where would you go, anyhow, should you manage an escape? Orphans haven't any family." Mrs. Finney moved to the washstand and poured water into the basin. "Not that you could hide from him if you did." She returned with a washcloth in hand, carefully unfastened the girl's damp gown, and exposed the girl's back. The woman's gasp rang out sharply in the silent room.

In her corner of the ceiling, where it was dark and cool, Hannah let shadows cloister around her, muffling color and sound and sensation. Time passed. She couldn't say how long. When the shadows thinned to wisps, Mrs. Finney was gone and the rain had softened.

Hannah watched the girl on the bed, huddled motionless beneath the green blanket. The girl's pale fingers lay curled near blank, open eyes. Slowly, slowly, as though tugged through a mirror, Hannah found herself pulled inside those eyes. Pale, pale green. No one else had eyes like hers. Only her beloved papa, who was gone. Gone, gone, gone.

Now, she stared through those eyes outward. Saw the girl's

fingers. Her fingers. White and curled. They twitched.

No. She didn't want to be here. She wanted the shadows, the ceiling. She wanted to float away again.

Pain wouldn't let her. It sang with a horrid vibration.

Mrs. Finney's words formed lyrics in accompaniment. *One day, he'll be gone.* The words chanted. Repeated. A song more dangerous than enemies, more foolish than the bravery of a stupid, desperate girl. *One day, he'll be gone,* they crooned. *One day, he'll be gone. And you'll be free.*

September 11, 1814
Lake Champlain, New York

JONAS SHOULD HAVE BEEN DEAD TEN TIMES BY NOW. TWELVE, if one counted the enraged husband who'd chased him with a cleaver and the enraged father who'd shot his hat clean off his head. But he never counted the incidents involving women and drink. Those were self-inflicted.

The truth was that Jonas Bartholomew Hawthorn was not meant to die. Rather, he was cursed to watch while others did.

"What's that ye're drawin' there, Hawthorn? Yer mother's titties?" Rollicking laughter followed the jest, blending into the creak of the frigate's hull and the snap of her sails.

Jonas glanced up from his sketchbook. The sun shone mirror-bright off the massive lake this morning. While carpenters scraped and hammered, and ill-trained infantrymen heaved cannons into place, he was taking a few blessed moments before battle to record the scene around him—miles of blue lake water, thick-forested shoreline, a flock of geese flying overhead.

Soon enough, death would come. For now, he would

harness something beautiful.

"No," he answered Bailey's taunt with a lazy half-grin. "*Your mother's titties are far more fetching. Care to have a look?*"

His fellow soldier's mirth turned sour. At twenty, Bailey was only a year younger than Jonas, but he'd seen one measly skirmish on the Continent before sailing to Canada with the Thirty-Ninth Regiment of Foot. Jonas had joined the Thirty-Ninth at sixteen. He'd survived muskets and cannon at Bussaco, goring lances at Albuera. He'd watched men like Bailey go blinding mad at Vittoria and collapse like stringless marionettes at Toulouse. He'd watched countless Frenchmen die by his hand. Today, he would watch Americans do the same.

Jonas was ancient, and death knew him well.

The ginger-haired Bailey raised his ginger-whiskered chin. "I don't let nobody insult me mam, you blighter."

Chuckling, Jonas blew away charcoal dust from his sketch, tucked the small notebook into his pack, and squinted up at his appallingly young antagonist. "Perhaps you shouldn't have let her cavort naked with the likes of me."

"What's cavort?"

"Dally."

Confusion turned to muddled wrath. "You never even met me mam. She's back in England."

"No, indeed. Though nothing amplifies a man's pleasure like anticipation."

Confusion returned. "What the devil are you sayin'?"

Jonas grasped the railing at his back and shoved to his feet. He moved slowly, as he'd always found being underestimated a valuable advantage. Likewise, he was tall, so he leaned back against the railing to reduce his height. Then, he grinned. "I'm saying it's best to avoid mentioning a man's mother altogether."

"That's what I said."

"Then, we agree."

Bailey scratched his gingered head. "I don't much like you, Hawthorn."

Jonas's grin widened. "Give it time, and you won't like me at all."

Another scratch. More frowning confusion. "When's the fightin' start?"

Jonas sighed and glanced behind him. They were passing the lighthouse on Cumberland Head. He expected the ships to begin firing before long, but dullards like Bailey lacked patience. They itched for a fight, even if it was with their fellows. Jonas only wanted to be left in peace.

"Not to worry, Bailey. Soon enough, you'll be swabbing blood from the decks. Likely your own. If you survive, you can go back to swilling rum and insulting the mothers of colonials."

"A fine one to talk of swillin'. I hear Lieutenant Phillips pulled your arse from gaol to board the *Confiance*."

Jonas crossed his arms and chuckled. "A misunderstanding. Happens an ensign's wife is not to be believed when she claims her husband shan't return for hours."

"You was in your cups."

"Every man in the Thirty-Ninth would be in gaol, were that the offense."

Bailey narrowed his eyes. "You was caught kissin' the lady in her husband's rooms."

"Hmm." Jonas smiled in remembrance. "Speaking of lovely bosoms."

Three more young infantrymen approached, flanking Bailey and squinting at Jonas with varying degrees of nervous tension.

"Last of the guns are in place," said the blond one, wiping sweat from his forehead with the back of a grimy hand.

"Bloody hell," said the tall one with the wine-colored mark over his cheek. "Never thought I'd be pining for Spanish dirt again."

Clayton, Jonas recalled. The man's name was Clayton. He'd

tried to avoid learning their names, but that birthmark was as vivid as Bailey's ginger hair.

"Aye," said the wiry one, shifting from one foot to the other as if struggling to hold his piss. "Lieutenant is speaking with Captain Downie. I expect we'll be firing soon."

Jonas turned his eyes aft. The smaller vessels of their squadron followed like lambs after a ewe. The *Confiance* was the biggest of them all—the biggest ship, the biggest target. Clouds momentarily covered the sun, coloring the water steel-gray.

He swiveled to look north beyond the prow. In the distance, a line of American warships waited to greet them with a booming welcome.

He eyed the men before him, part of a hastily assembled crew for an unfinished vessel. He looked down at the pitch-stained planks beneath his boots. The decks were constructed of green wood so rough the ship's massive guns initially had to be lifted into place rather than rolled. Even for a well-trained crew—which they were not—firing them was arduous.

He glanced up at the rigging, sensed the brisk wind weakening inside the great, white sails. Fought a queer, foreboding chill.

"I expect you're right," he murmured, straightening away from the railing. "Best get to it." He bent to retrieve his pack just as a squat beaver of an officer approached. Avoiding the man's bitter glare, Jonas shrugged on his pack. Obviously, the ensign was still sore about the incident between Jonas and his wife's lovely bosom.

"Take your positions, men," the beaver barked. "Make ready."

They moved below to the gun deck. Another chill snaked through him at the chaos—grizzled seamen barked commands at eight-man crews with too little experience. Even here, carpenters rushed about coated with shavings and weighed down by tools. Twenty-four-pound balls waited in racks to be loaded after the first volley.

A hand shoved his shoulder from behind. "Move your worthless backside, Hawthorn," the beaver snarled.

He wanted to ask if the ensign's wife thought his backside was worthless—she'd seemed rather impressed, as he recalled. But he didn't fancy being stuffed into a cannon and shot across the bay. So instead, he held his tongue and joined Clayton and Bailey and five other men at the seventh gun.

An officer with a Scottish brogue, blue frock coat, and wide epaulets prowled the line of cannons, hands at his back, eyeing the crews. He was younger than Jonas would have expected for a squadron commander—thirties, he would guess. But Captain Downie's eyes looked as grim as Jonas felt.

A third chill crawled up Jonas's neck.

"Prepare to scale the guns!" Captain Downie announced over the cacophony. Firing the cannons would signal the British army in the village of Plattsburgh to advance in a coordinated attack. "Whilst we win the battle in the bay, our soldiers shall claim victory on land!"

Jonas watched the captain, proud and straight, command respectful nods from the crew of inexperienced rabble and cast-offs from other ships. They all seemed to take reassurance. But to Jonas's eye, Downie did not look like a man about to win a battle. He looked like a man going to the gallows.

Another creeping chill took hold, turning into an itch along his nape. Jonas's gaze drifted to Bailey, feverish with anticipation. Beside him, the steadier Clayton appeared confident, though his throat bobbed on a swallow.

Upon the captain's signal, they scaled the guns. Each cannon recoiled several feet, stopped only by the ropes that secured the carriage. Jonas and the rest of the crew rushed to reload and heave the two-ton gun back into position.

His ears buzzed like insects.

The ship kept its course toward the Americans' flagship, the *Saratoga*. It might have been seconds or hours before the *Confiance* suffered its first hit—minutes, probably. When the blast struck, wood splintered and flew like bullets. The decks above shredded. Had his ears worked, he might have heard the screams of men dying. As it was, he couldn't hear much beyond the buzzing.

He could see, though. One of the lieutenants, face streaked with blood, shouted at Downie, who stood beside one of the guns. Jonas saw the lieutenant's mouth repeatedly form the words "lost" and "sheet anchor."

Despite his exertions heaving upon the cannon's ropes, Jonas's chill now pulsed thick inside him. Bloody hell. If they'd lost the anchor, they'd little hope of maneuvering into a proper position for battle, let alone turning the ship to avail themselves of fresh guns. He squinted through the gun port toward the *Saratoga*. The wind had died. Indeed, the *Confiance* seemed to have slowed to a crawl short of the position they needed for a full broadside.

The marine leading Jonas's crew gestured wildly, trying to convey the need to re-aim. Jonas seemed to be the only one who understood, so he shoved the frowning Clayton and the glassy-eyed Bailey toward the opposite side of the cannon's carriage. Showing them what was necessary, he rushed to the front and did likewise with two other men. The marine gave him a nod of thanks.

By the time the *Confiance* fired upon the Americans, she'd already taken fatal damage. Jonas had sensed it coming. The loss of the anchor, the dying of the wind. The ragged, inexperienced crew. Even the green wood of her decks. No one factor was responsible for the disaster that followed. Instead, individual drops of ill-fortune coalesced to form a tide.

One of the squadron's smaller vessels took damage early. It drifted like a child's toy boat between the *Confiance* and the *Saratoga*, denying them a clear shot.

They waited and waited for signs that their land forces had advanced and engaged the American strongholds. Signs never came.

Worst of all, no more than a half-hour into the fight, Captain Downie was felled by one of his own bloody cannons. Hit directly by a ball fired from the *Saratoga*, the massive iron gun flew from its carriage and crushed the grim-eyed Scot beneath its weight. His watch was flattened, too, marking the moment of his death.

The gun crews, already exhausted and desperate, sank into despair. Jonas and the marine continued shoving the other men into position. Kept shouting, though no one could hear. Kept gesturing to reload. Jonas kept heaving the cannon back into place, ignoring the slickness of pitch and blood on the deck. Ignoring death's foul odor, the bitter tang of gunpowder burning in a flash. Ignoring the listing of the ship as they took on water.

Another blast tore through the *Confiance*'s hull. Splinters of green wood flew, peppering his flesh like birdshot. He ignored it. Forced his boots to grip raw planks and yanked upon the cannon's carriage.

Losing was no excuse for giving up.

Another blast. Bright-orange streaked past Jonas's peripheral vision. Wine-stained horror wreathed Clayton's sweating face as he gaped down at the deck behind Jonas. Gripping Clayton's arm, he shoved him around to face the opposite direction.

No sense looking. Bailey was dead.

Probably better off. The wounded were being stashed in the decks below, where water was rising above their noses. Those who hadn't been blown to bits were about to drown.

Just load the gun, he thought. *Load the gun and fire.*

The crew to their left had been taken out in the last broadside. Half the crew to his right sat on blood-slicked decking, their eyes vacant and downcast, heads lowered in defeat.

Little wonder. The guns on this side of the ship were down to four. They'd lost a second anchor an hour past. Without anchors or wind, they hadn't a prayer of turning the ship for a fresh set of guns.

Despite the hopelessness, despite everything, he grasped the ropes and forced his crew to heave the cannon forward into the gun port. On the lieutenant's signal, Clayton lit the gunlock.

The shot shuddered the ship.

Immediately, his crew rushed to reload.

He clapped shoulders and offered nods of encouragement. He might not know their names. He might never see their faces again. But if they survived, he wanted them to be certain of one thing—the failure hadn't been theirs.

Sweat stung his eyes. Smoke singed his lungs. His shoulders were afire from the strain of hauling a two-ton gun into position over and over.

Clayton's wine-stained cheek caught his eye a moment before he saw a flash from the *Saratoga*. Where the boy's skin wasn't marked, it was white. White as the clouds above Lake Champlain.

He turned as though to ask Jonas a question.

Then his body went flying. Colliding. A hard, wine-stained skull cracked into Jonas's jaw. Flashes of light swirled and sparked. Thirteen stone of fellow infantryman flattened him like a weed beneath a plow. The force sent them both skidding across green wood and red blood.

For a time, he floated inside white and gray. He heard humming. At first, he blamed the ringing in his ears, which hadn't stopped since the firing began.

But no, this was musical. A soft, light voice. It wavered a bit, like lake water upon a pebbled shore. Timid, uncertain beauty. He wanted to capture it. To linger and bask.

In the sound, the shy warmth.

Land appeared before him, a rolling sprawl of pasture and sheep, barley and rye. Cottages, too. Thatched roofs in good repair. A larger house made of gray stone with, of all things, turrets on two corners. Like a castle in miniature.

He sat in a garden shaded by a draping willow taller than the house. Beneath his feet were square stones, and between the stones was thyme. The herb's fragrance filled his head, tasted like summer. Flowers spilled from urns nearby. A fountain splashed. He couldn't see it, for two sides of the garden were edged with high hedges, but he heard. Golden light slanted through the mist. It set everything aglow.

Wind came up. "Someday," it seemed to sigh.

No. Not someday. Now. He wanted to stay here, with her gentle voice washing him clean of death.

He tried to insist. Tried to speak.

"This is not how it ends," the wind breathed.

Amidst white wisps and golden light, just beyond the willow's weeping branches, he saw black silk fluttering. A bird's wing, perhaps? A raven. Shimmering black.

She hummed her tune.

"Not how it ends," sighed the wind.

Black slipped away between leaves. Fog swallowed the garden. Her song grew faint. Jittery. Frightened.

No! He wanted to stay. God, why couldn't he stay?

"Not how it ends."

He needed to stay. Needed to find this place. Find ... her.

White and gray faded into night. The buzz in his ears grew louder. A violent force shot him upward through a slit in the sky.

Black became red. Gingery red.

And wine.

And wood.

Something lay on his chest. Heavy. Couldn't breathe.

Shoulders hurt. Jaw ached. Ears buzzed.

His head rolled to the side. He allowed himself a single moment to close his eyes. Ignore the horror. Remember her song.

Breathe.

Then, he shoved. Rolled Clayton's lifeless body away. Sat up and looked at death.

Everywhere. Everywhere.

Ensign Beaver's big-toothed face appeared in front of his, clean but for a bit of soot. "Hawthorn," the man mouthed. "You alive?"

Devil take it. Yes. He was. As always, he was alive and surrounded by death.

It appeared to be his punishment, and a cruel one, at that.

Ensign Beaver mouthed something like "surrender." The gun deck was littered with the debris of war—bodies, blood. Parts that should have been men and no longer were. The creaking, broken ship listed sharply.

Jonas wanted to laugh. Absurdity usually did it. What a godforsaken farce to send men like Clayton and Bailey—infantrymen posing as sailors—to fight in an unfinished ship, then surrender only after the slaughter. They'd died for nothing.

No bloody thing.

Yes, he wanted to laugh. But he was covered in their futile blood.

And he could still hear her humming. Only a memory, of course, but it was sweet comfort. Someday, he would escape this vile world. For now, he would find pieces of beauty to keep him sane—green shoreline and blue lake water. Or a glimpse of shimmering black between willow branches.

Someday, he would have a place of beauty rather than war. He'd stand on stones that smelled of thyme, watch sunlight cut through mist, and know that he'd found home. A home no force in this world or the next could make him leave.

Chapter One

"A tedious ride on a lame mount holds more allure than a dance with you, my lord. Perhaps it is the company."

—LADY DOROTHEA PENWORTH to Malcolm Charles Bainbridge, Earl Bainbridge, in a letter expressing dissatisfaction with said gentleman's conciliation.

July 11, 1826
Primvale Castle, Dorsetshire

SEA-SCENTED WIND STREAKED PAST HANNAH'S CHEEKS WHILE her mount's galloping rhythm pounded as fiercely as her heart. Coastal soil flew. Tall grass rippled like water. Sunlight warmed her velvet sleeves.

Her rides were never easy. Even now, a year after she'd first climbed onto a saddle, her palm sweated where it gripped her riding cane. Rods of any sort tended to cloud her head. But, with help and time, she'd denied fear its victory.

Or nearly so, at any rate.

In the beginning, the best she'd been able to manage was a slow, rocking walk upon her gentle mare, and that only when her sister-in-law, Eugenia, was by her side, cajoling and challenging and insisting that she was strong. She wasn't, of course. Every moment had been filled with torturous dread. In time, she'd forced the queasy twist of her stomach to recede. She'd forced her grip to lighten on her horse's reins. She'd pushed herself, day by day, to trot then canter then gallop.

Now, every day after breakfast, she rode Astrea across her brother's vast lands. This morning, the sun glimmered upon the sea as she raced along the high bluff above Primvale Cove. Her legs gripped the sidesaddle's pommels, as Eugenia had taught her. She bent low over Astrea's neck, driving her mount—and herself—harder.

Speed was the thing. If she ran fast enough, it felt like flying.

Soon, Astrea's sides heaved upon harsh breaths. Hannah slowed their pace, guiding the horse inland, back toward Primvale Castle.

"We've done well today," she murmured, stroking Astrea's neck. Her voice trembled only a little. Scarcely noticeable, really.

She sat straighter and sighed. How she loved this place. Her brother possessed an extraordinary talent for cultivating gardens. As she passed through the orchards, she noted his newest variety of pear tree was beginning to fruit.

He would be pleased. Phineas Brand might be the Earl of Holstoke, but titles were not the source of his pride. He was a scientist, a horticulturalist. His passion for plants drove him to develop ever more resilient and prolific varieties, despite the Horticultural Society of London's continual denial of his application for membership.

How absurd. The mere fact that Phineas's mother had been evil incarnate should not signify one way or the other when it came to matters of science. Wasn't scientific inquiry supposed to be rooted in objective analysis? Alas, the Brand name would be forever tainted by the previous Lady Holstoke's murderous legacy.

Every day, Hannah felt thankful that woman was dead—for Phineas's sake as much as her own.

Fortunately, the new Lady Holstoke was a splendid woman. Hannah hadn't thought so at first. When Phineas had married Eugenia Huxley amidst a roiling scandal, Hannah had feared losing the bond she shared with her brother. He was the only family she had left, and after the hellish nightmare of her early life, his care and devotion had been her haven. But Eugenia hadn't stolen him away. On the contrary, she'd drawn Hannah close and become her sister in truth. She'd been relentless, ignoring Hannah's cold rebuffs, wearing away at her resistance until Hannah couldn't help loving her.

Now, as she guided Astrea out of the orchard and along a gravel path through the southeast gardens, Hannah smiled. Mad, blunt, hat-obsessed Eugenia. She'd missed her dear friend's company during her rides of late. But Eugenia was a new mother, and she'd insisted on nursing the babe herself. Hannah's nephew kept his parents busy, indeed.

Her smile grew into a grin. The mere thought of that precious little babe sent a glow through her chest. She'd never suspected one could feel so much love so quickly.

Winding around the square symmetry of Primvale Castle, she rode past the great fountain where a majestic griffin embraced a briar rose vine, and down the drive to the stables. Inside the stable courtyard, Primvale's head groom, the kindly Mr. Reynolds, offered no assistance as she dismounted, merely tipping his cap and wishing her good day. Taking care not to touch her, he waited for Hannah to step down from the mounting block and move several feet away before coming forward to claim Astrea's reins.

"How was your ride today, miss?" he asked with a warm, crinkled smile.

"Quite lovely," she replied, setting her riding cane carefully in his open hand before retreating several steps. "When the sun shines, there is no place on earth more beautiful than Primvale."

He nodded and tucked the cane out of sight. His eyes beamed gentle understanding. How she longed to return his warmth in kind. Reynolds was a good man, she reminded herself. He would never hurt her.

But she'd not yet found a way to persuade her body of what her mind knew.

Quietly, she thanked him before patting Astrea's flank and heading for the castle. Inside, she heard Eugenia laughing. The sound made her smile.

She found them in the drawing room—her brother, tall and lean with raven-black hair and pale green eyes. Her sister-in-law with her rich brown hair, tiny waist, and wide-brimmed hat topped with no fewer than three miniature fruits. And, best of all, her nephew, Griffin Brand, or Griffy the Fussbucket, as Eugenia sometimes called him. At the moment, Griffy was squealing with curious delight and giving the air repeated kicks beneath his long gown. He lay on the sofa, gazing up at Eugenia's hat with rapt fascination.

"He wants the fruit, Briar," Phineas remarked to Eugenia, calmly folding his newspaper. "I did warn you."

"Griffy knows dashing fashion when he sees it. Don't you? Yes, you do." Eugenia lowered her face to her son's belly and made funny kissing sounds. Meanwhile, Griffy clutched her hat's brim with determined focus. His mama laughed and gently retrieved it from the babe's fingers. "Now, now, my darling. Leave the obsessions to your papa." She slanted a wicked glance in Phineas's direction. "He's rather good at those."

Phineas's pale eyes—so similar to Hannah's own—lit with a secret glow. He rose from his chair, tucked his paper under his arm, and bent to kiss Eugenia in one smooth motion. His hand cupped the back of her head in a possessive gesture. Eugenia's hand cupped his cheek in a loving one. Their son gurgled and blew bubbles.

And Hannah's heart seized up with an ache as sharp as any blade. She dropped her gaze to where her blue velvet skirts gathered and fell. Her hands didn't know what to do, so she folded them there.

"I shall be in the greenhouse, Briar," Phineas murmured. "Whilst Griffin has his nap, you may join me there, if you like. I'm conducting a new experiment I believe you'll find ... edifying."

"Hmm. I do adore being edified by you, my love."

Hannah could nearly hear her brother's grin. Phineas had smiled and laughed more in the past year than in the prior six combined. Probably more than in his entire life. Hannah wouldn't know. She'd only met her brother seven years ago, when a mutual acquaintance—Eugenia's sister, as it happened—noticed their resemblance and introduced them.

Despite Hannah being their father's by-blow, Phineas hadn't hesitated a moment to take her into his home and embrace her fully. He'd protected her, sheltered her. He'd given her a home and a family.

Now, as he approached, she admired the man he'd become. He looked so much like their father. She remembered Papa visiting her and her mother in Bath, bringing her gifts and holding her on his lap. Before he'd been slowly poisoned by his viper of a wife, Simon Brand had been a good man, intelligent and patient and kind. Phineas shared those qualities along with an intensity that some found intimidating.

Around Hannah, he kept it carefully tempered, as he knew the effect it had upon her. Phineas was a protector by nature.

He paused just before reaching her side. Slowly, he extended his hand.

With her, Phineas always took the greatest care.

She hesitated only a moment before forcing herself to slide her hand into his. As usual, her reward was a gentle squeeze and a sense of relief. Phineas would never hurt her. She knew that. She did.

His eyes were full of tenderness. "You have a lovely bloom on your cheeks, Hannah. I trust you had a pleasant ride."

She nodded. "Astrea and I enjoyed a vigorous gallop above the cove. The breeze is warm off the water this morning. It feels like silk."

"I suspect we'll see a surge of heat this month."

"Your new pears are showing promise."

He grinned. "They are, indeed. I have high hopes for a September crop this year. I shall see you before dinner for our customary match, yes?"

They played chess every day, and every day he defeated her. But she learned more with each game. Last evening, she'd come within two moves of defeating him. Soon, she would triumph. She could feel it. She was an excellent player. "If you crave humiliation, then of course, I shall oblige," she said pertly.

He chuckled. "Until then." With one last squeeze of her fingers, he slowly bent to kiss her cheek.

She braced herself, holding still as she'd done often over the past seven years. In families, it was important to accept gestures of affection. Phineas was the only male with whom she'd managed such a feat, and he took great pains not to startle her.

"Go on with you, Phineas." Eugenia waggled her fingers in a shooing motion. "Your plants await."

As soon as he departed, Eugenia reversed her waggle and summoned Hannah to the sofa. "You must see this, dearest. I think Griffy is laughing." She tilted her head. "Or perhaps he is plotting to dismantle my hat."

Hannah sat beside her nephew and scooped him into her arms. He cooed and wagged his arms in circles. "Cleverness does run in the family."

Eugenia snorted. "He may do as he likes, so long as he continues sleeping soundly at night. Good heavens, I contemplated begging Phineas for a sleeping draught."

"For you?"

"For Griffy. The boy has a voracious appetite. It cannot be healthy."

Hannah grinned down into familiar pale eyes. "I think a strong appetite is an excellent sign. It means he's growing."

"Hmmph. This time next year, we'll need a cart and plow horses to wheel him about."

Running a fingertip over the babe's silky black hair, Hannah laid a kiss on his forehead. "Your mama is silly, Griffin. Surely a lad as clever as you will be walking on his own by then." Tiny hands snagged her curls where the black spirals dangled within reach.

"He adores you, you know."

Hannah smiled, refusing to take her eyes from his precious face. "And I him."

A long silence fell. When she glanced up, Eugenia was eyeing her with speculation, her fingers tapping her lips. "You should have one."

Hannah blinked. "One what?"

Eugenia nodded toward Griffin. "One of those."

Shock blistered her insides. For a long while, she could not speak. The ache she'd tried to deny—a pain that had grown sharper and deeper with each passing day—swelled and filled and demanded.

Eugenia was blunt by nature. The benefit of her candor was that one rarely had to wonder what she was thinking. The difficulty was that one was not always prepared to hear the truth.

Calmly removing her hat and placing it on a low table, Eugenia's direct gaze pinned Hannah to the sofa cushion. "To have one of those, you must first have a husband, of course. And there's the rub, is it not, dearest?"

Hannah couldn't form words, for none existed to describe her anguish. She could not tolerate Mr. Reynolds helping her down from her horse. She had to brace herself every time her own brother kissed her cheek.

A husband was impossible.

A man's face flickered in her mind's eye—square jaw, wicked grin, eyes that devoured her. She forced the vision away, but it cost her.

Eugenia's lovely face blurred into a liquid swirl.

"Please," Hannah whispered tightly. "Don't."

"I've held my tongue for months," she replied. Warm, brown eyes shone with compassion. "Would that I could wait a little longer. You've made wondrous progress, dear sister. But time is working against us now."

Hannah shook her head and cradled Griffy closer. His tiny fist patted her as though offering comfort. "I don't understand."

"This will always be your home. We will always be your family. Never doubt it." Eugenia caught her gaze and held it, strong and sure. "But you are three-and-twenty. If you are to build a family of your own, you must press forward past your fears."

"I cannot."

"Yes, you can."

"No. I am not ready."

Eugenia smiled and laid a hand on Hannah's forearm. "Ready or not, dearest, it is time."

Resentment roiled up inside her. "Perhaps age serves as a marker to *normal* ladies. A season at eighteen. A husband by twenty. A babe by two-and-twenty. One might as well be a clock wound by a master smith, chiming the hours by rote." Hannah raised her chin. "But I am not normal, Eugenia. Far from it."

Her sister-in-law's head tilted. "Do you wish to be?"

Another shockwave burst through her. God, sometimes she wished Eugenia would mince words. Just once in a while. But her honesty was also a comfort, as Hannah needn't fear deception. In return, she offered an honest reply. "More than anything."

Eugenia nodded. "As I thought." She squeezed Hannah's arm and stroked her son's fuzzy head. "You've too much love in your heart to keep it locked away any longer. We must formulate a plan."

"I don't want—"

"I know. But avoiding what you don't want stands in the way of what you *do* want. A husband. A babe of your own. Normalcy."

Her heart throbbed in a pounding panic at the mere thought. "How?" she whispered. "How am I to ... I cannot even imagine it."

"We'll approach this endeavor as we would any other. First, we establish our goals. Let's begin with normalcy. You are not as far from it as you may think." Eugenia leaned forward and poured them each a cup of tea from the tray. "Normal ladies drink tea. And you drink tea."

Hannah raised a brow.

Eugenia gestured toward the pianoforte in the corner of the room. "Normal ladies play music. So do you."

This time, Hannah rolled her eyes. "Normal ladies also sleep and eat, Eugenia. Shall we count these, as well?"

Laughing, Eugenia shook her head. "If it gives you solace, dearest, we shall count the use of a chamber pot."

"Nothing gives me solace. That is why it is impossible."

Eugenia clicked her tongue. "What a lot of rot. How do you suppose other ladies manage to appear normal?"

Hannah frowned. "Because they are."

"Wrong. These are simply behaviors. Other ladies learned to pour tea, to play their instruments. They learned to ride, the same as you have—by practice. Practice, practice, practice." Eugenia sighed. "Inside, we are all strange, you know. Strange creatures with peculiar natures. Some of us have too much fondness for hats. Some of us are endlessly curious about plants. Some of us are plainspoken and some reserved. Some merely tolerate children, whilst others ..." She covered Hannah's hand, gently stroking her knuckles. "Others cannot help but love them."

Hannah swallowed and looked down at where Eugenia touched her hand. She didn't even flinch any longer. She'd grown so accustomed to Eugenia's affectionate gestures, she scarcely paid them any mind, apart from the comfort they offered.

Perhaps Eugenia was right. Perhaps normal was merely a matter of practice.

She examined little Griffy's face. His eyelids were drooping; a nap was nearing. "I do want this," she conceded. "You're right about that much."

"Of course I am."

"What do you propose?"

"Lady Wallingham has invited us to visit her in Northumberland, a house party at Grimsgate Castle. My family is attending, including Maureen and Henry."

Maureen was Eugenia's sister—one of five Huxley daughters—and a dear friend of Hannah's. She'd been the one to introduce Hannah to Phineas, in fact. Henry Thorpe, the Earl of Dunston, was Maureen's husband, a dashing gentleman with a penchant for bold waistcoats and sharp daggers. He'd saved Hannah's life once. He was a good man and would never hurt her.

She released a shuddering sigh. "Having friends about should make our stay more pleasant, I suppose."

"Hmm. Helpful in the husband hunt, too." Eugenia had gone back to tapping her lips and eyeing Hannah with a speculative gleam. "My mother and sisters will revel in our little project."

"H-husband hunt? I thought we were only going to practice being normal."

"And we shall—whilst we find you a husband."

"This is your worst idea yet."

"Nonsense. First, we must teach you flirting. Pretend I am a gentleman."

Hannah glanced at the elaborate confection lying next to the tea tray. "No gentleman would wear a hat decorated with fruit."

Eugenia lowered her voice and her brows. "You are an exquisite creature, Miss Gray. I find you enchanting."

"Who says such things?"

Eugenia wagged her brows and leaned closer. "Verily, my beauty, I speak only the truth of your astonishing splendor."

"Well, do stop. It sounds silly. Griffy is more *enchanting* than I."

Eugenia broke character to chuckle. "As his mother, I quite agree. But gentlemen will not. You've the Holstoke coloring without the Holstoke severity. Such pure, delicate lines. No man will be able to look away. A hint of flirtation, and you shall hold them in thrall, vying for your favor in the most embarrassing fashion."

"But I don't want them in thrall. I don't even want them ... looking at me."

"Do you want this?" She nodded toward the now-sleeping Griffy.

Hannah's heart squeezed so hard, she felt like she was suffocating. "Yes."

"Then flirt with me."

"I don't know how."

"Simple. Step one, smile."

Hannah frowned.

"Wrong direction, dearest."

"Smiling is not the problem."

Eugenia sighed. A sad wince flickered over her features. "I know."

"Touching is. I cannot bear it."

"You couldn't bear riding either. Now you do it every morning."

Hannah stared at her sister-in-law, wishing she could explain how it felt to fight for one's sanity in the most ordinary of interactions. A polite press of hands. A close conversation. A dance.

"Would you know how to ride if you'd never attempted to mount a horse?"

Sighing, Hannah focused on her sleeping nephew. The tiny boy smelled of milk and sweetness. "No."

"Go on, then. Give us a smile." Eugenia demonstrated by beaming.

Hannah hesitated before following suit.

"Hmmph. An anemic effort."

"It is the best I can do."

"Perhaps we should skip the flirtation."

"I did warn you."

Eugenia tapped her fingers against her lips. "Let's narrow the field a bit. Husbands come in many varieties. Short ones, tall ones. Lean and fat. Pleasantly daft and darkly brilliant. What sort would you prefer?"

Swallowing her first answer, which was "none at all," Hannah considered the question. She sifted through recollections of the men she'd admired over the past seven years—Phineas, Lord Dunston, a gaming club owner named Sebastian Reaver, a duke's brother named Lord Colin Lacey. Another man stole through her thoughts, but she blocked the intrusion ruthlessly.

He was gone, dash it all. And he probably despised her.

"H-he would need to be kind," Hannah murmured. "Patient. I would need to feel … safe."

Eugenia nodded. "Naturally. I'll not have my sister married to a brute. What else?"

"A good father." The words nearly choked her, but they had to be said. "Above all things, he must love children and treat them well."

"Hmm. Should he be handsome?"

Again, a face appeared her mind's eye—a face with lips she hadn't been able to resist. She forced the vision away. "No," she answered. "Handsome men feel entitled to a woman's regard."

"True. However, I would advise keeping an open mind on the subject. Some of the best men I know are handsome as the devil and twice as charming."

This time, she had trouble banishing his image. Without meaning to, Eugenia had described him perfectly.

"What of height? Tall, medium, short?"

Hannah shook her head, still trying to force his image away. "He needn't be tall."

"Do you care anything for titles?"

"I should like him to be well settled," Hannah answered, stroking a finger over Griffy's plump cheek. "Able to provide a proper home for our children. But no, a title is the last thing I want." A titled man would expect his wife to function as his hostess, perhaps even traveling to London each season to attend agonizing rounds of entertainments. She would prefer to ride Astrea across the Channel wearing the sort of wool that gave her a rash.

"Sensible." Eugenia sipped her tea. "An abundance of unmarried, untitled, unthreatening gentlemen shouldn't be too difficult to find." She set down her cup and tapped her lips. "The challenge lies in finding one who will also please your brother. He will demand deep pockets and impeccable honor, as well as a facility with weapons."

Hannah frowned. "Weapons?"

"Hmm. Pistols, knives, swords. Fists, too. He'll need to be fit and strong. You may not care one way or the other about height, but Phineas will prefer a tall man."

"I don't understa—"

"I shall write my mother and Lady Wallingham this very day."

"Eugenia—"

Her sister cupped her jaw, the contact warm and gentle. "We will find him." Sparkling sherry eyes glowed with reassurance. "The man whose touch you will welcome. The man you may trust with your life, and more importantly, your heart." Her thumb swiped beneath Hannah's eye. "No tears, dearest. Trust that I would never ask more from you than I thought you could bear."

Hannah blinked away the annoying sheen of tears. She hated her weakness. Once again, she beat it back with the force of long habit. "Chess."

Eugenia's mouth quirked in amusement. "What about it?"

"He must play, and he must be good. I am an excellent player. I prefer a challenge in that regard."

Eugenia chuckled. "Leave it to me," she answered. "The men visiting Grimsgate Castle have little notion of the test they are about to endure."

Chapter Two

"You may be correct in stating I have demanded the moon and stars, my lord. But I find your counteroffer the equivalent of substances far more earthbound. I daresay one may inadvertently step in such substances whilst traversing London's filthier mews."

—LADY DOROTHEA PENWORTH to Malcolm Charles Bainbridge, Earl Bainbridge, in a letter exchanging offers of disparate value.

LONG BEFORE THE THIEF STRUCK, JONAS FELT HIS INTENTIONS as an itch. The crawling sensation slithered along his nape. He might have chalked it up to the sweltering heat of August in London. But he'd felt it before.

Every time death hovered near, the itch returned.

He kept his pace steady along Exeter Street, deceptively lazy, intentionally casual. Rounding the corner of a stench-filled alley, he calmly withdrew his blade from inside his oversized coat.

And waited for his fish to take the bait.

He did not wait long.

The thief gurgled, choked, and wheezed as Jonas's arm seized his throat. He thrashed against Jonas's hold, his heels sliding on the slippery leavings of animals and men.

"Thought you said you never strayed west of Temple Bar, Pickens." He muttered the taunt in the wily thief's ear then clicked his tongue in a mocking chide. "Should have kept to it. Mayfair nobs get a peculiar thrill from seeing shite like you hang."

Bertie Pickens clawed at Jonas's arm and twisted to work free his blade. After seizing the thief's wrist and applying a bit of pressure, the blade dropped to the ground with a ping. Jonas sent it skittering across muck-strewn ground with a kick. Then, he pivoted and plastered Bertie's face against sooty bricks.

"Eh! No call to bruise me up, Hawthorn," the thief whined. "What'd I ever do to you?"

Jonas plucked a purple velvet pouch from Bertie's pocket and dangled it before the thief's nose. "Not a thing, Pickens. My employer, on the other hand, would like her jewels back." Jonas tucked the pouch away and retrieved a leather cord to bind the thief's wrists. "Sentimental value. You understand."

"What's Bow Street want with a poor wretch what only works to feed 'is poor, 'ungry little childr—"

Disgusted, Jonas yanked Bertie away from the bricks and hauled him out to the street, where he flagged a hack. "Silence would be wise, Pickens." He tossed the vile creature up into the coach. The thief smelled musty, like mushrooms stewed in the same pot as sweaty breeches.

After a pained "ooph," Bertie scooted across the coach floor, avoiding Jonas's long legs. "I never stole nothin'. An' if I did, it was only what I 'ad to do for my poor little—"

"Lie to the magistrates, if you like," Jonas said flatly. "Perhaps they won't have heard how you sell your poor, hungry little children to depraved men when you're too bloody sotted for thieving."

They arrived at Bow Street within minutes. Relieved to be rid of the thief, he handed Bertie Pickens over to a constable known for dressing up prisoners in a bit of black and blue before their appointment with the magistrates.

Jonas shrugged out of his coat—a stifling but necessary evil—and retrieved the newspaper he'd begun reading earlier that morning, before one of his informants had alerted him to Pickens's whereabouts.

He weighed the purple velvet pouch in his hand. Loosened the drawstring. Diamonds winked up at him like stars flickering in the dark. Pearls glowed like moonlight.

"Bloody, bleeding hell, Hawthorn." The grumbled epithet came from the hound-faced, middle-aged runner approaching from his right. Deep grooves had worn their way into the other man's face. To be expected, he supposed. Drayton had already been at Bow Street a good decade before Jonas had become an officer.

Calmly, Jonas sat behind his desk and picked up his paper. "Who pissed in your ale this time, Drayton?"

"Pickens was mine."

"Seems to me the reward was offered to anyone who retrieved the goods." He plopped the velvet pouch on the desk and nudged it with his knuckle. Then, he grinned. "I'm anyone as much as you are, eh?"

"I needed that job."

"We all need the jobs." None of the Bow Street men lived like kings. If they wanted better pay, they had to go hunting rats like Bertie Pickens.

Drayton limped to a nearby chair and sat, rubbing his leg as though the old bullet wound pained him. "I saved your arse not more'n a year past, Hawthorn."

"And I bought you the Black Bull's finest ale for your trouble, did I not?"

"Bloody ingrate. What do you need the reward for, anyhow? All you wear is rags. You've no mouths to feed but your own."

Jonas leaned back, surveying the bleary-eyed drunkards, petty thieves, prostitutes, and laggards crowding the Bow Street police office. Some were criminals waiting to go before the magistrates. Some lingered to learn the fate of their kin or conspirators. Others were newspapermen scribbling notes, or wives wringing their handkerchiefs.

He'd watched the same scene from the same play every day for nine years. Longer, if he counted his time as a soldier. Patterns repeated and repeated and repeated, as inexorable as an infection of the bone.

"You like it here, Drayton?" he asked softly.

The hound narrowed his eyes. "Bow Street? There's worse places."

Half-smiling, Jonas nodded. "Suppose so." He picked up a pencil and tapped it against his newspaper. In summer, when the nobs fled to their country estates, jobs with generous rewards grew scarce. "Better ones, too, I reckon."

"Aye. But for the likes of us?" Drayton shook his head and snorted. "Finest thing we can expect is a good pint after a long day."

Christ, what a depressing thought. Perhaps Drayton was content to collect human rubbish for a pittance, a pint, and the poor satisfaction of keeping men like Bertie Pickens from fouling civilized society. But Jonas meant to have more. Another year or two, and he'd have the funds to leave Bow Street behind for good.

"Would have liked the Pickens job, though," Drayton

muttered, scratching his grizzled jaw. "I've almost saved enough to purchase a new stone."

A wormy pang crept through Jonas's chest. "Stone?"

"Aye. For my sister. Some evil sod defiled the churchyard last month, broke up her marker with a hammer." A small, grieving smile haunted the hound's face. "Betsy deserved better."

He shouldn't care. Hell, hadn't he learned by now that everybody had a sad tale to tell? Dead sister. Dead mother. Bad leg. Bad lot. If he didn't fight for his own piece of ground, he'd never claim it, let alone keep it.

This was why it didn't pay to form attachments.

One of the young boys Bow Street employed for errands squirmed between two constables and rounded the desk, breathless with an eager gleam. The boy was new. Jonas estimated the gleam would disappear within a month. "Letter for you, Mr. Hawthorn!" The boy extended the envelope and adjusted his cap. "It has one of them fancy seals."

Jonas took the letter, noted the fine, swirling script, and dismissed the boy with a nod. The boy didn't take the hint. Instead he hovered in place, bristling with curiosity.

Drayton leaned forward to pat the boy's shoulder. "Off with you, now, Tommy. You've more tasks before the day is done."

The boy nodded and dashed off through the throng of human refuse.

Jonas broke the seal and unfolded the fine paper. "Why do you bother learning their names?" he murmured.

Drayton's answer was a long pause, a hard stare, and an echo of Jonas's earlier words: "They're anyone as much as you, eh, Hawthorn?"

He shook his head. The boy wouldn't last six weeks. Eight, if he toughened up.

"Who's that from?"

Frowning, Jonas quickly finished reading the letter. Then,

he read it again. Then, he unfolded the additional page that had been included with the missive.

A shockwave rang through his body. As Drayton would say, bloody, bleeding hell.

"Hawthorn?"

"The Dowager Marchioness of Wallingham."

Drayton's shaggy brows arched. "The dragon? What's she want with you?"

"A task." Jonas collapsed back against the chair, stunned by the sketch, astounded by the coincidence. He rubbed his jaw and blinked. Then he read the letter a third time. "One of 'unutterable urgency,' or so she claims."

"Does she mention a reward?"

An incredible one. Had the old woman added three zeros and a thousand acres without realizing? She hadn't appeared senile last time he'd seen her. "Aye," he muttered. "But she demands I travel to Northumberland at once."

Grunting, Drayton shifted in his chair and rubbed the ache in his leg. "Best be warned what you're takin' on, Hawthorn. They don't call her 'dragon' because she has scales."

Jonas shot the man a wry half-grin. "I've survived her ladyship's fire before."

"Nah. Might have been in the vicinity, but not square in her sights." Drayton gave a full-body shudder. "Better off working for Blackmore."

The formidable duke had employed Drayton for various tasks over the years. He paid well, but anybody who worked for him earned his coin thrice over.

Jonas had little doubt the dragon would be worse. But the reward ... his heart kicked harder at the mere thought of it.

He'd be done. Done scraping. Done hunting. Done with rich nobs and their precious baubles. Done with London's refuse and desperation.

One final job—one—and he'd be free.

The thought drove him to his feet. He plucked up his coat

and pencil. He tossed the newspaper in Drayton's lap and donned his hat before sidling past the other man's chair.

"Hawthorn! Forget somethin'?"

He glanced over his shoulder.

Drayton nodded toward the velvet pouch he'd left on the desk.

Jonas settled his hat tighter. "Nah." Shrugging on his coat, he shot the older man a warning glance. "Clark and Sons does shite work. Talk to Harris. He'll make your sister a proper stone." He shoved through the crowd and out onto Bow Street.

Within ten minutes, he'd reached his lodgings. The rooms weren't much—the upper floor of a two-story house on a forgettable side street. The plaster was neither gray nor brown, but rather a distant memory of white. The bed was narrow and whined every time he turned over. The single window looked out on an alley. The place was clean—he preferred clean over filth—but empty. He also preferred empty.

Quickly, he dug in his lowest coat pocket to retrieve his knife. Then, he dropped to his knees and pried at the third floorboard to the right of the window, just beneath the plain, scarred washstand. He shoved the washstand aside with his shoulder and, using his fingertips, worked the board loose and lifted it free. Finally, he pulled a small box from the crevice.

The box had been old when he'd bought it at a pawnshop the previous year. Small brass hinges protested whenever he opened the lid. But he only bothered to look inside when darkness gouged too deep, when need overcame his resistance. Besides, the size of the box was just right—small enough to fit in his pocket and big enough to keep what needed keeping. And the lining was silk. Snowy, pristine silk.

He ran a thumb over the carved wood surface, a relief of moon and stars. He opened it. Tucked Lady Wallingham's letter and sketch atop the dreams he'd sketched himself. Then, he closed the lid, slipped the box into his pocket alongside his knife, replaced the board, and shoved the washstand back into place.

After gathering up his few possessions, he left his rented rooms and made his way outside. One of the girls who plied her trade between his street and Covent Garden leaned against the side of the house. She brightened with a calf-eyed smile. "A fine day to you, Mr. Hawthorn," she cooed, working her shoulders to plump her bosoms above their confines.

He tipped his hat in his usual dismissal and continued past her without a word, but she persisted.

"Care to take me upstairs? I'd not charge you." She sauntered after him, her hips twitching back and forth in an exaggerated sway. "Come now, Hawthorn. Never seen you bring a woman home. Man like you—strong and 'andsome. You 'ave needs, aye?" She fluttered her lashes and trailed fingertips across his shoulder blade. "I'd even let you be a bit rough, if you'd care to."

She'd offered her services many times before, and he'd never accepted. For one thing, the girl was too young—eighteen, perhaps. For another, she was all wrong. Blonde hair instead of black. Dark eyes instead of light. Buxom instead of slender.

Ordinarily, he'd show more patience. He'd disguise his true nature with grins and harmless banter. Reject her brazen offers by suggesting she'd find more receptive customers in a tavern on a scorcher like today. But why bother? He was leaving. With luck, he'd never see her or this place again.

Lifting her wrist away with his thumb and finger, he tilted his head and let her have a good look at the man she'd invited to slake his hunger with her.

The prostitute swallowed visibly, withdrawing her hand. Caution replaced brazenness.

Without a word, he left the girl behind. Left his rooms behind. Soon, he would leave London behind, and everything would change.

Automatically, his hand traced the box in his pocket. Yes, everything would be different now. All he had to do was complete one small task for a dragon.

GRIMSGATE CASTLE TOWERED ABOVE FLAT, OPEN FIELDS LIKE a ship of the line on a quiet sea. Rather than white sails, however, the sprawling pile of stone occupied a knoll at the edge of the water, square towers looming dark against a feathery sky.

Jonas knew he should have slept a few extra hours at the last inn. His ride to Northumberland had taken only two days, but his eyes felt like dry gravel. He smelled of horse and sweat. His stomach protested the brick of bread he'd eaten at his last stop.

Well before noon, the early-August heat was sweltering, despite a goodly breeze off the water. He hoped like hell Lady Wallingham would demand he bathe and shave before soiling her furniture. Imagining her wrinkling that imperious nose at his dishevelment almost made his misery worthwhile.

He guided his hired mount up a winding gravel drive past the old towers of the gatehouse. By the time he stood inside Grimsgate's grand hall, surrendering his dust-stained hat to a stiff-necked butler, he'd decided his first purchase would be boots that fit his feet without blistering.

"This way, sir," the butler said, waving toward a set of arches at the rear of the cavernous hall. The castle was grand, he'd grant that much. A vast sprawl of multiple towers encircled by a stone wall, the complex of structures and gardens occupied an entire hilltop. Inside the main keep, stone walls were enriched with square-paneled wood, massive fireplaces, and high, beamed ceilings. Everywhere, signs of old bloodlines and titled influence were prominently displayed—portraits, tapestries, shields painted with the Wallingham crest. Equally, the castle itself, with its abundance of windows and polished stone floors, spoke of immense wealth. Upkeep on the windows alone in a place like this must cost hundreds of pounds per year.

The butler led him through a set of doors into what he assumed was a drawing room. The enormous space boasted several large carpets, two fireplaces, multiple red-draped windows, dozens of furnishings ranging from gold-striped chairs to a black-and-white marble chess table.

And one purple-clad dragon.

She set her teacup in its saucer with a clink and arched a white brow. "I trust there is a sound reason for your delay, Mr. Hawthorn." She sniffed and angled her chin upward, even as her mouth curved down. The twin plumes tucked into her white coiffure bobbed their agreement. "Waylaid by a vagrant who forced you to wear his garments, perhaps?"

He gave her brief bow. "I left London the day before yesterday, when I received your letter, my lady."

"Hmmph." She gestured to the chair opposite hers, a winged leather piece that probably cost six months' rent. "Do sit down, boy. You're giving me a pain in my neck."

He shrugged out of his coat, draping it over the arm of the chair before sinking onto the seat.

"Are you quite accustomed to informality, Mr. Hawthorn?" Her tart tone disapproved.

He glanced at his shirtsleeves before grinning. "Aye."

"Here, we call such impertinence rude."

His grin widened. "Aye."

She snorted. Was that a smile fighting to take hold of those old, wrinkled lips? He thought so. "Fortunately for us both, I do not require a *gentleman* but an investigator. One of some skill, if no manners whatever."

"Your letter mentioned a missing item."

"Items, Mr. Hawthorn. A trunk. Its contents are extremely valuable."

He nodded. They must be to justify such a colossal reward. "When did it go missing?"

"Recently."

"Can you be more specific?"

"No."

"Where did you last see it?"

"Here."

"In this room?"

"In this castle."

"Don't you have a bloodhound that could track—"

"Humphrey was laid low during the period surrounding the disappearance. Ill-advised consumption of meat pies from the rubbish pile, I'm afraid. Dreadful mess. By the time he recovered, there was no scent to be followed." She sniffed. "I trust you'll exhibit greater restraint, Mr. Hawthorn."

Sighing, he narrowed his eyes upon the old woman. She was tiny—more like a bird than a dragon. But her voice carried far beyond her size, not loud but clear. She spoke the way field generals spoke, so as to be heard above gunfire.

"What did the trunk contain?" he asked.

"Nothing a thief would find alluring."

"Was the trunk itself valuable, then?"

"It is a trunk, Mr. Hawthorn. Wood and leather. Well crafted, perhaps, but hardly worth stealing."

"Then, the contents must be costly."

"They are of infinite value to me."

"But you refuse to tell me what they are."

"Find the trunk. That is your task."

Grinding his back teeth, he tried another grin and leaned back against buttery leather. "Might a servant have mistakenly moved the trunk without your knowledge?"

Jewel-green eyes sparked with a hint of indignation. "My servants do not so much as swallow their supper without my knowledge, Mr. Hawthorn. Or they are not my servants for long."

"But if they had—"

"They did not," she snapped. "Someone has stolen my possessions. It is your task to find them and bring the thief to me. Now, do you intend to sit there with that insufferable male grin you mistake for charm and continue asking doltish questions? If so, I shall summon Mr. Drayton at once. *He*, at least, will have the good sense to wear a proper coat whilst he wastes my time."

Her hands, he noted, clenched the arms of her chair. Fragile fingertips dented the leather. Lady Wallingham was a formidable woman, but she rarely exhibited tension. Too superior, he supposed. Other signs—carefully controlled breathing, tightened cords in her neck—added to his conclusion that her distress was both acute and real.

He leaned forward to hold her gaze. Deliberately, he dropped his "insufferable male grin" and let her see his resolve. "I will find your trunk, my lady," he said quietly. "Of this, I can assure you."

Several breaths passed while they gazed at one another— gauged one another. Finally, she nodded, her plumes bobbing. "I trust you will. Within a fortnight, young man. Or I shall reconsider my decision to hire you instead of Mr. Drayton. Perhaps hounds are superior trackers, but a wolf hunts for his survival. In all things, motivation matters."

He frowned. "Am I the hound or the wolf in this analogy?"

"We shall see, Mr. Hawthorn. Results will tell." She gave him leave to question her staff and search the estate. Then, she informed him that he was to conduct his investigation discreetly, as she was hosting a house party.

He cursed beneath his breath. Bloody hell, this was all he needed—tracking down a lost trunk amidst a sea of aristocratic guests, all of whom would likely bring trunks of their own.

"I assume you bathe upon occasion," Lady Wallingham said

tartly, waving her fingers in his direction. "Despite appearances."

Once again, he gathered his patience and nodded.

"Splendid. My butler, Mr. Nash, will show you to your chamber."

"That's not necessary, my lady. I've taken a room at the inn—"

"Do you *enjoy* infestation, Mr. Hawthorn?"

He blinked. "Pardon?"

"Biting insects one scarcely sees. Rats with a taste for human flesh. Do you crave such discomforts?"

"No. I can't say that I—"

"Then, I suggest you accept my generous offer and follow Mr. Nash. Luncheon is at two. You will wish to bathe and don a proper coat."

This time, he frowned. Luncheon? What the devil? "Are you suggesting I dine with you and your guests?" He asked only because the idea was absurd, and he wished to see her horrified reaction. This should be amusing.

"Precisely." With a calm lift of her brow, she rang a bell and granted him a small smile. "Wear a fresh shirt. Doubtless everyone at my table will be appreciative."

He started to inquire if her cup was filled with brandy rather than tea that morning, but the stiff-necked Mr. Nash arrived to lead him from the room in proper stiff-necked fashion.

Bloody hell. Why on earth would she want him mingling with her guests? Did she suspect one of them of filching her trunk? He'd have to wait to ask. The dragon dismissed him in favor of her lorgnette and correspondence.

Nash led him back along the lengthy, windowed gallery toward the grand hall. "Her ladyship has asked that the staff cooperate fully with your investigation, Mr. Hawthorn. If you require assistance in any regard,"—the butler coolly eyed Jonas's boots and coat—"anything at all, you have but to inquire."

"Her ladyship wants me to join her guests at luncheon."

"Indeed, sir."

He watched the man's face, waiting for signs of incredulity. "Any idea why?"

"She wishes your presence, sir."

"A Bow Street officer. Dining with lords and ladies at a marchioness's table."

"We have arranged a bath for you, as well as suitable attire."

Jonas stopped. "Nash."

The lean, rust-and-gray-haired butler halted and turned on his heel, hands clasped at his back. His face showed only the discipline of his profession. "Yes, Mr. Hawthorn?"

"What has luncheon to do with finding her trunk?"

"So far as I am aware, nothing at all."

"She gave me a fortnight to complete my investigation. Luncheon wastes my time and hers. Makes no sense."

"It is as her ladyship wishes, sir. Her reasons are her own." Nash lowered his chin to a slightly less pompous angle. "However, in my experience, one is well advised to assume her reasons are sound."

Old dragons were not to be questioned, apparently. "Very well. Lead on. The sooner we dine, the sooner I can finish what I came here to do."

"Indeed, sir."

As they neared the grand hall, voices echoed along the gallery. A man and woman. Accents that spoke of money and entitlement.

"... invited us to his annual hunt in November." The low, masculine voice sounded through the arches. "She may certainly wait until then to find a husband. Or next year, for that matter. Your urgency baffles me."

"That is because you are a man, my darling," replied a wry female.

"What has sex to do with it?"

"Lord Muggeridge could still father children, should he find a blind woman desperate enough to accommodate him. And he is older than Lady Wallingham. A woman's time is more limited."

"My sister is hardly in her dotage. A year or two will make scant difference—"

"Think of it in plant terms. Perhaps that will make more sense to you."

"How so?"

A feminine sigh of exasperation. "Some plants need no more than sunlight and rain to bloom the entire summer through, correct?"

"Yes."

"Others are more delicate. Orchids, for example. They bloom only when a very particular set of conditions are met. Miss your chance, and you may not get another."

"Briar, have you been reading my horticulture texts again?"

"Only browsing the pictures. Lovely sketches, you know. More than one bonnet has been designed with your little plants in mind. Additionally, I have listened to you droning on about plant reproduction whilst we romp about the gardens—"

The flinty, masculine voice deepened. "Perhaps you are feeling drowsy, love. We should retire to our chamber."

"What are you on about? I feel fine." A pause. "Oh! Yes, well." A chuckle. "I suppose one does feel a bit winded after a ride."

Nash reached the center arch ahead of Jonas. The butler stopped and bowed to the guests. Light brightened then faded as a door opened and closed.

That was when he heard it. A voice as cool and soft as snowfall.

"I should like to ride along the beach tomorrow, Eugenia."

Jonas slowed. Drifted toward the sound.

"Of course, dearest," the first woman said, a smile in her voice. "But I must insist you wear your red habit. A gown is not truly yours if you refuse to put it on."

He waited for her reply. Braced a hand against the gallery wall and clenched his teeth tight.

What in bloody hell was she doing here?

God, he needed to hear her. One more time. A tiny taste of snowfall to see him through.

What a fool he was. After everything that had happened. A damned fool.

His hand fisted. His head fell forward as he waited. Wanted.

"You don't think the red too bold?"

"Don't be silly. Every male within ten miles will suddenly declare it his favorite color. Mark my words."

The tall, pale-eyed Earl of Holstoke and his petite, plainspoken countess strolled past Nash, turning toward the grand staircase without looking in Jonas's direction.

A woman followed.

The woman.

Midnight hair and moonlight eyes.

Snowfall voice and fresh-cream skin.

She wore blue velvet. She wore the bearing of a queen.

Untouchable. Haughty. Serene.

He thought she'd pass without seeing him. Better that way, he supposed. Snow Queens shouldn't have to acknowledge the low, wild creatures below their station.

But while her brother and his wife continued toward the staircase, something slowed the Snow Queen's steps.

She halted at the edge of the third arch. Her shoulders stiffened and shivered as though she'd caught a draft.

Then, she turned, her slender neck tight, her delicate chin lifting.

Stunning, ice-green eyes landed upon him. Flared in recognition. Alarm.

Creamy cheeks bloomed rosy pink.

He'd seen the reaction before. A year ago, the first time they'd met, she'd stood in her brother's London drawing room defying Jonas with a Snow Queen's hauteur—and turned the very same color. She'd looked at him the very same way, as though he were a wolf and she his supper.

The assessment wasn't far off.

He stared at her now, moonlight and midnight. Small waist, delicate jaw. Dainty nose, rosebud lips. He looked his fill. For, that was all this would ever be—looking and wanting.

She was an earl's sister. A by-blow, but still miles above his reach.

No, he would never have her. But he could have this. A moment. A slow grin that he knew would make her cheeks flare brighter, her breath come faster.

Ah, yes. There it was.

Just like the first time.

Just as he'd dreamed every night since he'd first set eyes upon the exquisite, elusive Miss Hannah Gray.

Chapter Three

"A handsome man expects ease when luring an ordinary woman into forgetting herself. But I have never been ordinary. And I never forget."

—LADY DOROTHEA PENWORTH to Malcolm Charles Bainbridge, Earl Bainbridge, in a letter explaining why some expectations are destined to be thwarted.

THE FIRST TIME HANNAH EVER SET EYES UPON JONAS Hawthorn, her skin had fairly lifted from her body. Glowed. Tickled with the sensation of lightning charging the air—part fear, part awareness, part pleasure.

Their acquaintance had begun the previous year when she and Phineas had traveled to London for the season so that he might find a wife. Since Phineas's mother had been a notorious murderess, and he had a rather "peculiar nature," as Eugenia put it, his search had been a trying one. Respectable young ladies feared him, though their avoidance had been hysterical nonsense. Phineas was the best sort of man she could imagine, kind and honorable.

Still, Lydia Brand, the late Countess of Holstoke, tended to ruin every life she touched, even in death. Phineas's reputation had suffered for being her son.

Matters had worsened considerably when two women who'd rejected Phineas's suit were poisoned. Phineas had become a suspect in the murders, and the ladies' families had hired a Bow Street runner to investigate.

He'd called at Holstoke House on Park Lane shortly after five. She remembered because she often practiced her music at five, and she'd been at the pianoforte when their butler, Sackford, had asked if she would receive a visitor.

"Who is it?"

"Mr. Jonas Hawthorn, miss. An officer with the Bow Street police office. He is here making inquiries regarding dreadful attacks upon two young ladies."

She considered turning him away. Inquiries from Bow Street men were better left to Phineas. But the incident involved young women.

Hannah had been a victim once. She'd had no one to defend her, no one to help. If answering a few questions prevented other girls from suffering similar horrors, then she would do it gladly.

So she squelched her usual response to unusual circumstances—a fizzing belly, a tightened chest—and nodded her assent. "Send him up. Thank you, Sackford."

Rising from the pianoforte, she smoothed her skirts and her hair, glancing at her reflection in the large mirror above the fireplace. She wandered to the chair at the center of the room. Her hands drifted nervously to the curved wooden frame before she forced them to still. Then, she folded them at her waist and waited.

She'd thought herself prepared. She wasn't.

Her first glimpse of Jonas Hawthorn stunned her speechless. She held very still while the dark-haired, gray-eyed, square-jawed wolf prowled into her brother's drawing room, scanning the entire space in a single glance. Then, like the hunter he was, he fixed upon her.

He moved like he wanted to be missed—fast pretending to be slow.

He dressed like he wanted to be mistaken for a vagabond—clever pretending to be feckless.

He grinned like he wanted to be welcomed—dangerous pretending to be charming.

His eyes sharpened upon her. Brightened with a silvery gleam.

She scarcely breathed while he crossed the room. Long strides were deceptively lazy as they carried him closer. Too close. She didn't like men to come near her, particularly men like him. Tall. Strong. Capable.

He tilted his head down and to the side, giving her a crooked grin that crinkled the corners of his eyes. An incisor faintly overlapped a neighboring tooth, she noted. The rakish imperfection drew her to his mouth.

"Miss Gray, I presume."

Swallowing the bewildering urge to smile in return, she greeted him as steadily as she could manage. "Mr. Hawthorn." Blast, she sounded like a breathless ninny. But her heart was pounding—*flutter and pound, flutter and pound.* "I understand you're here regarding an incident."

"Aye." She liked his voice—a bit graveled, a bit rough. His accent was difficult to place, mainly London with a patchwork of inflections from Norwich to Devonshire. "Two young ladies appear to have been poisoned." He shifted his weight so that one shoulder was higher than the other. It put him very close to her. "I'd hoped to speak to Lord Holstoke."

"As Mr. Sackford informed you, my brother is not at home."

"No, indeed." The weight of his gaze wandering over her face made her retreat a step. His grin reappeared, wider this time. "Perhaps you can help me."

She held that silvery gaze as long as she could bear before turning away and gesturing to a settee six feet away from her chair, separated by a low table. Then, she took her seat.

But he did not. Instead, he stood in place, smiling down at her, a wolf intrigued by a misbehaving meal. He withdrew a small notebook and a pencil from inside his black wool coat. "Where is Holstoke now?"

Blinking, she answered truthfully, "Attending a dinner."

"With whom?"

"The Huxley family."

"The Earl of Berne's residence, then. Grosvenor Street, if I recall."

"That's right."

He nodded as though this confirmed something. Tapping his pencil against the cover of his notebook, he gave her a mischievous boy's endearing grin. "Why did you not accompany him?"

"How is that relevant to your inquiry?"

"Indulge me." The way he spoke those two words sent her heart spinning. They were a playful tease. A secret caress.

Tingling like bubbles in a glass, her reaction froze her in place. She needed him to move away. She needed him to stop looking at her. "It occurs to me I've indulged you quite enough by granting a man of your sort an audience in the first place, Mr. Hawthorn."

His playful gleam turned sharp. She'd intended him to take umbrage. To back away. He did neither. Instead, he moved directly in front of her and lowered into a crouch, his eyes now level with hers. "Two women have been murdered, Miss Gray," he said softly. "When such evils occur, men of your brother's sort hire men of my sort to hunt down answers. Even when men of my sort must sully the fine air of a lady such as yourself."

She swallowed, her heart thundering a protest: *Too close. Too close. Too close.* "I will thank you to take your seat," she murmured.

"I will thank you to answer my question."

"I was feeling unwell. I elected to remain here for the evening."

"Unwell?" For the first time, his infernal smile disappeared entirely. "You are ill?"

"That is none of your concern." In fact, she was suffering, but she would never tell him why. Her courses came with harsh pain and deep fatigue every month. Phineas usually prepared her one of his medicinal teas to ease her symptoms. They helped a little, but she'd not felt well enough to enjoy an evening with the boisterous Huxley family.

"Hmm." His gaze caught on her hands. "Where was he this morning?"

"I did not ask."

"What time did he leave Holstoke House?"

"After breakfast. Nine or so."

Silvery eyes came back up to meet hers. "Are you acquainted with Lord Glencombe's daughter Lady Theodosia?"

"Lady Dunston has mentioned her."

"Lady Dunston. One of the Huxley daughters, yes?"

She inclined her head. "Lady Maureen Huxley, before her marriage."

"You are friends?"

"Yes."

"Then, I am flummoxed."

His refusal to move away from her, as well as his barrage of questions, chafed her already shortened temper. "Little wonder," she snapped. "Perhaps you would find greater clarity if you focused upon your task rather than bothering those courteous enough to tolerate your impertinences."

He chuckled as though she were an amusingly disgruntled kitten. "Am I bothering you, Miss Gray?"

Yes. Profoundly. More than any man in recent memory. "Ask your questions, Mr. Hawthorn. Then leave."

"Why are you not with your brother at Berne House?"

"Because I don't wish to be."

"Why not?"

Her temper ignited. "We've discussed this already."

"Are you ill?"

"I wished to stay here. That is all you need know."

"Have you been at home all day?"

"Yes."

"Because you are feeling poorly."

"Because I feel positively wretched, Mr. Hawthorn. And you are *not* improving matters."

His eyes fell to her hands once again. This time, he caught her clutching her lower belly. His brow—which she hadn't realized held tension—relaxed. He nodded. "Indeed." His grin returned, revealing the perfect imperfection of his overlapping tooth. "So, you've no idea where your brother has been, either this morning or, with certainty, right now."

"I told you—"

"You told me what he told you. But, you've been here, not with him. For all you know, he might have been visiting his mistress."

Her skin went hot. She wanted to stand and force him from the room. She wanted to slap the smile from his face. She wanted to scream that the next words he spoke had best be an apology for his rudeness.

But she did nothing of the sort. Instead, she sat very still and held that gray gaze for long seconds, gathering calm around her in a seamless shell. "My brother has no mistress. He is in town seeking a wife. Now, if you are quite finished insulting me—"

"Oh, no insult intended, I assure you. Merely trying to

ascertain whether Holstoke murdered Lady Theodosia." He smiled. "That's all."

"Murdered?" All the heat in her body dissipated beneath a flood of weakness and ice. "Sh-she was murdered?"

"Poisoned." He tilted his head in that wolfish way. "How old are you, Miss Gray?"

Still reeling from the news of a second poisoning death— the first had happened days before, another young lady Phineas had briefly attempted to court—she answered without thinking. "Two-and-twenty."

His eyes touched on her hair, her throat, her hands. "You seem both younger and ... older. Interesting."

"Wh-when was she—"

"Today around noon. She was discovered an hour or so later."

Her mind reeled. "Phineas—my brother would not kill anyone. He is a good man."

"You are his half-sister, isn't that right? Your mother was the previous Lord Holstoke's mistress?"

She nodded.

"Your loyalty to your brother is heartening, Miss Gray. But then, his lordship has been rather generous," he murmured, his eyes drifting over the drawing room. "It's not every earl who keeps his father's by-blows in decadent luxury, be they male or ... the loveliest of females."

She stiffened. "My brother cares for me. And he is not a murderer." Despite her acute discomfort at his nearness, she shoved to her feet, which put his face inches from her skirts. "If you truly wish to find the man responsible for poisoning Lady Theodosia, I suggest you leave Holstoke House at once, for you shan't find him here."

"But I've found you." Silvery eyes lifted to hers. Teasing. Challenging. "Time well spent, I daresay."

She moved away several steps, unable to bear this any longer. He was too handsome. Too forward. Too close.

He unfolded from his crouch and stood. Then, his smile faded, leaving only a subtle hunger. His posture emphasized his height. His size. His strength.

Her head started lifting and spinning. She swallowed her alarm. Retreated behind the settee.

He followed, frowning. "Miss Gray. You've gone white as sails. Are you all right?" He reached for her elbow.

She jerked back, her head floating away, now. "I should like you to leave." Someone else spoke with her voice, remote and colorless.

The wolf in the room with her dropped his hand. Tucked his notebook and pencil inside his pocket. Gave her a hard stare. "Assure me you're all right."

For a moment, she couldn't speak. God, how he frightened her. More so when he wasn't smiling, when she glimpsed the real man. Her head wanted to fly away and hide. She forced herself to stay. "I predict I shall improve immensely upon your departure, sir."

He winced and rubbed his jaw as though she'd struck him. Then, his grin returned. "Begging your pardon, miss. Men of my sort aren't often permitted to tarry in the presence of such splendid beauty." He bowed in exaggerated fashion, his oversized black greatcoat tightening across wide shoulders. "Forgive a lowly hound for begging scraps, hmm?"

Hound. Preposterous. No, hounds were tame. He was a wolf through and through.

She crossed the room to pull the bell cord. "Mr. Sackford will show you out. If you have further questions, you may address them to Lord Holstoke."

"What if my questions are for you, Miss Gray?" His tone was teasing. Light. She assumed a man as handsome as Jonas Hawthorn used flirtation as a method of ferreting information from unwary females.

But Hannah was warier than most.

"I suggest you curb your curiosity, Mr. Hawthorn. My

brother will not be pleased by your presumptuous behavior where I am concerned."

"Two women are dead. Holstoke has bigger concerns."

Her temper surged again, pressing her to defend Phineas again, to attack the wolf before he attacked her brother. But before she could do either, Sackford arrived to escort him from the house.

She'd watched through the drawing room window as his long strides had carried him out onto Park Lane. Tracing the glass with trembling fingers, she'd strained to control wild surges of panic interlaced with unfamiliar yearnings.

He'd walked away that day, leaving her reeling.

But the effect of the wolf's presence hadn't left her. Not later that evening as she'd rushed to Berne House to warn Phineas. Not in the following days as her brother had battled to defend his innocence.

Nor any other day.

The wolf had entered her life, tempting and challenging and wanting. He'd risked his life for her, ridden to Dorsetshire like a man possessed while bleeding from wounds her enemies had caused. He'd nearly died. To warn her, protect her.

And if the real man with real hunger in his eyes hadn't terrified her down to her craven soul, she would have made that wolf her own.

Instead, she'd made him hate her.

Now, here in Grimsgate Castle's grand gallery, she turned and found silvery eyes devouring her as though not a day had passed, let alone a year, since she'd watched him climb into a coach and disappear from her life.

She felt the same. Skin lifting and glowing. Heart reaching and pounding. Fear rising and choking.

She saw her wolf—ragged, dark, hungry—and wished with all her heart she could be different for him. Better.

But she couldn't. So, instead, she did what she'd always done when the fear took hold. She turned and walked away.

JONAS WAS WELL ACCUSTOMED TO SHAVING HIS OWN WHISKERS. But he had to admit having someone else perform the task was one luxury he didn't mind.

Still, he would have preferred a woman.

"There you are, sir." Lord Wallingham's valet, a tidy little man who smelled like a French perfumery, dabbed at his jaw with a towel. "A fine improvement, indeed."

Lord Wallingham—the dragon's son—had lent Jonas both his clothing and his valet. What the marquess thought of dressing up a Bow Street man in a dandy's garb and parading him around like a girl's pet pony, Jonas couldn't say. He assumed the dowager had methods of pressuring her son that didn't require explanations.

The valet retrieved a length of linen and wrapped the thing around Jonas's neck in an elaborate series of puffed folds he insisted were certainly *not* a bow. Next came the coat—snug through the shoulders, but lightweight and comfortable. Jonas and Lord Wallingham were similar in height and frame, according to the valet.

All in all, he found being trussed and brushed, pampered and primped like a princess's pony not altogether unpleasant. When a bottle of perfume appeared, however, Jonas drew the line. "No scent," he said. "The shaving soap was bad enough. I'll not trot about smelling like a whore's corset."

"Oh, but, sir—"

"Brindle—"

"It is Wendell, sir."

He braced a hand atop the valet's shoulder. "Right. Some men fancy a strong scent." Angling his head to catch the shorter man's eye, he grinned. "Disguises a number of sins, eh? A decaying tooth. A fondness for cognac. A recent tryst in the larder."

The valet's eyes grew wider with each passing sentence. On the word "larder," his throat bobbed on a swallow.

Jonas patted his shoulder. "Other men—me, for instance—prefer our disguises less aromatic. You understand."

"H-how—how did you ..."

He straightened and searched for his coat. The valet had stashed it in a chest of drawers. "Your jaw is swollen on one side. I noticed while you were shaving me." He dug through his old coat's pockets for his notebook and pencil. "The cognac I could smell on your breath. Have a fondness for the stuff, myself, though not the coin to afford it." He searched his borrowed coat's interior for pockets. Only one. Blast.

"A-and the ... larder, sir?"

He tucked away his notebook and pencil in his single measly pocket then strode past the valet. "Bit of a guess, that one." Opening the bedchamber door, he grinned back at the man. "Though, you may want to dust the flour from the front of your trousers before his lordship notices."

Jonas left the valet frantically swiping while he found his way along the corridor to the grand staircase. The dragon had put him in one of the guest chambers, a large room with a large bed and large swaths of brown velvet and blue silk. He still did not know why she was treating him as a guest. Just as he did not know why fate had put him in the path of Hannah Gray again.

Damn and blast, he needed to forget her. This was about finishing a job. That was all.

He found his way to the dining room as footmen carried trays of sliced meat out of the room and toward the gallery. Nash stood in the doorway, directing his troops.

"Please tell me I missed luncheon," Jonas muttered.

Nash raised a starchy brow. "Her ladyship has decided luncheon will be served in the garden, sir. I believe she is there now with several guests."

His gut tightened. "Holstoke."

"Yes, sir."

He debated the merits of refusing to play pony for aristocrats' entertainment. But he bloody well needed this job. So, a pony he would be, at least for the next hour.

Following a footman, he found his way outside through the gallery's glass doors. The gardens matched the castle in scale with hedges, flowers, paths, and lawn spanning acres inside the old stone walls. A gravel path led to a large fountain where seven tables had been decorated with white cloths and flower-laden urns. Lady Wallingham examined one of the blooms through her quizzing glass while the black-haired, pale-eyed Earl of Holstoke explained its structure.

Holstoke did like his plants.

"Mr. Hawthorn?"

He turned. A pretty woman with laughing brown eyes grinned up at him. Five peacock feathers waved from her green silk bonnet.

"Lady Holstoke." He smiled and inclined his head. "A pleasure to see you again." It was, in fact, a pleasure. The first time he'd met Lady Eugenia Huxley, she'd strolled into the Bow Street police office, bold as you please, and pronounced herself Holstoke's mistress, and thus, his alibi for the murder of two women. A transparent lie, of course, embellished with improbable claims about Holstoke's stamina. But Jonas had been charmed.

Holstoke, on the other hand, had been incensed. He'd married the brazen chit with such haste, Jonas had concluded the man must have been waiting for an excuse. Later, when Jonas saw them together at Primvale Castle, his suspicions were confirmed. The Earl of Holstoke was mad for his wife.

Now, Lady Holstoke's eyes danced as she took in Jonas's new attire. "My, my. How dashing you look in properly fitted clothing. What would your fellow officers say if they could see you now?"

He chuckled. "Something vulgar, no doubt. We're a rough

lot, my lady."

"Hmm. Have you spoken with my husband yet?"

"No."

She nodded in the direction of the tables. "He will be gratified to see you looking so well." Her eyes darted to his shoulder and leg. "When you left Primvale, we hoped your injuries mightn't trouble you too much. But you appear to have recovered fully."

"That I have," he lied. The arrows that had torn apart his shoulder and thigh had been mere pinpricks in comparison to other wounds. Those hadn't healed at all.

He glanced around the garden, noting the guests wandering toward the tables. Two young fops whose cravats nearly swaddled their ears. A tall matron on the arm of a shorter man in a bright-yellow waistcoat. A dark-haired gentleman with silver at his temples and a build similar to Jonas's. This was Lord Wallingham, accompanied by a blonde woman who affectionately brushed lint from his sleeve.

None of them had silken hair dark as a raven's wing. None of them glowed like moonlight on water. None of them were ... her.

"... my sister, Maureen, and Lord Dunston arrive tomorrow. Mr. Hawthorn?"

He returned his attention to the woman in front of him. "Last time I saw Dunston, he was handing me twelve guineas for the pleasure of losing a wager. He might still be sore."

"Dunston is the affable sort. Not one to hold grudges."

"The wager involved archery and brandy consumption. He may have been misled as to my true capacity in both arenas."

"Misled by whom?"

He answered with a grin.

Her lips pursed. "Hmmph." With a glint of determination, she claimed his arm and tugged him forward. "Come. You must speak with Holstoke."

"About?"

"Something pleasant, preferably. Be honest. But not too honest. Don't lie. Necessarily. And do try to get on with him. Best behavior, now."

"Hmm. Good of you to remind me. I had thought to remove my trousers and splash about in the fountain. Without a woman to manage me, 'tis a wonder I get by in polite company."

"Oh! That's another thing. Curtail your sarcasm. We wish for him to like you, not merely tolerate you."

He frowned down at peacock feathers and green silk. "Why, precisely?"

She tugged harder, dragging him forward. "If the conversation takes a sour turn, ask him about plants. That should mollify him for a time."

"Mollify?" He frowned. The woman was dizzying.

"Are you a good shot, Mr. Hawthorn?"

He didn't remember her being mad. A bit unusual. Forthright, certainly. Flamboyant in her choice of headdress, perhaps. But not a lunatic. Perhaps he'd missed something.

She assessed him from beneath her bonnet's brim. "You are, aren't you? A superb shot. I'd stake all my red ribbons on it."

"Lady Wallingham didn't tell me she'd be serving wine this early. Point me to it, my lady. I could do with a glass or two."

"How are you with blades? Knives, swords, that sort of thing."

He stopped, which forced the lunatic clinging to his elbow to stop as well. "Are you anticipating a siege?"

"Answer the question."

"I'm capable of slicing ham into polite pieces if that's what you're wondering."

Her eyes flared when he mentioned her favorite food. "You remember?"

He shrugged. He remembered a lot of things. Too many. "If you're thinking of hiring a runner, I recommend Mr. Drayton. I can vouch for his marksmanship, and he's not much for sarcasm."

"I don't wish to hire you."

"Then, what is this about?"

She released a sigh. "You must trust me."

In his experience, a man's biggest mistakes started with just such a plea. He patted the countess's hand and gently removed it from his arm. "It has been a true pleasure seeing you again, my lady. Do give my regards to Lord Holstoke, hmm?"

He'd taken three strides back toward the castle when a shimmer of black caught his eye. It was ... her.

She wore white. Sheer, white layers of muslin with a satin sash in softest green. No bonnet. No gloves. She sat on a bench near a rosebush.

And in her arms was a babe.

Freezing in place, Jonas riveted upon the sight. She gazed down at the little mite with a heart-melting smile. If the moon had suddenly turned pink and blazed brighter than the sun, he could not have felt deeper shock.

Then, he examined the babe. A few months old, perhaps. Raven-black hair. Palest green eyes. As beautiful as the woman whose love shone impossibly bright.

His legs stiffened. His gut burned.

God Almighty. Was this the secret she'd been guarding? Had she saved her heart for another? Given her body to another? Let another touch her while she shied away from Jonas at every turn?

It would explain a great deal. Her rejection. Her coldness. If she'd been carrying another man's child a year ago, Jonas might have been nothing more than a nuisance. Merely another pathetic mongrel begging at the feet of a Snow Queen.

Everything inside him seized. He fought to remain still. Not to charge forward. Not to make demands.

She owed him nothing, for she'd promised him nothing, he reminded himself. He'd never even kissed her. Granted, he'd nearly died trying to protect her. But she hadn't asked it of him. He'd done it because ... bloody hell, he didn't know why.

A servant—her lady's maid, by the look of it—approached carrying a straw bonnet with green ribbons. Hannah didn't glance up when her maid spoke. Instead, she murmured a reply but kept her eyes upon the babe, rocking gently from side to side while tiny fingers clutched her thumb. The maid placed the bonnet on the bench beside her mistress then strolled away.

Jonas didn't know what drove him forward. He should ignore her. Getting tangled up with this untouchable woman again was pure idiocy.

His legs didn't care. His chest burned with the need to know. To hear her voice. Perhaps snowfall would affect him differently this time.

"Miss Gray."

Her rocking stilled.

He found himself drawing close, gazing down upon silken black and creamy white, hoping for a drift of her scent. Wanting. God, how he wanted.

Slowly, thick black lashes lifted. Stunning eyes the color of frosted leaves found him. The only sign of disquiet was quickened breathing. Otherwise, she was a seamless composition. "Mr. Hawthorn."

He wanted to curse at his body's reaction. It seemed snowfall would always make him burn. "I assume it is still 'Miss Gray.'" His eyes flickered to her bare hand. "Or am I mistaken?" A babe in her arms but no ring. Had the man died? Had he been imprisoned?

If not, perhaps one or the other could be arranged.

"Why should my name be different?"

Her answer was so cool, her expression so shuttered, he thought for a moment she was mocking him. But Hannah Gray's nature was remote, not sardonic. A small crinkle between her dark brows indicated genuine confusion.

His eyes fell to the babe in her arms. Acid was eating his insides, so rather than answer, he shrugged.

"I am ... surprised to see you here," she said. "Northumberland is a long way from London."

"Lady Wallingham needed a hound to track her belongings." His mouth twisted into a smile. "It seems I will do."

The babe grew restless, grunting and waving its arms. Hannah jostled the child a bit, stroking downy black hair with delicate white hands. "You look well," she murmured, her eyes roaming from his waist to his forehead. Not by a flicker of a lash did she reveal anything approaching interest. Yet, he sensed something beneath the surface—a disturbance she was controlling with great will. "When you left, I ... well, you'd only just begun to recover." She pulled her gaze away from his and back to the babe. "Did Phineas's physician visit you in London?"

"Aye. Not to worry, Miss Gray. A hound's injuries are hardly worth a moment's thought. Ladies of your sort have better things to do than sully themselves with mongrels, eh?"

Her shoulders stiffened then, oddly, trembled. Delicate muscles along her jawline rippled. She stroked the babe's head again. "I saw your wounds. I sat at your bedside while they tried to claim your life. Perhaps you've forgotten."

He watched her reaction, confused by the tone. Her words were soft, but in anyone else, he would have sworn they were on the edge of being shouted. She had, indeed, sat with him for hours. Days. Each time he'd flickered into consciousness, she'd been there, pale and perfect. Waiting and watching.

When he'd finally regained enough strength, he'd reached for her. She'd flinched away as though scalded.

"I don't forget much." He gave her a grin. "A blessing and a curse, you might say." Nodding toward the child, he felt his mouth twisting, his jaw tightening. "This I don't remember."

She blinked. "Oh, well, you wouldn't. Griffin was born in March."

He traced the lines of her waist, the soft curve of her

breasts, both unchanged since the last time he'd seen her. "You, too, appear well recovered."

"Recovered?"

"Who is the father?" The question escaped without his consent. He shouldn't be asking. He had no rights to her. She'd made that clear.

"I'm not sure I understand your question."

"Where is he now?" He should shut his mouth. He should walk away before he made a fool of himself again. But he wanted to know. Burned to know. "More to the point, where is his ring?"

Those extraordinary eyes flared. "Are you—are you implying ... that Griffin is mine?"

"Isn't he?"

The child began squirming. The little face scrunched. Then, he let out a squawk, several grunts, and a full-scale wail.

Jonas frowned. That had turned rather quickly.

From behind him came a feminine chuckle. "Heavens, it appears Griffy the Fussbucket would prefer to dine earlier than the rest of us."

Lady Holstoke slipped past him to claim the baby, who calmed as soon as she scooped him into her arms. She brushed her nose against the boy's then tickled his belly with her finger. "Griffin Brand, you are your father's son." She laughed then grinned at Jonas. "I must feed him or we shall all suffer his wrath. But you and I did not finish our conversation, Mr. Hawthorn. When I return, I expect we will do so." With a pert nod, Lady Holstoke carried the black-haired infant away, cooing and calming in a motherly fashion.

Because *she* was his mother.

And Phineas Brand was his father.

And Hannah was his aunt.

Blast, it hadn't taken long for Jonas to play the fool again, had it?

Hannah rose from the bench and calmly donned her

bonnet, tying the green ribbon beneath her chin. "The assumption was natural," she said. "He has my coloring. You saw me holding him." She focused upon him with a level stare. "And we haven't seen one another in some time."

She was right, but he still felt like an idiot. He rubbed his jaw with his knuckles. "A year," he agreed.

"More."

He frowned.

"A year and thirteen days," she clarified. "You look well, Mr. Hawthorn."

She'd already said so. Was her breathing faster? And had she been *counting* the bloody days? *He* was the fool who did that. She was the one who'd sent him away, refusing to look at him as he'd climbed into the coach.

He moved closer but stopped when her neck stiffened. "The coat is borrowed."

Darting a glance across his shoulders, she murmured, "It fits you handsomely."

"You noticed. Careful, Miss Gray. You'll have me blushing."

"I scarcely recognized you without that black wool sack you always wear."

She'd obviously been spending a lot of time with Lady Holstoke. The bluntness was catching. "I favor pockets," he replied, glancing at his sleeve. "This has only one."

"Why did you ask about Griffin's father?"

More bluntness. A surprising change when she'd always been so reticent before. "Curiosity," he answered. "A hound's affliction, I'm afraid."

"Stop calling yourself a hound." Soft lips tightened. "It doesn't suit."

"What should I be called, then?"

"Your name."

"And what is my name?" He was only half teasing. He wanted to hear his name on rosebud lips.

Her eyes, for all that they stopped a man's heart with their beauty, gave him nothing. In all his days, he'd never seen a woman so opaque. She was as cool and pristine as mirrored glass in a moonlit room. But for a split second, something flickered beneath the surface. A shadow, then a spark. Fear followed by defiance.

"Jonas," she whispered. "Jonas Bartholomew Hawthorn."

He couldn't speak. Couldn't move. Couldn't breathe. Bloody hell, in three words, she'd lit him afire.

Her gaze slid to his chin, his neck, his waist. "I am glad you are well," she said, her voice small and tight. "I have never been so glad of anything."

Her maid came to fetch her. A light breeze blew across his skin as she gave him a polite nod and walked toward the castle. Distantly, he heard the fountain splashing. Birds calling. Guests chatting. Lady Wallingham crowing.

But all he could do was stand there with the sun warming his back.

She knew his name. He'd never told her the middle one. Perhaps she'd learned it from her brother or Lord Dunston. Perhaps the physician had mentioned it. One thing was clear— a woman who bothered to learn his middle name and speak it back to him was not as indifferent as she'd have him believe.

Chapter Four

"My sister insisted I speak with you. She did not specify
politeness. Neither did she insist your coat remain unsoiled.
But, then, she knows me rather well."

—LADY DOROTHEA PENWORTH to Malcolm Charles Bainbridge,
Earl Bainbridge, in a letter of non-apology for a confrontation at an
otherwise civilized party.

SHE HUDDLED IN A BLACKENED CORNER, GASPING FOR AIR.
With clawed hands, she tore away her bonnet so she might
breathe.

She'd done it. She'd been normal.

With *him*.

She'd spoken his name. Held his eyes. Felt herself falling

into him like warm, clear water.

Stifling her mouth with both hands, she collapsed onto an old, dusty surface.

Earlier, when Hannah had confronted Eugenia about Jonas Hawthorn's unexpected presence at Grimsgate, her sister-in-law had flatly refuted Hannah's accusations of betrayal. "You are choosing a husband, dearest. Offering you the option of the man you truly want is the opposite of betrayal."

"Why did you not tell me?"

"Because you would not have come."

"He complicates everything. I cannot choose him, Eugenia." She hadn't been able to disguise her anguish. "You know why."

"Yes. But your choice must be made in full awareness of what you're rejecting. And whom."

"Why must it?"

"To weaken the regret you may feel one day." Eugenia had explained how she'd received word that Lady Wallingham intended to hire a Bow Street runner to track down a lost trunk. She'd promptly encouraged the dowager to hire Jonas Hawthorn and orchestrate the "happy coincidence" of a house party and his arrival at Grimsgate.

Then, to give Hannah the "best possible chance" of making a proper decision, Eugenia had made her practice being normal. Hannah had run through scenarios a hundred times since this morning. How to greet him. How to control her reactions. How to converse like a normal lady with a man she ...

What? Dash it all, what was he to her? Their connection remained murky. He'd saved her life. She'd refused to let him die. He'd reached for her. She'd run away. Sent him away.

But the longing—oh, the longing remained.

Her lips trembled against her fingers as she rocked back and forth.

Good heavens, he was handsome. When she'd seen him in that green wool coat, his brown hair trimmed so neatly, his lean, square jaw freshly shaven, her bones had turned to molten gold. How could he be handsomer than before? It seemed impossible, and yet there he'd been, a wolf in gentleman's clothing.

He scared her silly. Even now, she thought pieces of her might break loose and fly away.

Griffy had been a comfort, an anchor. But there, at the last, she'd felt herself slipping.

A soft knock sounded at the door. She closed her eyes.

"Mistress?"

It was Claudette, her lady's maid. Probably come to fetch her back to luncheon. But Hannah had burned up every ounce of normal to speak with him. She had none left. Only the fear, and it threatened to break her apart.

The door creaked open. "Mistress? His lordship—Lord Holstoke, that is—he is waiting for you." Her young maid slipped into the old stone chamber. Claudette was small and gentle. She carried a lantern. She came to sit beside Hannah, setting the lantern on the floor. Then, she rested her open hand on the surface between them.

Slowly, Hannah forced her hand away from her mouth. She lowered it into Claudette's palm. The girl stroked her knuckles with her thumb.

"We shall take a moment to repair your skirts, mistress," the maid murmured. "It is very dusty in here."

Hannah glanced around. It was a cellar. Cool and dark, tucked away below ground in a corner where even servants rarely ventured. Hannah had found it on her first day at Grimsgate Castle. She liked hidden spaces. "I suppose it is."

"Lady Wallingham offered me a position again."

Hannah squeezed her maid's hand. "Did she? This is the fourth time, is it not?"

"Third. I do not count the last one, as she was dismissing her previous maid at the time. I think she meant to torment that poor girl."

Gradually, with Claudette's cool hand holding hers, she

managed to quell the forces trying to pull her away. She took a breath. Then another. "Would you—would you consider it?" Hannah forced herself to meet Claudette's eyes. They were pure kindness. "Leaving me?"

"No, mistress." Her thumb stroked the back of Hannah's hand. "So long as you want me to stay, I will stay."

She couldn't manage a smile. She felt it. Wanted to respond with the gratitude she felt. But all she could do was nod.

What a fool she'd been to listen to Eugenia. *Everyone treats you like wet paper,* her sister-in-law had once scoffed. *You are stronger than anyone I know.*

Foolishness. She wasn't strong. She was broken.

"Come, mistress. Let us clean you up and return to the garden. Lady Wallingham is serving peach tarts."

Peach tarts were her favorite. Finally, after long seconds, Hannah nodded.

Claudette was an excellent lady's maid, so she had her mistress dusted and repaired and returned to the garden in minutes. Hannah spotted Jonas instantly, conversing with Lord Wallingham near the fountain. She drifted toward him without thinking but caught herself before she'd gone farther than the hedge that circled the fountain. There, she hovered and tried not to stare.

A man approached from her right. Handsome. Golden. Tall. He smiled at Hannah with affection lighting his blue eyes.

She couldn't help smiling in return. He'd been her champion, her teacher. After the bad time and before she'd found Phineas, he'd been the one man she'd known was good, for he was the one who'd brought the bad time to an end.

"Lord Colin," she exclaimed. "How lovely it is to see you."

"And you, Miss Gray. It seems an age since our last visit."

"A month or two at least," she agreed. "I fear Eugenia has kept me occupied with her new millinery shop in Weymouth." Hannah glanced around for his wife, who was usually by his side. "Is Sarah ...?"

"Waylaid by two pint-sized ruffians, who have demanded a ransom of five peach tarts each. Good behavior grows costlier by the day," he observed with a fond papa's wryness. "I expect she'll return momentarily."

Colin and Sarah Lacey had two daughters, three-year-old Rebecca and four-year-old Abigail. Both were mischievous imps too adorable not to spoil, though they looked like perfect cherubs with their father's blond curls. Hannah sometimes plaited their hair into fanciful halos when she visited them in Devonshire. Their home, Yardleigh Manor, also housed the school Colin and Sarah ran together. Hannah had attended St. Catherine's Academy for Girls of Impeccable Deportment for two years before she'd gone to live with Phineas.

Lord Colin had taught her to love music. He'd helped her learn to dance. He'd offered her a sense of safety during the time she'd needed it most. And in the years since she'd left the school, he and his wife had become dear friends.

He tilted his head closer. "I've been told you may be seeking a husband," he said with an approving smile.

"Who told you?"

"First Sarah, then Reaver." Colin grinned, blue eyes sparking with his usual humor. "I should warn you, between him and me and Dunston and Holstoke, any gentleman seeking your hand will have a devil of a gauntlet to run before he'll be deemed worthy."

She smiled softly. "I am thankful for every one of you."

"Have you met anyone who strikes your fancy?"

Instinctively, her eyes shifted to Jonas. He was glaring at Lord Colin with the oddest expression.

"It is early yet," she murmured, fighting a queer twist in her midsection. "Not all the guests have arrived."

"A few interesting ones have, though."

With effort, she pulled her gaze away from where it wanted to be and back to her friend. "Eugenia insists I must make an informed decision."

"Hmm. Quite right. Though I must say, sometimes one simply knows. It was that way for me."

She frowned up at him. "With Sarah?"

"I was half dead when she found me. Should have been fully dead, by all rights. I awakened in an angel's arms and thought by some clerk's error, I had been sent to heaven rather than where I truly belonged. She didn't know me at all, yet she refused to leave me. Refused to let me die."

"Sarah has a kind heart. You must have been grateful for her care."

Sky-blue eyes glowed with the love he felt for his wife. "Yes, but I was also grateful to her mother," he noted wryly. "And I did not move heaven and earth to marry Mrs. Battersby, charming though she is." His expression grew thoughtful. "It took some time to accept, you know. I was damaged goods. How could I ask Sarah to take me on?"

Confused, Hannah shook her head. "But, your injuries healed."

"My body, yes. But I'd damaged myself beyond forgiveness long before Sarah found me. I didn't want her to know the terrible things I'd done. I thought she deserved a better man, one who hadn't made my mistakes. And so she did." His smile was wistful. "But she had different ideas on the subject. To her mind, we are all damaged in one way or another. The ones who truly love us don't judge us by our scars but by who we've become as a result."

Her scalp tingled as she realized what Colin was trying to tell her—that he understood. He understood how frightened she was to ask someone to share the burdens of her past. But even Colin, who had been tortured by the same hand as she, could not comprehend the extent of the damage she'd be bringing to a marriage. Further, no one—not Eugenia or her brother or her friends—knew why Jonas Hawthorn was both her greatest risk and her greatest temptation.

Carefully, she laid a hand upon Colin's arm. "She is a wise woman, your wife."

He grinned and started to reply, but a commotion beyond the hedge interrupted their conversation. Deep barking and a resounding howl echoed past greenery and over lawn. Childish giggles followed. Then, "Over here, Humphrey! Chase me!"

Hannah and Colin exchanged amused glances then wandered around the hedge to see a floppy-eared, deep-wrinkled brown dog loping after a young boy with dark hair and a gleeful grin. The sight sent happiness beaming through Hannah like sun through a window.

Lady Wallingham's hound, Humphrey, might be getting on in years, but when her grandsons were about, the dog romped like a pup. The oldest boy, Earl Bainbridge or Bain for short, sprinted around the fountain and dashed between the tables. He was followed closely by Humphrey and two smaller boys, his brothers Christopher and William.

This was why Hannah had allowed Eugenia to push her into a husband hunt. This was what she would risk everything for—the pleasure of watching children play and laugh and run, the joy of pouring her heart into a babe of her own. Perhaps she should thank her sister-in-law. Normal wasn't easy for Hannah, and likely never would be, but Eugenia had been right—it was her one chance at having a family of her own.

Drawing a deep breath, she searched the growing crowd for Eugenia.

But her eyes snagged on green wool and a rakish grin. He wore his usual disarming expression, the one that revealed his overlapping tooth. The one that could charm a lady out of her petticoats. But this time, it was not directed at Hannah.

It was directed at a lady she'd never seen. Beautiful. Hair the color of morning light. The woman beamed up at him, fluttering long lashes and blushing sunrise pink. She had an open smile and large bosoms. She had full lips and a vividly blue gown.

She had, in other words, everything Hannah did not. Of particular concern, however, was that she had *his* attention.

And like a wave pulling sand from beneath Hannah's feet, something powerful flooded in. It pushed against her skin. Flushed into a hot prickle.

Jonas laughed at something the woman said. He leaned in close as though to confide a secret.

The heat worsened. Hannah's throat burned. Her hands clenched. What was this? She hated it. Hated the feeling. Hated the woman. Hated him.

"There you are. I've been looking everywhere." Eugenia greeted Colin as he left to find Sarah. Then she clasped Hannah's arm. "I have two gentlemen you must meet. Both untitled. Both mild as blancmange. Not too handsome, though not repulsive, either. I think you'll be impressed."

He was standing so close to her. And she looked at him with such ... flirtation.

Hannah had never flirted with him—with anyone, really. Eugenia had forced her to practice, but she remained dreadful at it. She simply could not simper or flutter her lashes or pretend interest in hunting properties without thinking how very foolish it all was. This woman, by contrast, seemed talented in the art. Shameless, even.

"What the devil are you staring at, dearest?" Eugenia leaned sideways to align her head with Hannah's. "Oh. I see."

"Who is she?" The question emerged from nowhere. Well, perhaps not *nowhere*. But certainly somewhere dark and unexplored.

"Clarissa Meadows. Lady Darnham's granddaughter. Quite pleasant, really. Spent years as a wallflower. This past season, she managed to climb down off the shelf and turn herself into quite the popular figure. No engagement yet. I expect she's enjoying the attention after all those years sitting next to her grandmother whilst other girls waltzed away toward matrimony."

Jonas said something that made Miss Meadows laugh. The woman's pink color deepened. Hannah's insides turned jagged.

"What did you suppose might happen, dearest?" Eugenia's tone was gentle. "He will not keep forever."

"I want him to stop. I want her to leave." Hannah's breath quickened. She clenched her fists over and over. "What can I do, Eugenia? This is ... I hate it."

"These feelings you're having, they're unpleasant, hmm?"

"I don't like them at all."

Eugenia snorted. "Imagine feeling them for your sister," she muttered before waving the thought away. "Never mind that. You asked what you can do. Think of Mr. Hawthorn as a chair you would like to claim for yourself, a prime perch at a lovely feast with acres of ham and peach tarts. If that perch is desirable to you, it must naturally be desirable to others. Leave it unoccupied too long, and you've forfeited the chair to other ... sitters, as it were."

"Speak plainly, Eugenia. Riddles do not suit you."

"Hmmph. Feeling prickly, aren't you? Very well." Eugenia squeezed her arm and leaned close. "Take your seat, dearest. Show Miss Meadows and any other roaming female that this particular perch is *occupied*."

"What if I cannot?"

"Then, you must cede your perch to someone else. Unlike a chair, Mr. Hawthorn has feelings, too. And he deserves to be treated fairly, wouldn't you agree?"

Hannah swallowed. Yes, fairness was important. But, at the moment, her least noble impulses had her in their grip. Watching him flirt with someone else was a pain she'd never felt before—and she'd thought she'd experienced every sort of pain there was.

"Come. Glaring daggers at them will only make matters worse." Eugenia tugged her toward a group of gentlemen chatting between two tables. "Let me introduce you to my two blancmange candidates. They may be less enticing, as perches go, but perhaps they'll offer you a new perspective."

MISS MEADOWS WAS A CHARMING WOMAN. SMALL YET voluptuous. Polite yet lively of humor. Breathlessly talkative yet endearing. Splendid, really.

Had Jonas not been an utter fool, he might have pursued her—but he was, so the point was moot.

Blast, he'd missed half of what the chit had said. Of course, she packed ten-stone of talk into a two-pint jar.

"... arrived early because Grandmama insisted on leaving Ellery Hall fully three weeks ago. I told her it was only two days' travel, but she claimed it would be cooler in the north. A miscalculation, I daresay ..."

Who was the man Hannah had been standing with? Jonas's height. Blond hair. Highborn handsomeness that brought to mind winged gods in Florentine paintings. Hadn't some of those gods plummeted to their deaths after their wings melted? He thought so.

"... in any event, that is why we arrived before everybody else. Lady Wallingham has let us ramble about hither and thither, and it has been lovely. Simply lovely. The beach, the gardens, the library. Oh! And the horses. Magnificent. Lord Wallingham keeps a superb stable. What was your question, again?"

He cleared his throat. "Did you see anyone leaving when you first arrived? Perhaps carrying a trunk."

"Not that I recall. Everything was a bit hectic, as we were not expected to arrive so early. The Grimsgate staff has shown us the utmost courtesy ..."

Perhaps Lady Holstoke would know who Hannah's fair-haired god was. She seemed to know everyone here, as if she'd penned the guest list for Lady Wallingham herself.

"... did you say you were from, Mr. Hawthorn?"

He gave the chit a smile, noting how her cheeks pinkened every time he did. "London," he answered, shrugging. "Largely."

"You must find Northumberland a relief. London is stifling in summer. Though, I had a marvelous time in town during the season. I don't recall seeing you there."

He widened his grin and leaned in close. Most people found such a move disarming—usually females. "Would you remember me if you had, Miss Meadows?"

"Oh!" she breathed, fluttering her lashes and turning pinker. "Yes. Yes, I certainly would."

There. Now he needn't explain how she wouldn't have seen him prancing about Mayfair ballrooms because he was a lowborn Bow Street runner who fetched thieves for a living. He straightened. Above the woman's blonde curls, he spotted Nash. "I do beg your pardon. I see an old acquaintance I must speak to."

"Perhaps we will converse again?" Her tone was hopeful.

He inclined his head. "'Twould be a pleasure."

She said something else, but he'd already started across the lawn toward the man who might have the answers he wanted.

"I need a name, Nash."

The butler turned and raised a salt-and-rust brow. "Only one, sir?"

"For now." He swiftly scanned the crowd, spotting the de-winged god conversing with a honey-haired pixie. "There. Who is he?"

Nash frowned. Peered past the fountain and tables. "That is Lord Wallingham, sir."

"For the love of God, Nash. I know Wallingham. I am wearing his coat."

Squinting, Nash tried again. "The sizable fellow with the spectacles? That is Mr. Reaver. He is the owner of a gaming club in—"

"I also know Mr. Reaver," Jonas snapped. "Blue coat. Gold hair. Looks like he tumbled out of a painting."

"Ah. Lord Colin Lacey. Younger brother to the Duke of Blackmore."

A duke's brother. Bloody hell. It figured she'd smile at him and put her hand on his bloody arm. They'd be perfect together. Moonlight and sunlight. Aristocratic bloodlines and unnaturally beautiful offspring.

"Lord Colin arrived shortly after you did, sir." Nash sounded amused. "With his wife and their two daughters."

"Wife?"

"Indeed. Lady Colin is there with him, now." Nodding toward the woman with the child-swollen belly and spiraling honey hair, the butler didn't bother to disguise his smirk.

If Lacey was married, then why had Hannah gazed up at him with such ... fondness? Had he promised her a position as his mistress? Was that why she smiled sweetly at him then turned to ice with Jonas?

"Lord and Lady Colin run a girls' school in Devonshire. Miss Gray may be able to tell you more. She attended the school some years ago and has maintained a friendship with the Lacey family."

Sanity began to seep back into his thick, muddy head. Blast. He shouldn't be concerning himself with the Snow Queen. He shouldn't be asking about the men for whom she saved her smiles or what about Jonas sent her scurrying.

He was here to do a job. That was all.

"My lord." Nash bowed.

Jonas frowned at the butler then saw the shadow approach from behind him. He turned. "Holstoke."

The earl stood an inch or two taller than Jonas, but it was his stillness more than his height that made him an imposing presence. Most people shrank or fidgeted beneath that icy-green stare.

Jonas was not so easily intimidated.

"My wife wants me to speak with you."

He remembered the cold, flinty voice, the impenetrable

expression. The man's demeanor was one reason Jonas had considered him a suspect in the poisoning deaths of two women. That and the fact that his mother had employed similar methods to kill many of her victims.

Eventually, Jonas had rejected the probability of Holstoke as the perpetrator, but not before the earl had decided to dislike him. Understandable, really. No one enjoyed being accused of murder, particularly when one became the real murderer's target, along with one's wife and sister.

They'd worked together the previous summer when saving Eugenia and Hannah had lit them both with a killing fire. But Holstoke's dislike remained, visible as the man's emerald cravat pin.

"Your wife made a similar recommendation to me," Jonas said now with a smile he knew would irritate the earl. "Puzzling, that."

"Yes. Puzzling." He fell silent, studying Jonas's face.

Jonas waited. Long, empty seconds. Nothing. "Well, now," he said finally. "Stimulating conversation, my lord. Perhaps we should do it again at the next house party where I'm tasked with finding lost things." He started to leave but halted at Holstoke's next words.

"My sister is not an option for you, Hawthorn."

Slowly, he pivoted.

"She never will be."

"Who says I want her?"

Holstoke raised a brow. "Who says I wanted Eugenia before we wed?"

Grinning, Jonas rubbed his jaw with his knuckles. "Anyone with eyes, man."

"Precisely."

Jonas's grin faded. "Put away your dueling pistols, Holstoke. I am not here for her. I'm here to do a job. That's the beginning and the end of it."

"She has little experience with a man like you," the earl

continued as though Jonas hadn't spoken. "What seduces some women frightens others. If you give a damn for her, I suggest you keep your distance."

Shock prickled his nape. "Frightened. Of *me?*" He shook his head. "That is pure shite. She knows I would bloody well die for her." He hadn't meant to say it aloud—and certainly not to Hannah's overprotective brother.

"Indeed. You almost did. We are all grateful for—"

"There's no need to lie, man. I know what you're after."

"Do you?"

"Aye." He invoked Southwark and Norwich and Dorchester to hammer his point. "Somebody tha' don't 'ave to borrow 'is coat for a foine par'ee such as this. Ain't that so, m'lord?" This time, his grin accompanied a taunting bow. "Nevah say Oi ain't quick." He tapped his temple. "Me 'ead's fick, but me eyes see righ' enough."

Holstoke tilted his head at an analytical angle. "Then, you'll no doubt see the wisdom of remaining out of sight and letting her find a husband better able to give her what she needs."

Against his will, he felt his own mocking mouth curl into a snarl. "Husband?"

"That is why she's here." Holstoke said the words calmly, as though he hadn't just swung a hammer at Jonas's knees.

Once he caught his breath, Jonas asked softly, "And what is it she needs?" He laughed, but there was no humor in it. "Let me guess. Something to do with pockets and the contents therein."

Holstoke frowned and seemed about to reply, but Jonas was done.

Done with the conversation.

Done with bloody aristocrats.

Done with Snow Queens who wanted a husband—any husband.

Except Jonas Bartholomew Hawthorn.

As much as he wanted to be done with her, however, his

body had other ideas. Late that night, it wanted to remember.

He'd spent the afternoon chasing details about the missing trunk and searching the castle and grounds. After his rushed ride from London to Northumberland and the long day of fruitless hunting, he should have fallen asleep easily. He didn't.

Instead, he lay in the dark upon an oversized bed that didn't creak, surrounded by brown velvet and blue silk. A cool breeze blew through the open window, caressing his skin with the scent of sea and summer.

His eyes felt dry, but they wouldn't close. They wanted moonlight. They wanted to see her.

With a curse, he sat up on the edge of the bed and ran a hand down his face. He'd walked away from her before. It had hurt. Badly. But he'd done it. No reason he couldn't do it again.

But the thought of how they'd parted sent memories surging.

The first glimpse of her, composed and solemn in the light of her brother's London drawing room, had caught him off guard. She'd worn a gauzy pink gown. Daylight from the windows had shone through its layers, outlining slender hips and a small, round bosom.

He'd found her beautiful in silhouette. Then, he'd met her eyes—extraordinary, icy green. And it had been all he could do not to stare. She'd been pure propriety, chin high, gaze cool and opaque. But a blush had touched those pale cheeks. Rosebud lips had parted on the faintest sigh. Thick, black lashes had fluttered.

He'd been driven closer, wanting to find something to weaken his sudden fascination. Her coldness should have done it.

It occurs to me I've indulged you quite enough by granting a man of your sort an audience in the first place, Mr. Hawthorn.

God, he'd wanted to kiss her. He'd had a job to do, a murderer to catch. But he'd wanted to follow that blush where it led. Melt coldness into heat.

He'd never reacted to a woman that way. Most succumbed

easily. Most fell for his grin, gave him too much too quickly. He'd always rewarded their generosity with pleasure, but that was all it had ever been—passing pleasure. He didn't bother with innocents, let alone haughty, remote innocents from aristocratic bloodlines.

She was different. More. From the beginning, he'd seen it— the crinkle of concern when he'd mentioned the two murdered women. The reaction to his nearness, as though he both flustered and tempted her.

Now, he rubbed his eyes and forced himself to remember the rest. He'd gone back to Holstoke House several times. At every turn, he'd questioned himself, cursed his damned fascination. The pretext had been his investigation into the poisonings, of course. But he'd gone there for her.

To hear her say, "Good day, Mr. Hawthorn," in that cool, soft voice.

To watch pink bloom in those cheeks while ice-green eyes flitted to his mouth and over his chest.

To listen to her amusingly haughty insults.

When did you say Lord Holstoke would return?

I did not.

Mmm. I thought you had.

You thought wrong, Mr. Hawthorn. One has the impression it is not the first time.

Her spark had sunk into him like a hook—the contrast of her heated reactions and perfect calm was a mystery he hadn't had the fortitude to resist.

Then, Holstoke had taken her back to the safety of Dorsetshire while Hawthorn had hunted the man poisoning women who surrounded the son of Lydia Brand. His blood had thrummed with hard urgency. He'd been focused as never before. Relentless.

He'd followed the poisoner's tracks into a back street near Covent Garden. Discovered a connection to Hannah that suggested she was the poisoner's next target. Everything inside him had roared with the need to find her. Protect her.

Then, he'd been blindsided by two arrows, one through the shoulder and the other through his thigh. Drayton had found him. Taken him to Dunston's house, where a surgeon had removed the arrows and stitched his wounds.

But something inside him would not let him stop. He'd ridden to Dorsetshire with Dunston and Drayton. He'd been out of his head by the time they'd reached Primvale Castle.

His body remembered, though. That snowfall voice telling him he was not permitted to die. Ordering her brother to do whatever was necessary to keep him alive.

He remembered pain. Heat. Opening his eyes to see her, midnight and moonlight, sitting at his bedside in the pink light of dawn, in the yellow light of day, in the blue light of night. Sometimes, he'd catch her watching him, odd yearning in her eyes. Other times, he'd thrash awake to feel her almost touching him. She would murmur his name and order him to rest, then read to him while snowfall gentled his fever.

Once, he'd thought she might have kissed him. But he must have dreamt it.

Days later, when his fever had finally broken, he'd found her standing at his window, gazing out upon her brother's gardens, still as a statue. He'd croaked her name. Reached for her. She'd drifted close, her expression shuttered. She hadn't taken his hand.

He'd demanded to know everything—had she been hurt? Had they found the poisoner? Then, he'd asked his final question—why had she stayed with him?

Her only answer had been silence. But he'd known. Pity. The obligation one felt for a crazed man who'd risked his life for a woman he scarcely knew.

She'd left the room. Left him alone with his conclusions.

After the poisoner had captured her, Jonas had been too bloody weak to help, though he'd managed to drag his arse from the bed and organize a search. Ultimately, Holstoke,

Dunston, and Drayton had killed the blackguard and saved both Hannah and Eugenia.

In the following days, she'd frozen harder, her indifference a seamless mirror. At breakfast, she'd scarcely looked in his direction. When the time had come for him to leave, she'd fled to her bedchamber to avoid even the courtesy of a proper farewell.

He'd felt like a dog cast out into the street. But the message had been as clear then as it was today—she wasn't meant for him. Hannah Gray would marry someone with better blood, better manners, a better coat.

She'd marry a man with wealth and land and servants. Not a soldier-turned-Bow-Street-man with nothing to offer but his wits and his body.

Sitting on the guest bed in a grand castle in Northumberland, Jonas linked his fingers behind his nape, hung his head, and repeated what he already knew. *I must forget her, damn it. Forget her, forget her, forget her.*

It rarely worked, and it didn't now. His body demanded the memories. Creamy, blushing skin. Pale, curious eyes. Rosebud lips he wanted to kiss.

With a foul curse, he gave in. Shoved to his feet. Found his coat and the hinged box he kept in the lowest pocket.

He lit a candle. Stood naked and hard and hopeless as he opened the box decorated with the moon and stars.

Then, he pulled out the sketches drawn by a desperate man. Exquisite. Untouchable. Pristine. He let himself imagine her cool hands upon his face, her soft lips upon his mouth. He permitted himself one last moment of delusion. Then, with a shaking hand, he lowered the paper to the candle's flame. Watched it catch. Watched it burn.

And threw an idiot's dreams into the fireplace, where they could end the way they'd always been meant to—in ashes.

Chapter Five

*"Do not feed me gruel and expect me to take it for ambrosia.
I am neither sufficiently famished nor sufficiently foolish
for such inadequacies."*

—LADY DOROTHEA PENWORTH to Malcolm Charles Bainbridge, Earl
Bainbridge, in a letter responding to said gentleman's faint praise.

HANNAH LET THE CONVERSATION IN LADY WALLINGHAM'S
drawing room swirl around her, a light breeze of feminine
sound. Meanwhile, she pondered the flavor of unearned
victory. It tasted like blancmange.

"Mr. Winstead seems remarkably ... sensible," proclaimed
Maureen. "I never knew steeping the same tea leaves four
times could trim one's expenses so markedly."

Meredith Huxley, the warm, round Countess of Berne, huffed a protest. "After the second steeping, can it rightly be called 'tea'?"

"No," answered Lady Wallingham tartly. "Nor can the man suggesting it rightly be called an Englishman."

"I must say, I preferred Mr. Brown," commented Sarah Lacey, resting a hand upon her swollen belly. "He appeared most taken with Miss Gray."

Annabelle Conrad, the eldest of five Huxley daughters, chuckled. "How could you tell? He spoke not a word—not even when he backed into the urn."

"Perhaps he is clumsy," offered Jane, the Duchess of Blackmore and the second-oldest Huxley daughter. She nudged her spectacles and sipped her coffee. "One should make allowances. We are not all born graceful, you know."

The fiery-haired, freckled Charlotte Chatham, Marchioness of Rutherford, raised a finger. "As one who was not, I can confirm Mr. Brown is, indeed, smitten and not merely a habitual toppler."

The exquisite, raven-haired Viola Kilbrenner, Countess of Tannenbrook, giggled. "Oh, Charlotte. Now, you simply must tell us how you know." Seated between the exceptionally tall Lady Rutherford and the somewhat tall Augusta Kilbrenner, Viola resembled a tiny, sparkling fairy guarded by two red-haired Valkyries.

Not that she needed protecting—Viola's husband, Lord Tannenbrook, was the same size as his mountainous cousin, Sebastian Reaver. Whose real name was Elijah Kilbrenner and whose wife was Augusta. Which made Viola and Augusta cousins-in-law.

Didn't it? Keeping everyone straight had become a chore. All she knew was that remembering names and titles was part of appearing normal. So, over the past four days since the garden luncheon, she'd resorted to tying small labels around chess pieces—white for ladies, black for gentlemen—to memorize names and connections.

She'd quickly run out of pieces.

"We bumblers are rarely surprised by our mishaps," Charlotte replied. "Chagrined, perhaps, but not surprised. Mr. Brown was positively dumbstruck."

Augusta, whose regal self-assurance and dark-russet hair Hannah had long envied, glanced over Viola's head at Lady Rutherford. "Charlotte, didn't you say your cousin, Mr. Farrington, plans to visit Chatwick Hall soon?" Chatwick Hall's lands neighbored those of Grimsgate Castle.

"He arrived this morning," Charlotte confirmed before turning to Hannah with a warm smile. "Andrew will inherit my uncle's baronetcy one day, so he shan't remain forever untitled, I'm afraid. But he is the dearest man, Hannah. I suspect you will find him charming when you meet him tomorrow." Briefly, the flame-haired marchioness glanced between Viola and Hannah before arching a wry brow. "I am certain he will find *you* enchanting."

Hannah blinked. She didn't understand the reference, but that was nothing new. How to reply? Responses flitted through her mind. The odd silence lengthened, and she knew she must say something. "It—I will be—I should be happy to meet him."

Dash it all, that had not sounded normal. She must try harder. Thus far, she'd done nothing but fail in what Eugenia called the Normalcy Project. Surely her dissatisfaction would ease once she improved her technique.

It was not as though Eugenia had failed *her*. Quite the contrary.

Over the past four days, three gentlemen had been served to Hannah upon a tufted pillow. All three were safe, untitled gentlemen who were well settled, unmarried, and not overly handsome. To arrange such a selection, Eugenia had solicited help from the ladies presently assembled in the drawing room: The dowager Lady Wallingham and Julia, the current Lady

Wallingham; Lady Berne and her five daughters, Annabelle, Jane, Maureen, Eugenia, and Kate; Sarah Lacey and Lord Colin's sister, Victoria, Viscountess Atherbourne; and, of course, Charlotte and Viola and Augusta. Most were titled ladies with vast connections. Some knew the details about Hannah's past, while others knew only generalities. All were kind and wanted only to help Hannah find happiness.

Hannah *should* have been happy. She had some of the most powerful women in England working on her behalf—women who had not merely navigated the marriage mart but mastered it.

Unquestionably, she was fortunate.

Undoubtedly, she could choose any of the gentlemen Eugenia had selected and be married before autumn.

Unexpectedly, she did not feel frightened by the prospect. She felt bored. It was the strangest, most confounding thing.

The first of Eugenia's blancmange men, Mr. Winstead, was a half-inch taller and a half-shade whiter than Hannah. His wispy hair might be considered light brown or dark blond, she supposed. To her, it looked like ash. He spoke in hushed tones as though God were listening, and he dared not offend the Almighty's ears with anything louder than a murmur. During their conversations, she'd gathered frugality was his favorite virtue.

"Spices such as mace and cinnamon are best reserved for Christmastide," he'd remarked as they'd stood exchanging pleasantries during the garden luncheon. "If it cannot be grown near one's kitchen door, I daresay, the expense may empty the rest of one's larder in a trice."

His smile was pleasant enough, his eyes brown and kind. Eugenia had assured her he owned a prosperous Yorkshire estate near Blackmore Hall, where Jane lived. Additionally, while he was not himself a Quaker, he employed many believers and had grown sympathetic to their philosophies. In short, the man would sooner bury himself in cinnamon than raise a hand to anyone.

Safe, prosperous, kind—Mr. Winstead should have been perfect.

Then, she'd met Mr. Brown, a physician from Nottinghamshire. Taller than Mr. Winstead by three inches, Mr. Brown suited his name. His hair, his eyes, his coat, and his trousers were all the same shade of brown—approximately the color of dry clay. She did not know what he sounded like, for he hadn't spoken aloud. Rather, he'd gaped at her with round-eyed wonder and, as Annabelle had noted, promptly stumbled backward and toppled an urn.

Hannah had been bewildered by his behavior. Not frightened. Not startled. Simply puzzled.

Eugenia had suggested he'd been overset by her beauty. Hannah had scoffed. Viola was far more beautiful. Augusta and Charlotte were more striking, with their rich, red hair. Witty, vivacious Kate Huxley was more charming. Clearly, the man was a bit touched.

But the deciding moment in Mr. Brown's disfavor had come when Lady Wallingham warned her against using a double surname in the event they married. Gray-Brown was comically close to Mr. Brown's actual coloring. Once evoked, she hadn't been able to put the image of toppled urns and silly surnames away.

The last of the blancmange men was also the tallest at four inches short of six feet. A mathematics tutor at Cambridge, Mr. Keeble had amassed a sizable fortune through speculation. He had a shy smile, flushed a bit about the cheekbones whenever she spoke, and hid a lovely pair of blue eyes behind thick spectacles.

She quite liked Mr. Keeble. They'd played chess the evening before last. She'd beaten him soundly. After six matches, out of mercy, she'd pled drowsiness and left him to examine the board.

Now, as she sat amongst the women strategizing on her behalf, she could only sigh. None of this was working. She'd tried to be normal, and sometimes she achieved a semblance of it. The blancmange men were all pleasant in their way, and every one of them had appeared to find her attractive. That was something, she supposed.

But she'd tried to imagine each of them gazing at her across the breakfast table. She'd thought about tending them when they were weak with fever, kissing them because she felt a compulsion strong enough to shove her out of her chair. She'd pictured holding their babes, seeing Mr. Keeble's blue eyes or Mr. Winstead's wispy hair or Mr. Brown's gray-brownness in a child she'd helped create.

The visions wouldn't come. Nothing worked. Nothing.

She glanced now at Eugenia, who was unusually quiet, sketching a new hat near the fireplace while the other ladies chatted and laughed. Hannah did not know how to tell her the truth. She barely knew how to tell herself.

"Time to offer dear Hannah our best advice, ladies," announced Lady Berne, giving Hannah a merry wink. "Let us share our secrets in service of a greater cause."

"A man offers a woman two of life's necessities," Lady Wallingham trumpeted. "Three if he has adequate night vision."

Lady Berne coughed. "Dorothea, perhaps you should abstain from the advice portion of our meeting."

The dowager harrumphed. "Rubbish and rot. The girl must know sooner or later, Meredith. Now, listen closely, Miss Gray. Husband management is no minor endeavor to be undertaken by moonstruck lambs. If you are diligent, you will have the first two necessities in short order—offspring and a house of sufficient size to afford you a chamber of your own. The first makes the second all the more essential. As to the third necessity—"

"Dorothea—"

"—I daresay if a man lacks talent or stamina or girth—"

"Oh, dear. Dorothea!"

"—then, pray, do not lie back and accept mediocrity as your lot." The old woman raised her chin. "Some men have natural advantages." She sniffed and glanced at Charlotte, whose mouth quirked in a secretive smile. "Their wives are most fortunate." The dowager's gaze returned to Hannah. "For others, there is only instruction and repetition."

"Gracious me," murmured Sarah.

"Mother," Julia said, casting a dubious look at her mother-in-law. "Are you suggesting a man should be trained like a hound? Surely I have that the wrong way round."

Lady Wallingham arched a white brow and sipped her tea. "I fail to see the affront. A trained hound will heel and lie down wherever suits you. An untrained hound will mistake mauling for affection and clean skirts for an invitation to cause havoc."

Maureen was covering both cheeks. Annabelle was stifling a laugh. Julia blinked. Sarah looked bemused. Lady Berne frowned. Victoria whispered something to her best friend, Jane.

Jane, the plump, bespectacled Duchess of Blackmore, cleared her throat, opened her mouth several times, then said, "She is right."

Shock filled the room. Lady Wallingham was the first to recover. "Of course I am."

All eyes focused on Jane, who had long struggled with shyness. She reddened in what Maureen and Eugenia called the Huxley Flush. As all the Huxley daughters had milky skin and brown hair, the red was noticeable. "I—I only mean that husbands cannot always know what pleases us. It is in our interest to offer ... insight."

Lady Wallingham snorted. "I believe *instruction* is the term you seek."

"Guidance," Viola interjected. "Yes, I think it's true. Men do much better when they know what we want. Otherwise, they are left guessing. And that may end any number of ways, some good and some splendorous."

Warming to the topic, Lady Berne added, "I've found parsnips a most effective deterrent for undesirable behavior."

"And fish," said Victoria. "Quite persuasive."

"Encourage him to set aside time for vigorous exercise," advised Augusta. "Sebastian's mood goes positively black when he stays too long behind his desk."

"Yes," agreed Charlotte. "I, too, find exercise helps immensely. Whatever he prefers—riding or walking or farming. Especially farming."

Maureen sat forward, her golden-brown eyes dancing as she joined in the spirit of the conversation. "Don't forget to spoil him every now and then. You might be surprised at what a bite of his favorite cake or a little praise for his skills can do."

Annabelle, looking warm and wry, patted Maureen's hand, adding, "Quite right." She gave Hannah a smile that spoke of storms weathered and battles both lost and won. "Always remember, dear Hannah, whomever you choose to stand by your side stands upon the same ground as you. Whatever you do to undermine that ground likewise undermines you. Whatever you do to strengthen it likewise strengthens you."

Of all the advice she'd received, much of it useful, some of it amusing, this felt the truest.

Then, Eugenia spoke. "Laugh together," she said, her expression oddly serious. "Even when you feel silly about it. And tell him the truth, dearest. Trust is the soil. Love is the bloom."

Hannah drew a shuddering breath. "What if the truth is a burden he has no wish to bear?"

Eugenia did not smile. She did not offer false hope. Instead, she gave Hannah no less than what she'd asked. "Then he is not strong enough to carry it. You need somebody strong."

Several hours and a great deal of advice later, Hannah wandered through the gardens alone, thinking about chess and blancmange and men who toppled urns. A soft breeze blew through her skirts. It smelled of the sea.

She missed home. At Primvale, everything was known—the gardens, the beaches, fields and pastures. She awakened at seven, had breakfast at eight, went riding at nine. She spent most mornings working with Eugenia on making hats and strategizing ways to improve their millinery shops in Bridport and Weymouth. Luncheon was at two. Her walk was at three. At five, she practiced the pianoforte. At six, she played chess with Phineas. Dinner was at seven. All the gardens were flawlessly maintained, and there was not an inch she hadn't explored. All servants had been chosen particularly for their kindhearted nature, including Claudette, who was often by her side.

Here, at another castle by the sea, albeit on the opposite end of England, most things were unknown. Anything could happen. Humphrey might bolt after a squirrel. Lady Wallingham might insist on discussing male anatomy again. Mr. Keeble might trounce her in their next match—unlikely but possible. Charlotte's cousin Mr. Farrington might charm her silly.

So, why was she ... bored?

She blew out a sigh and followed stepping stones around another hedge. Inside a small, square courtyard were more urns brimming with ivy and topiaries. One of them looked like a fish.

"I expected you would be playing your music."

She spun to find Phineas beneath the trellised arch at the courtyard's entrance. "Is it five already?"

He nodded, wandering closer, hands clasped behind his back in his usual posture. "How is the project going?"

"Eugenia's selections are superb. I could not have asked for better."

He went quiet then drifted to a topiary shaped like a swan. "She has worked tirelessly on your behalf," he murmured, examining the ivy at the swan's feet. "When Eugenia loves you, she will not cease until she has brought about your happiness."

"She is an extraordinary friend."

Again, he fell silent. This was Phineas's thinking pattern—it meant he was trying to untangle something in his mind. "I take it you haven't yet settled on a favorite."

"A favorite?"

"Of the men she invited."

"Oh, the blancmange gentlemen. Not entirely, no."

Phineas turned to face her, his brows drawing together. "Blancmange."

She nodded. "That is what we call them. Because they are mild and ... safe."

His frown deepened. "Blancmange is what nursemaids feed to invalids."

Just then, she realized what lay beneath her discontentment. She hadn't recognized it, for she'd only begun to feel it with regularity since seeing ...

Oh, heavens.

Phineas stepped closer, his hand hovering several inches from her elbow. "Perhaps we should sit."

He took the greatest care with her. He always had.

As one would with an invalid.

Weak and broken and dependent.

Someone who must be surrounded by kindhearted servants and approached with gentle caution. Someone who must be fed the equivalent of half-sweet milk.

Eugenia, by contrast, had insisted she was strong. From the beginning—even when Hannah had resented her bold new sister-in-law's intrusion into her life—Eugenia hadn't minced words. She'd taught Hannah to ride. She'd pushed her to use her business mind, to speak openly and accept the touch of a friend without flinching.

Without thinking.

Without fear.

Eugenia, through sheer determination, had made Hannah normal. At least, normal with her.

They laughed together. They told each other the truth. Always.

Trust is the soil. Love is the bloom.

Everyone treats you like wet paper. You are stronger than anyone I know.

In all the years Hannah and Phineas had played chess together, she'd won a single game against her brother. Her satisfaction had lasted approximately thirty seconds—the length of time it had taken to realize he'd let her win. Everything inside her had deflated, turned sour, gone cold. She'd carefully explained to him why handing her a victory was not kindness but an insult. He'd never repeated the error.

But she remembered the feeling well enough to recognize its likeness now.

She did not want to be an invalid.

She did not want to be fed blancmange.

"Phineas," she breathed. "Take hold of me."

"Pardon?"

"Grasp my shoulders. Or my elbows. Or my hands. But, please, do it quickly. Not carefully, as you usually do."

"Hannah—"

"Please, Phineas. I need you to do this for me."

He came closer, frowning fiercely and obviously confused. But he did as she asked, grasping her shoulders with a light grip.

Fear's slithery chill crawled between his hands and her shoulders, spurring the familiar impulse to pull away. But instead of giving in, she stood still and looked into her brother's eyes. Her eyes. Their father's eyes. Griffin's eyes.

Phineas held her steady as she fought her battle.

"N-now pull me in tight," she said. "No hesitation."

He drew her into his chest and closed his arms around her back.

For a moment, she couldn't breathe. Her fingers clawed against her brother's waist.

"Hannah, please. You're shaking. Let me release you."

"No," she said against his coat. "No. I am all right."

He laid a kiss on the top of her head. "God, little one. I cannot bear for you to be afraid."

"Tighter," she rasped, her heart knocking. "Please."

His arms squeezed her gently. At first, she felt the same suffocation she'd grown accustomed to. Her head spun and threatened to detach. But she forced her eyes open and saw Phineas's emerald cravat pin.

He wore it often, as Eugenia found it pleasing. She breathed deep and recognized the faint aroma of lemon balm. She focused upon the weight of Phineas's arms across her back, the strength he always—*always*—tempered for her.

And love flooded all her usual impulses. The fear. The suffocation. The sensation of breaking apart and floating away.

Love for her brother, who had given her everything.

She breathed. And breathed. And let love dilute the remnants of pain.

Then, she held her brother in return, tighter than she'd ever done. "Thank you, Phineas," she whispered. "This is how it shall be from now on. Do not be cautious with me. You understand, don't you?"

He kissed the top of her head again. "Are you certain?"

She nodded against him. Held tighter. "I am strong, Phineas."

"I know you are, little one."

She felt him sigh. Heard the solid thud of his heart—a stout reassurance.

"You've always been strong," he murmured. "Though I wish down to my very bones you didn't have to be."

Chapter Six

"Hounds fetch what is lost and eat what is discarded.
Which is where their usefulness ends."

—LADY DOROTHEA PENWORTH to Malcolm Charles Bainbridge,
Earl Bainbridge, in a letter of disagreement over the value
of a loyal hound.

JONAS HAD RIDDEN TO THE MIDDLE OF BLOODY NOWHERE FOR no bloody thing. It was the second time that day. This particular nowhere had more trees than the last and a pleasant vista of the surrounding farmland, but it was still merely an outcrop of sandstone jutting out of rolling Northumberland hillside. Both nowheres seemed like oddities left behind after a flood had worn away the rest of the land. Both were caves.

Both shared the same legends about St. Cuthbert, a hermit monk from Lindisfarne.

Both were empty of everything but wind.

Behind him, coming up the hill, he heard Henry Thorpe, the Earl of Dunston, chatting amiably with his companion. "I cannot imagine what the rush might be, Humphrey." Dunston paused, pretending to listen to the hound. "Yes, it could be the need to piss, but one would suppose that could be done anywhere. Behind a tree, onto a rock, into the grass. Well, you understand perfectly, don't you? It's not as though a cave is the only proper receptacle." More pretense of listening. "Ah, yes. Perhaps he did eat too much fruit at breakfast. Fruit, heat, and exertion. That is quite the formula for urgent digestive complaints, I must say."

Jonas arched a brow. "Nobody asked you to come along," he called down to the climbing earl. "If you cannot keep up—"

"Never had trouble on that score, old chap." Dunston grinned as he reached the mouth of the cave. "A hound does require water and rest upon occasion, however. Horses too, oddly enough."

Humphrey, huffing merrily while his long ears swung to and fro, wandered to the rear of the cave. The crevice wasn't particularly large, so Jonas let the dog sniff.

Hands on hips, he glanced around. Nothing but stone and moss and ferns. "Fool's errand, this. Another bloody day wasted."

"Well, now, let's not be hasty. We've had a pleasant ride. Explored a bit of ecclesiastical mythmaking."

Jonas glowered at Dunston, whose mood never seemed to deteriorate, regardless of the sapping heat or pointless wandering.

"Incidentally, how does one become a saint simply by having one's dead body carted by one's fellows all over the countryside? I must look into this. One never knows when such a measure might prove useful."

The dapper lord had every appearance of a dandy. Reddish-brown hair was trimmed neatly, his blue coat flawlessly tailored to lean shoulders and a trim torso. His waistcoat was a brilliant shade of emerald—Dunston preferred a bit of flamboyance in that quarter. Everyone thought him both affable and fashionable.

Jonas had recognized a kindred creature from the first. Affability was an effective disguise for deadliness. So were grinning charm and disarming gestures and a lazy stride.

He should know.

"The maid did say it was St. Cuthbert's Cave, did she not?" Jonas hadn't slept in two days, so the question was a real one. Perhaps he'd imagined it.

"That is what she said. Though, to be honest, she struck me as—well, let's put it kindly. I have used sharper instruments to scoop marmalade."

Jonas rubbed the back of his neck. It was soaked with sweat.

"You should dispense with the coat."

"I need the pockets."

Dunston sighed. "If you're carrying an arsenal in there, Hawthorn, I assure you, you're going about this whole clandestine crime hunter business wrong."

Jonas moved to the entrance and leaned against the rock. An insect scrambled over the back of his hand. He didn't care.

"The trick," Dunston continued, "is to focus upon a singular weapon. Daggers are both lethal and conveniently sized, particularly useful when wielded in tandem." He withdrew twin daggers from inside his well-fitted coat. "You see? No need to perish inside a sweltering hell of misshapen black wool."

"Why would she claim something so specific as St. Cuthbert's Cave?"

"Why do women do anything? They are mercurial."

Jonas had spent the past four days interviewing Grimsgate's vast array of servants—Nash, the army of footmen, a half-

Prussian housekeeper who spoke with her teeth clenched, gardeners and scullery maids and stable boys. Everyone. Nobody had answers until a trembling chambermaid had given herself away before he'd even reached for his notebook. She'd begun weeping when he'd inquired about the last place she'd seen the trunk.

The watery, spoon-sharp Miss Allen had developed a habit of sneaking into Lady Wallingham's dressing room to try on her ladyship's slippers. The trunk was routinely stored there, locked and close at hand.

The morning Lady Darnham and Miss Meadows had arrived early for their visit, the staff had been in an uproar. The half-Prussian housekeeper had sent the girl to the village on an urgent mission to obtain oranges. A man had approached her.

"A dark man, 'ee were," she'd exclaimed as though describing an encounter with a ghostly apparition.

He'd frowned. "Dark?"

"Aye. 'Air like yours."

"Brown, then."

"Aye."

"How tall was he?"

"'Ow tall are you?"

"Six feet."

"Aye. That's it."

"And what of his frame? Heavy? Thick? Or lean?"

She'd eyed his shoulders. "Lean, I'd say. But 'ee could lift three trunks like 'er ladyship's all on 'is own, I've no doubt. Appeared quite fine."

"Fine."

"Aye. 'Andsome."

"Miss Allen, are you describing the man who you believe stole Lady Wallingham's belongings?" He'd had to ask, as the girl had not ceased staring since she'd stopped crying.

"Oh, aye."

He'd had his doubts about the maid's reliability, but he'd asked her what the thief had demanded.

"'Ee wanted the trunk."

"No, I understand that's what he wanted. What did he say?"

She'd lowered her voice to a mockery of maleness. "'I know what you been doin', Miss Allen. And you'd best 'elp me or I'll tell yer employer.' Only 'ee mighta called me Elly."

"Why would he call you that?"

"'Tis my name."

He'd blinked, gathering his patience. "Yes, but why would he know your Christian name?"

She'd shrugged. Then, her eyes had widened. "D'you suppose 'ee's a gypsy? I met one at the fair in Alnwick once. She claimed she could tell 'oo you were to marry from the shape of your 'and." She'd thrust her palm under his nose before retracting it for her own examination. "She said as my 'usband would be tall and 'andsome. Dark, too."

In the end, he'd managed to coax sufficient details from the girl to set him on his present course. The thief had threatened to expose Elly Allen's surreptitious slipper fittings if she did not provide him entry through a door near the kitchens. He'd described the trunk to the maid then blackmailed her into telling him where it was stored. If everything was as she claimed, the trunk had indeed been the target.

She'd begun weeping again when she confessed to letting the man kiss her. Jonas had found that bewildering, but she'd sobbed that he'd returned on another three occasions to kiss her more, and in his "moments of passion" had told her where he was keeping the trunk—St. Cuthbert's Cave.

Jonas had asked the maid to describe the man while he drew his face.

Now, with his shoulder propped against cool stone in the second empty St. Cuthbert's Cave, he reached into his topmost pocket and withdrew the sketch.

Dunston came over to examine it. "This is her thief? Looks

like you, Wallingham, and Atherbourne defied the laws of all
things holy to spawn offspring."

Jonas rubbed his jaw. Blast. He needed a shave. "Either she's
smitten or she's lying. I haven't determined which." He glanced
behind him to where Humphrey investigated a half-scorched
fern. "The trunk isn't here, that much is certain."

Dunston clapped his shoulder. "Take heart, man. Perhaps
she is mad. A mad maid with wild fantasies about being
ravished by a highwayman." He took the sketch from Jonas's
hand. "Who, coincidentally, looks like you and Wallingham,
only handsomer."

"Bloody hell, Dunston. This is not helpful."

"This is what you get for taking my twelve guineas."

"I need to be done with this task."

"Why the rush?"

"A castle full of nobs gives me hives."

"I think that may be your coat, old chap."

He glared at Dunston then shrugged out of the greatcoat,
draping the heavy wool over his arm. "Happy?"

Dunston's dark-blue gaze turned assessing. He refolded the
sketch and handed it back to Jonas. "Have I ever told you
about my pursuit of Horatio Syder?"

Jonas retrieved his water flask from one of his pockets
before replying, "Syder. I remember the name." He took a
drink of water then wetted a handkerchief and wiped his nape.
"When I first came on at Bow Street, it seemed he was behind
every thieving ring and gaming hell in London."

Leaning back against the wall of the cave, Dunston crossed
his arms and glanced out at the wide, rolling landscape. "He
was behind a great deal more than that."

Indeed, every low creature and poor wretch east of Mayfair
had whispered the name Horatio Syder as one might speak the
name of the devil. Once an obscure solicitor, the man had
amassed a vast empire of illicit businesses—brothels catering to
the wickedest perversions, hells built on cheating and

exploitation. Syder had ruled the city's darkest quarters, bribing officials to remain free of punishment, controlling his empire through fear. Some had called him the Butcher, for he'd been fond of torturing and killing those who defied him inside a Whitechapel slaughterhouse.

"I hadn't realized you helped Drayton take him down," Jonas said. "Makes sense, though. Half of Bow Street had taken payment from Syder. An outsider would have been necessary, I expect."

For years, Dunston had secretly worked with the Home Office to pursue particularly elusive criminals within England. Jonas had assumed Holstoke's mother, a murderess and a traitor, was the earl's primary target. But apparently, he'd been tasked with bringing down the Butcher, as well.

"More accurately, Drayton helped me, but yes." Dunston slanted him a glance. Half his face lay in shadow. The other half was harder than stone. "He was a monster, Hawthorn. Every day that I failed to stop him, innocents suffered. Yet, I could do nothing but follow threads, one by one."

Jonas understood the feeling. Often, petty thieves like Bertie Pickens were his quarries. If their crimes went unpunished, some wealthy nob lost a ring or a pretty bauble. But last summer, when the only thing standing between Hannah Gray and death was his ability to stop a murderer, he'd known what desperation truly was.

"How did you do it, in the end?" he asked.

"He prized his businesses above all," Dunston explained. "His wealth protected him. His brutality made finding turncoats within his employ near impossible. A direct attack would only ricochet, and I had other targets to concern myself with."

"Lady Holstoke."

"Indeed, though I didn't know it was her, at the time. I didn't even suspect the Investor might be a woman."

"Investor?"

Dunston gave him a hard stare for long seconds. "That is what we called the figure who initially funded Horatio Syder."

Jonas recoiled. "Bloody hell. They were connected?"

"He started as her solicitor then became her protégé and, eventually, her partner." Again, Dunston went silent, examining Jonas's face as though making a calculation. "They had a falling out. She wanted him to kill a mother and child, you see."

Jonas frowned. "The Butcher balked at killing?"

"Oh, the mother he dispensed with readily enough. But the child, yes. He grew ... fixated upon her. Took her as his ward. Kept her as a hedge against his former benefactress."

A dark chill slithered up his spine. A child in the hands of such a man—the thought was grotesque. "So, you chased Syder to get to the Investor."

Dunston nodded. "Drayton and I went after his businesses piece by piece. We sent a man into one of his worst hells to gather information. That man was later tortured for my name, but he refused to give it. Another of my contacts at the time, a man I'd worked with whilst pursuing the Investor, obtained his release. But he was in a bad way." Dunston's head swiveled to look out at the hillside. "In time, he recovered. Married. Then, Syder took his wife. The blackguard cut her throat whilst this man watched, and the man gutted Syder for it. Understandable, really. I would have done worse." Dunston released a sigh then rolled his head back in Jonas's direction. "Remember the house in Knightsbridge?"

Jonas frowned and nodded. The previous year, when he'd hunted the villain responsible for a string of murders centered on Holstoke, a final victim had turned up in an empty Knightsbridge townhouse. She'd been a Covent Garden prostitute known as Midnight Mary for her black hair and light eyes. The resemblance had not escaped him.

"That house is where Syder met his end." Dunston's eyes were hard as a steel blade. "A just end, if an inconvenient one."

"Inconvenient?"

"He was killed before I could use him to find the Investor. I was a few minutes late to Knightsbridge, it would seem."

This explained why the prostitute had been placed there. The poisonings, as it turned out, had all been an "offering" in Lady Holstoke's supposed honor. Placing one of the victims in the house where the murderess's former partner had died would have seemed appropriate to the lunatic responsible. He glared now at Dunston. "Might have been useful to know about Syder's connection to the place last year."

"By the time I knew the Knightsbridge murder occurred, you were full of arrows and half out of your mind—"

"That's a load of shite. You should have told me."

Dunston sighed. "Perhaps. My point is it took nearly two years following Syder's death to learn who the Investor was. So, you see, Hawthorn, some investigations simply take longer than others. The threads remain stubbornly hidden and must be coaxed to the surface. Have patience. At least Lady Wallingham's trunk cannot feel pain."

Again, Jonas felt the cold slither. He took another long drink, mulling what Dunston had told him. "What happened to the ward?" he asked.

When he met the other man's eyes, they were no longer hard—they were sad. Dunston took a long time to answer. "She survived. But not without scars."

The water in his belly churned. He wiped his mouth with his wrist.

A low, grumbling whine sounded near the fern. Humphrey snuffled and trotted over to Dunston. In his mouth was something purple.

Dunston pulled it free with a pat on the dog's head. As he turned it over, it caught the light—black spangles and purple velvet.

"Bloody hell," Jonas breathed as he realized what this was. What it meant.

Grinning wide, Dunston extended the fanciful slipper out to the sunlight to get a better look. "You see, Hawthorn? All you need is a bit of patience." He gave Humphrey a pat. "And a boon companion by your side."

Chapter Seven

"I find you tolerable."

—LADY DOROTHEA PENWORTH to Malcolm Charles Bainbridge,
Earl Bainbridge, in a letter expressing newfound affection.

HANNAH LIKED HIM. MORE THAN SHE'D EXPECTED. MORE THAN she wanted to. Andrew Farrington was everything Charlotte Chatham had claimed, only better.

His hair was the precise color of the sand in Primvale Cove after the tide had gone out. His handsomeness was the sort unlikely to form expectations. His eyes danced when he laughed. He was shorter than Charlotte by two inches, which put his chin even with Hannah's forehead.

And the first thing he said to her was, "Has anyone

complained yet about the shortage of peach tarts? That is the only reason to attend one of these picnics, you know. Peach. Tarts."

He'd made her smile. He'd put her at ease. He'd charmed her silly.

Now, she watched him greeting his tall, flame-haired cousin, who promptly knocked his fawn hat from his head with an inattentive gesture. He caught it midair and tossed it end-over-end before putting it back on as though performing a well-practiced trick. Charlotte laughed and kissed his cheek.

Hannah laughed too, surprising herself. Mr. Farrington slanted a dimpled smile her way and gave her a wink.

Goodness, charming was right. His face was wide open. His thoughts lit his eyes bright—even his enchantment with her was plain to see. Why he should find her enchanting remained a mystery, but the interest was there if she wished to pursue it.

She could love him, she decided. She could. Given time and effort, it was possible.

Charlotte's oldest son, Jameson, came over to inform his mama that his papa was searching for her. The boy rolled his extraordinary turquoise eyes. "Margaret ruined her dress *again*. Strawberry jam *again*. Papa has made it worse by trying to clean it. *Again*." Every "again" had the long-suffering tone of a brother who had little desire to play messenger.

As Charlotte left them, Mr. Farrington placed a hand on the boy's shoulder. "How many peach tarts did you hide?"

The boy's gaze took on a cunning gleam. "Well, now, that depends, Uncle. What are you willing to give me for them?"

Mr. Farrington narrowed his eyes then removed his hat with a flourish. "I'll let you wear it for, say, a half-hour."

The boy raised a single brow and folded his arms. He looked so much like Lord Rutherford in that moment—sable-haired, calculating, and sardonic—that it was like seeing an echo come to life. "An hour. For two tarts."

"An hour for four."

"Done." The boy held out his hand, and Mr. Farrington held it above his reach.

"Your mother taught me very early to collect my purchases before delivering payment."

Jameson sighed. "Very well. Stay here."

When he ran off toward the castle, Mr. Farrington chuckled and donned his hat again. "He loves nothing better than a good negotiation. A trait he inherited from both Charlotte and Rutherford, no doubt." The words were full of affection.

Hannah tilted her head and examined the man at her side. "You enjoy children," she observed.

"I do." He smiled. "Probably because I am one, at heart."

That must have been why she felt so comfortable around him. He was full of boyish energy.

"I enjoy them, as well," she said, hoping her conversation sounded normal. "My nephew was born this spring. Griffin. Though he is but an infant, I can already see his intelligence. So much curiosity about the world."

"My younger brothers are twins, and while they share some traits, their personalities are quite different. As boys, you could see Freddie was the more assertive and Edward the more thoughtful of the two." He cast her a sidelong glance. "Do you believe we are born with a certain character, Miss Gray?"

She nodded. "In many respects, yes. Though, the things that happen to us may reshape who we are." She glanced toward the east garden wall that overlooked the sea. "Sometimes drastically."

He went quiet then asked if she played chess.

Minutes later, they stood on a giant chessboard formed of flat, gray flagstones and squares of lawn. The chess pieces were large-scaled, as well, made of painted wood. Her game with Mr. Farrington lasted an hour.

Of course, they were interrupted twice, once by Jameson delivering the peach tarts—of which Mr. Farrington offered her two—and the other by Phineas, who asked if he might observe.

Hannah let the game go on longer than necessary. She could have trounced Mr. Farrington in the first five minutes. But the large-scaled chessboard was in a part of the garden that overlooked the water, and she was enjoying herself immensely.

By the time Mr. Farrington conceded defeat and bid her farewell, she'd decided she simply must have a similar chessboard in her own garden—wherever that might be.

"You could have defeated him seven times before you did." Phineas came to stand beside her while she gazed out at the water. "Is he who you want, little one?"

By all rights, he should have been. Andrew Farrington was not blancmange, to be sure, but his manner was so lighthearted her fear had faded to a mere hum rather than a constant roar. He liked children. He played chess, albeit with more exuberance than foresight.

He hadn't touched her, of course. That was the true test. But as a beginning, their hours together showed promise.

Except that her chest would not stop aching.

"Hannah?"

She blinked faster and focused upon the sea. In the distance, blackening clouds stacked into mountains.

"What is it?"

"No," she whispered. It felt as though the truth were being ripped out of her by the wind. "He is not."

For all his easy charm, Andrew Farrington was not the man she wanted. No, the one she wanted rarely put her at ease. Rather, he challenged her. Fired her senses. Drove her to the very precipice of her control.

Phineas sighed. "Do not tell me—"

"I want ..."

"Bloody hell."

She looked at her brother, whose frown was fierce. "I want

Jonas Hawthorn." It felt good to say it. The pressure inside her chest lightened. Then changed. Then started to glow. She released a breath. And another. Before she knew it, she was smiling and little tingles were climbing her spine to her scalp. They tickled her skin.

Phineas shook his head. "Blast. She told me you would do this. I insisted you were far too sensible."

"Eugenia knew?"

"She's been trying to persuade me to like him. Now I understand why."

Hannah chuckled at Phineas's grudging tone. If Eugenia ever acquired the patience to learn chess, Hannah suspected she'd dominate them both.

"You realize the man hasn't the funds to purchase a decent coat," he said, "let alone provide for a wife and children. He lives like an impoverished miser. God knows what he's doing with all the bounties he collects."

"I have funds. More than enough."

"You shouldn't have to use them."

Her chin went up. "This was no easy decision, you know."

Ignoring her point, he blew out a breath and propped his hands on his hips. "He lives in London. You hate London. He is a Bow Street runner tasked with apprehending thieves and other criminals. That is a dangerous occupation for a man with a family."

"He risked his life to save mine."

"He frightens you. I can see it."

It was true. No man was more dangerous to her heart than Jonas Hawthorn. But no other man had seized her heart as his sole possession, either. No other man had suffered two arrows through his body then ridden two days, bleeding and dying for her.

Yes, he terrified her. With him, she risked more than pain. But they went hand-in-hand, didn't they? The risk and the prize.

"I want the sort of love you share with Eugenia." She swallowed the lump forming in her throat. She must stay strong or Phineas would believe her too frail to survive the ordeal she was about to undertake. Her own doubts were difficult enough. "Your love has immeasurable power, Phineas. It makes you willing to bear anything for her sake. Pain. Fear. Death." She rested her hands upon the ancient stone wall, rough beneath her fingers, and looked out upon the darkening water. "The things I must overcome will require just such power. Sensible is safe, but it is far too weak. I don't need sufficient funds. I need sufficient force."

His hand covered hers. She only flinched a little.

"If he hurts you, I will deliver punishment that will make him wish those arrows had ended his existence."

"But you will not stand in my way?"

Eyes the same as hers focused upon their hands. "No. I won't stop you."

"Will you ..." She swallowed. "Will you help me, Phineas?"

His eyes came up, fiercely lit with the intensity he usually softened for her sake. "I will give you anything you require. Always, little one."

Seeing his love for her unveiled was difficult to bear. But, just as she'd worked at climbing on a horse and holding a riding cane and letting Eugenia hug her, she practiced allowing the resistance to rise then move through her. She pictured it as a membrane that must pass. A membrane of dread—unpleasant, to be sure. But eventually, with time and repetition, it would erode and she'd hardly feel it at all. She must believe that. She must.

With a deep, shuddering breath, she asked her brother for advice. "I—I need to know ... what might ... tempt a man."

Eyes like hers flared with alarm. Phineas reeled back and paced ten feet away before turning. "Good God, Hannah. Perhaps I should have specified I'd give you anything except advice on—"

"I am dreadful at flirtation, Phineas. Eugenia has been teaching me, but—"

"Damn and blast."

"—I require a man's perspective. You are the only one I trust."

He stared at her for several seconds, then looked around and closed all but the last two feet between them. "You won't have to flirt with him," he muttered.

She frowned. Had Eugenia been wrong?

"He already wants you. All you must do is convey to him that you are ... open to his suit."

"I want him to be my husband, not my suitor."

"Perhaps we should fetch Euge—"

"It must happen immediately. Before he returns to London." And before she lost her courage. "I haven't time to experiment."

Phineas pinched the bridge of his nose. "Make him an offer."

"Of?"

"Marriage."

Her mind went blank. Offer marriage? Just like that?

"The man looks at you like you're the first meal he's seen in a decade of famine. Make marriage the price to dine."

"Yes, but surely it cannot be that simple. What of wooing?"

"What of it?"

"Won't he need persuasion?"

"No."

She blew out a breath, thoroughly exasperated. "I don't believe you. I think you are trying to sabotage me."

"Don't be ridic—"

"This is just like the trap you set for my queen two nights ago. I sweep in for the kill, and next thing I know, you are crowing checkmate."

"You must—I did not—devil take it, Hannah. Just trust me."

"Thank you for your advice, Phineas." She sniffed. "I shall ask Eugenia."

He pinched the bridge of his nose again. "That's what I tried to—"

She spun on her heel and went in search of her sister-in-law, who was certain to give better counsel than proposing marriage to Jonas Hawthorn without so much as a fluttering eyelash.

She searched the gardens first but found no sign of Eugenia. She did, however, discover the butler, Mr. Nash, quietly instructing a footman to find the missing peach tarts. Mr. Nash did not know where Eugenia had gone.

Rounding a hedge, she then encountered Benedict Chatham, Lord Rutherford, the source of little Jameson's sable hair and hooded turquoise eyes. He was lifting a squealing boy of perhaps two years onto his shoulders.

Tiny legs kicked the marquess's chest as the boy bounced and demanded, "Ide, Pa. Ide."

She assumed he meant to say, "Ride."

Rutherford grinned at her, demonstrating what Charlotte must have found irresistible in her husband. "Miss Gray. My son tells me his peach tart scheme proved quite lucrative."

She smiled at Jameson's younger brother as the little boy reached for her from his high perch. "Indeed. He persuaded Mr. Farrington to surrender his hat with scarcely a volley of negotiation."

"His mother's influence." Turquoise took on an admiring glow. "Charlotte has a keen understanding of supply and demand."

She asked if he'd seen Eugenia, and he pointed in the direction of the castle, saying he'd seen her with Maureen a short while ago.

Minutes later, she found Maureen inside the gallery—but no Eugenia.

"Lady Wallingham demanded her consultation on a new bonnet," Maureen informed her. "It seems she is torn between three ostrich feathers and five."

Hannah blew out a sigh. Blast.

With a tilt of her head, Maureen asked, "Oh, dear. That sounded melancholy. May I be of help?"

Blinking, Hannah examined her friend. With sweet, soft features and sunlit brown hair, Maureen Thorpe was the prettiest of the Huxley sisters. She might not be as plainspoken as Eugenia, but she'd had several successful seasons before marrying Lord Dunston. She'd even enticed Phineas to offer marriage. "Yes. Perhaps so." Hannah glanced around as two footmen passed carrying a tray of peach tarts. She gestured toward the drawing room, which, fortunately, was empty. She asked her question just as Maureen sank down on the sofa next to her. "How does one induce a man to propose marriage?"

Maureen's mouth rounded. "Induce?"

"Compel. With urgency."

"Oh, my. Have you decided upon a suitor, dearest? It is Mr. Keeble, isn't it? He does have lovely blue eyes."

"It is not Mr. Keeble."

She nibbled her lower lip. "Oh. I fear I must confess, when I called Mr. Winstead sensible, I was attempting to be kind. Reusing tea leaves is an appalling—"

"It is Mr. Hawthorn."

Maureen's hand fluttered to her bodice. "Oh," she breathed. "Oh!"

Hannah waited. And waited. "So, how did you persuade Lord Dunston to marry you?"

"How did I ... oh, yes. Henry and I were very much in love. But he led a dangerous life because of ..." Maureen's eyes saddened. "Well, you know."

Hannah nodded.

"In any event, he'd convinced me that his affections were merely friendship. To keep me safe from ... you know. Then your brother began to take an interest, and I liked him very much. Phineas is such a good man."

"Yes, he is."

"Mmm. But my heart was always Henry's. He was all I wanted. And, in time, he came round to see things the same way."

Hannah sat forward. "What changed his mind?"

"Well, Henry may appear to be a perfect dandy, but he is a bit ... possessive. I suspect it was all the standing about pretending to be my bosom friend whilst other gentlemen expressed an interest—"

"Did you flutter your lashes?"

"Pardon?"

"Your lashes. Did you flutter them?" Hannah demonstrated.

"Oh, dear. No. That looks a bit like an insect flew into your eye."

She slumped. "That's what Eugenia said."

Maureen's expression softened. "Dearest, what is this about?"

"Flirtation is something normal ladies do. I am inept at flirtation. Yet, I must flirt if I am to persuade Mr. Hawthorn to marry me."

Her friend's golden-brown gaze turned wry. "When I last spoke to Mr. Hawthorn, he did not appear blind."

Hannah frowned.

Maureen clarified, "You are beautiful, Hannah. I doubt flirtation will be necessary to gain his interest. Perhaps you should simply speak to the man."

She blew out a gust of frustration. "And say what, precisely?"

"Well, start with, 'Lovely day, Mr. Hawthorn.' Then give him a smile."

"It doesn't work."

"What?"

"My smile."

"You have a lovely smile."

"Not with ... him. I am too anxious. My belly fizzes." Her

hand moved there. Even now, she felt the bubbles starting.

"That is excitement, darling." Maureen whispered the words like a secret. Then, she clicked her tongue. "Here is what you must do. Are you ready?"

Hannah nodded, hoping for proper instruction this time.

"Your first task is to locate Mr. Hawthorn. Your second is to approach him. Bid him good day. Speak of the weather, perhaps. Next, inquire after his health."

"His health."

"Indeed. Or his horse. That works equally well."

"I'm not sure that I—"

"Then, you must suddenly lose control of some element of your apparel."

What in blazes? Had Maureen gone mad?

"Your handkerchief, for example. Or your bonnet. Even a slipper will do. Ask for his assistance. This will put him in proximity. Now, I know this may be difficult for you, but proximity is necessary in matters of this nature."

"I have trouble with normalcy, Maureen. Not basic knowledge."

"Now, the final step is critical. Are you listening?"

Hannah wanted to roll her eyes. But there was a tiny, near-infinitesimal chance that Maureen might say something useful. So, instead, she nodded.

"He must help you reapply whatever article of clothing you have lost. And when he moves near enough to do so, you must look directly into his eyes. Hold his gaze as long as you dare, then let your eyes fall to his lips. His chin works, too. They cannot tell the difference." She waved a hand in a sweeping motion. "The point is to lower your gaze. And that is when you say, 'My dear Mr. Hawthorn, I should be a fortunate lady indeed to have a gentleman so dashing as you in my life.'" Maureen sat back, looking quite impressed with herself. "He will melt faster than butter in a hot pan."

"Did you employ such measures with Dunston?"

"Oh, no. Henry knew I felt as he did almost from the first. We were enchanted with one another. Had certain ... matters been different ..."

"Lady Holstoke. You may say her name."

"Yes. Lady Holstoke."

"So, did you apply this stratagem to Phineas, then? Or other gentlemen?"

Maureen shook her head. "I read about it in a periodical some years ago. I may have missed a step here or there. But the concept sounded quite effective."

Drat and blast and devil take her best hat. Was there nobody at this house party who might teach her to flirt properly?

"Ah, there you are, pet." Dunston strode through the drawing room door, looking wind-tossed and handsome in a blue coat and emerald waistcoat. He grinned a greeting to Hannah but moved directly to his wife to steal a kiss. "I have been looking for you."

"Mmm. I thought you'd return much later. Did you discover anything useful?"

Dunston chuckled. "Only that Hawthorn is surly as the devil when he's a trifle overheated. I'm tempted to send him to my tailor for a new coat. But he already has my twelve—"

"You were with Mr. Hawthorn?" Hannah interrupted.

He raised a brow. "Yes, since daybreak. Why do you ask?"

"Where is he now?"

Dunston looked to Maureen, who nodded as though giving permission. "He was headed to the village. The inn, I think."

She stood and made for the doors, her belly tingling and bubbling. Her breath came faster, and she wondered if she wasn't a bit mad.

Of course she was. But if she did not go to him now, she greatly feared that she would lose her nerve.

"Hannah," Maureen called softly.

Hannah turned.

Maureen clung to her husband's hand, and he appeared to give her a reassuring squeeze. "Good luck, dearest."

Though he smiled, Dunston's eyes flashed with a hard glint. "If he troubles you, remind him that I am much more proficient with knives than archery."

Hannah returned his smile with one of thanks. From the moment he'd discovered her existence, long before he knew her name, Dunston had fought to save her from harm. But this battle—her hardest battle—was one she must fight alone.

Chapter Eight

"An incidental resemblance does not imply kinship.
One might as well decide sheep give birth to clouds.
Or Lord Muggeridge fathers sheep."

—LADY DOROTHEA PENWORTH to Malcolm Charles Bainbridge,
Earl Bainbridge, in a letter expressing doubt about the parentage
of a handsome Thoroughbred.

"LOOKS A MITE LIKE YOU, EH?" THE GRIZZLED OLD INNKEEPER
scratched his head and squinted at the sketch in Jonas's hand.
"No. Haven't seen such a man hereabouts."

"It would have been several weeks ago. He might have had
a trunk with him. Black with brown trimmings."

The innkeeper shook his head. "Regret to say I cannot help

ye. Pr'aps me barmaid will remember somethin' different." He nodded toward a redheaded woman with round hips and a ready grin placing bowls of stew before two large men.

Jonas ran a hand over his neck then tucked the sketch away. "She doesn't. I've already asked her."

"Ah, well. If she don't recall 'im, then he weren't here."

Nodding, Jonas thanked the man and went back to the table where his tankard sat, half-empty. He drained it and picked up his hat.

What a devil of a day. After finding Lady Wallingham's stray slipper in St. Cuthbert's Cave, he and Dunston had ridden back to Grimsgate, only to discover that Elly Allen had disappeared. No one knew where the maid had gone—not the half-Prussian housekeeper, not the disgruntled Nash, not any of the other maids.

Further, no one recognized Jonas's sketch of the man she had described as the thief. Probably because he was a figment of her imagination. But, then, why had the slipper been where she'd claimed the trunk was hidden?

Bloody useless, all of it. And, after two nights fighting lust-fueled dreams about midnight hair and moonlight eyes, the exhaustion wasn't helping.

He turned toward the inn's door.

And froze.

Hardened.

His hand clenched the back of a chair.

God, was he imagining her? He blinked. No. She was there. Wearing an evening gown of layered red silk with tiny sleeves and no gloves. Standing in a humble country inn when she should be inside the castle walls, particularly as the sun neared setting.

Ice-green slowly swept the dim interior, catching on the barmaid before finding him. For a moment, he wished he'd taken time to change his clothes, perhaps shave and wash after the long day of riding to the middle of nowhere.

Her eyes flitted between him and the barmaid. Then, that sweet, stubborn chin elevated, and she moved toward him. Graceful. Every step, every breath this woman took was graceful.

He clenched his teeth. Gripped the chair until the grain of the wood impressed his palm.

She came to stand before him, her expression smoother than glass, cooler than the moon. Her scent was roses and the threat of rain. She said nothing, simply examining him as her brother might examine a leaf. Her breathing was a bit fast, but he suspected that was due to her walk into the village.

With effort, he loosened his grip on the chair, folded his coat over his arm, and donned his hat. Then, he tugged the brim and pasted on a grin. "Miss Gray." More effort, and he ordered his legs to move. They carried him past her and out the inn's door.

What was she doing there? It was no fit place for—

Bugger all, he needed to stop wondering. She was not his and never would be. Her whereabouts were none of his damned business.

"Mr. Hawthorn."

The soft call nearly stopped him. But he forced himself to keep going. Across the inn's yard. Down the rutted lane. Out of the tiny village. Past fields filled with ripening grain and wildflowers.

By the time she caught up with him, wind was moaning off the water and clouds had darkened the sky to the color of plums.

"M—Mr. Hawthorn!"

A drop splashed on his hand, cool and ominous. Without stopping or glancing her direction, he warned, "Best return to the castle, Miss Gray. Storm is coming. Shame for that gown to be ruined."

"I must speak with you."

He kept his eyes forward, his strides long. "Then, speak."

She stopped. He kept going.

A moment later, something soft hit his hat, knocking the thing off his head. He halted. Turned. Looked at her, standing in the middle of the road, cheeks pink, soft breasts heaving on rough breaths. Then, he glanced at the ground near his boots.

A slipper. Silver satin with red tassels on the toe, lying in a dusty rut.

"What in bloody hell are you doing?" He glowered at her, then at the shoe she'd obviously thrown at him. When had the haughty Miss Gray begun throwing things at men? For that matter, when had she begun seeking him out for conversation? As he recalled, she preferred to be the one walking away.

"I need to speak with you."

"I got that bit." He bent to pick up her shoe. The sole was leather but thin and light. It was a wonder she hadn't injured herself on a sharp rock. He crossed the distance between them with purposeful strides. With each step, her breathing quickened and her shoulders stiffened. Inches away, he offered her the shoe and a warning. "Throw this at me again, and you'll be walking back to the castle without it."

Her delicate jaw flexed. "You must help me ... reapply it."

He tilted his head and wondered at the strange creature before him. She didn't appear sotted. A bit more flushed than usual, certainly, but not mad or confused. "Must I? Perhaps I missed some rule of etiquette, Miss Gray. I hadn't heard the one about aiding women who accost you with slippers."

"It slipped from my hand."

"It should have been on your foot."

"It required adjusting."

"And happened to fly in my direction."

"Do you intend to help me?"

"No."

A little crinkle appeared between dark brows. "Why not?"

"You struck me with your shoe."

"You refused to stop."

He extended the slipper. "Take it. Put it back on."

Rosebud lips tightened. "You must help. It is the gentlemanly thing to do."

He lowered his head until his eyes were level with hers. "Ah, but then, I am not a gentleman, Miss Gray."

"Nevertheless, I insist."

"Do you, now?"

"It is a lovely day, don't you agree?"

He glanced to the sky, which had begun sending down fat raindrops to plop and splash onto dry dirt. Then he watched her shiver as a seaborne gust chilled her bare arms.

"I have neglected to inquire about your horse," she said.

"My horse."

"Yes."

She must be sotted. True, he saw no signs of it. Her eyes were clear, her balance fine, her words soft and crisp. Her aim certainly could not be faulted. But there was no other explanation. The woman was in her cups.

"The only horse I have is hired, and he's cross with me for pushing him too hard today. As for the weather, we are about to be drenched, Miss Gray." He spoke slowly through gritted teeth, for she'd pushed him to the edge of his patience. "So, for the last bloody time, take your shoe and put it back on."

The flush in her cheeks abruptly faded to white.

Oh, God. Was she going to be sick?

Ready to put distance between himself and the trajectory of any violent upheavals, he reached for her hand, intending to place the slipper back in her possession.

Her reaction was violent, but she didn't cast up her accounts. Rather, she reeled backward before his fingers did more than brush her skin. Her lips went tight, her breathing labored. The woman whose grace was innate stumbled and caught herself.

He frowned. Was this the drink? She'd reacted similarly once before, though he'd been feverish and half-dead at the time. He'd reached for her, the only beautiful thing in a world of pain, and she'd backed away as though he'd repulsed her.

Now, he watched her gather her composure, her hands flattening over her abdomen.

Ah, yes. Rebelling stomach. Chancy balance. Sudden confusion. Her reactions were simply the drink. They must be. Perhaps she'd gone off kilter and stepped on a pebble.

Or perhaps she still felt repulsed by a man she considered beneath her.

His mouth twisted with a new understanding that felt a year old. "Good enough to kneel at your feet. Not good enough to touch you, eh?" He tossed the slipper across the few feet between them, surprised when she caught it easily. "Go back to the castle, princess. You've no business out here where the peasants roam."

He turned and left her there, pale and panting. She'd feel better after she cast up her accounts. He'd inform Holstoke about her condition when he arrived at Grimsgate. She would be fine. It was not as though she could miss the castle. The massive thing loomed over the countryside like a gargoyle.

He'd gone perhaps twenty paces when idiocy began to take hold. The rain was coming in earnest now. She'd be soaked. She'd catch a chill.

He should leave her. She'd found her own way into the village, and she could find her own way back. He'd be a fool to stop now.

But his idiocy slowed him down. It allowed her to catch up.

She spoke, close behind him, out of breath. "P-please, Mr. Hawthorn. Please. Wait."

He stopped, cursing his own stupidity.

She moved in front of him, opaque and exquisite. Her skin glistened with rainwater. Her lips trembled. "I—I have a proposition."

A hundred devilish things burned through his mind, all of which he'd dreamt in scorching detail over the past year.

Ruthlessly, he forced them back. She didn't want him. And he didn't want to be tangled up with a Snow Queen.

How many times did he have to remind himself?

"Let me guess," he said with a half-grin. "You lost a bauble."

"No."

"Hmm. You wish to hire me to—"

"I don't wish to hire you."

He folded his arms, wondering what the tipsy little woman imagined she wanted. "What is it you would have from me, then? Apart from going to my knees, of course."

She swallowed. Her color had returned. "Phineas said I should simply make my offer. Other advice has not proven effective. So I am left with no other choice. You must brace yourself, Mr. Hawthorn."

This made him smile. By God, she was amusing when she was drunk. "Fully braced, Miss Gray."

"I wish for you to ... to become my ..."

He waited. She was panting again. "Your?" he prompted.

"Husband."

Of all the things he'd anticipated—investigator, guard, companion for tea, pony—husband wasn't anywhere near the list. She was clearly intoxicated, so he didn't take her seriously, of course. But his cock did. It turned to steel inside a single heartbeat.

Damned unthinking thing. All it took was the suggestion that she might be his, and he was throbbing for her. He cursed the day he'd walked into Holstoke House. She was nothing but torment. Beauty and torment.

His anger rose, bitter and hot. What was she doing? Was this a lark? She'd never seemed the sort, but nobs did strange things when boredom took hold.

"Did you hear me?"

"Aye, I heard you well enough."

"And what is your answer?"

"Doesn't matter."

Confusion crinkled her brow. "How could it not?"

"I could promise to carry you to Hades on my shoulders, and you wouldn't remember a damned word."

She appeared to take offense. "I have an excellent memory."

"I'm certain you do. When you're sober."

Startled, she took a moment to answer. "I've had nothing more intoxicating than peach tarts, I assure you."

"Right. That's why you're standing in the middle of a rainstorm in your evening gown and tasseled slippers, proposing marriage to a Bow Street runner you ordinarily wouldn't grant so much as a smile."

"I am not in my cups, Mr. Hawthorn. I am asking you to marry me."

"Take my advice, Miss Gray. Avoid propositioning men of my sort." He leaned closer and grinned. "Never know when we might take you at your word and ... well, *take* you."

Her blush deepened to full-bloomed rose. Her eyes dropped to his mouth. Then, her entire body shivered.

His grin faded to a frown. Blast, rain was truly pouring, and she was truly drenched. The woman needed looking after. Where was her overprotective brother, anyway? Against his better judgment, he unfolded his coat and offered it to her.

She took the heavy thing as though she'd never seen wool before. Then, fumbling as the liquor obviously affected her fingers, she struggled to drape it over her shoulders.

"Here," he said impatiently, "let me." He grasped his own lapels and resettled the wool around her until the garment swallowed her whole.

She went utterly still. Her eyes fixed upon his mouth. Or was it his chin? He couldn't tell. All he knew was that she smelled like roses and rain. And she was the most beautiful thing he'd ever seen.

Drunk.

Drowned.

Devastating.

God, he was an idiot.

"I intend to kiss you now, Mr. Hawthorn." The statement barely registered, so matter-of-factly was it spoken.

He chuckled. "Of course you do."

"Hold still, if you please."

"Certainly. Are there two of me?"

"No," she whispered. "There is only one of you, Jonas Bartholomew Hawthorn. Only one." And, with that, she rose up on her toes.

Craned her neck.

And tilted her head to align their mouths.

Even as he felt her breath—peach-scented and sweet—against his lips, he didn't believe it.

No, that took contact. The brush of a rosebud mouth. Trembling.

The sensation of soft woman leaning into his body. Aching.

And the realization that nothing had ever touched him before the untouchable Hannah Gray pressed her lips to his.

She kept her eyes closed.

She didn't smell of wine or brandy or liquor of any sort.

Tiny tremors shuddered through her. Then, soft hands fluttered upward like fledgling butterflies, landing upon his chest. He felt her warmth through his shirt. Sensed his coat slipping from one of her shoulders.

Couldn't move.

Didn't want to.

Only wanted this—moonlight touching his mouth.

"M-Mr. Hawthorn?" Thick, dark lashes remained pressed to her cheeks, almost as if she were afraid to look at him. "Am I doing this properly?"

He would have pushed her away—should have, by all rights—if he'd tasted the drunkenness he'd suspected. If his senses hadn't exploded at the first tingling contact. If she hadn't asked him her question with such uncertainty.

Instead, he answered, "No, love. Allow me."

Then, in one swift motion, he slid his arms around her and took her mouth with his. She jolted against him, but she didn't withdraw. And, dear God, her mouth was soft. Sweet. Her breasts flattened against him. His arms cinched tighter, and she moaned in her throat.

Fire pulsed through his veins, demanding he go deeper. Show her what kissing really was. Obeying the order, he slid his tongue along the seam of her lips, which had gone still beneath his. But she did not withdraw. She didn't push him away. She stayed within his arms.

Then, he felt her move. First, her lips trembled again, responding to the slow glide of his tongue. Opened for him.

God, yes. He took her surrender. Invaded and made her his. Tasted sweet peaches and hot woman. Another moan. Yes. He pulled her tighter against him, feeling her body soften, discovering every flare and curve and exquisite line of the woman who'd been made for his pleasure.

Soon, their mouths were fused and grinding, her moans softer and throatier, her hands clinging and climbing to circle his neck. Slender hips turned demanding, writhing against his thighs and cock as her tongue tentatively stroked his.

Firing hotter than a forge, his arousal was both agony and force. His hands gripped, wanting contact with her skin. He tore away wool. Felt wet layers of silk. Groaned into her mouth. Clutched at her slender thigh to draw it up along his hip. Needed. God, he needed her.

Her mouth and her skin and her hands upon his neck. He needed more.

More and more and more.

Rain soaked them both. He didn't care. Loved the wet of her skin, the panting breaths between them, the surprising strength of her fingers digging into his muscles. She fisted his shirt, forced her lips and her hips tighter against his, tangled his tongue and melted into his skin.

His head spun. He needed air, but he needed her more.

Couldn't relinquish his hold on her or she might turn back into ice.

How could this be his Snow Queen? Demanding his mouth and seeking his cock like a flower hungry for sun. Hard nipples and soft, wet breasts. Heat and heat and heat. God, there was nothing cold about this woman. Her fire burned him alive.

The force between them was too strong. In his dreams, she'd been coolly sensual, challenging him to find the right tricks to please her. In reality, she was shaking with desire, her innocence obvious.

Bloody hell, was he the first man to kiss her? The thought started at the base of his spine, winnowing upward, curling and finally detonating inside his head.

He was. She'd never kissed another man. Only him.

His cock swelled and hardened until he wondered if he might lose control of himself. Lift her wet skirts and take her virginity in the middle of a muddy road.

Virgin. Yes. It shouldn't matter, but it did. Just like her heat mattered. The desperate, needy moans in her throat and the desperate, needy grasp of her fingers along his jaw.

He needed to see her. Needed to see those moonlight eyes blazing for him alone.

It was the only thing with the power to pull him away.

Needed to see those eyes. Lighting for him. Melting for him. Only him.

She kept them closed, her lips swollen and panting with little, hitching gasps of desire. Rain slicked her creamy skin. Wetted her raven hair.

"Open your eyes, love," he said, scarcely recognizing his own voice. "Open for me."

Her lashes fluttered. Her hands slid down his shoulders to his chest. For long moments, she didn't move, didn't lift her eyes. Simply breathed with him. Clung to him.

"Hannah."

She squeezed her eyes closed. Her shoulders shook. Her

mouth moved in an airless repetition. He couldn't make out what she was saying, but it looked like, "Must do this. Must do this."

Finally, those extraordinary eyes opened. Lifted.

And whatever she saw in his face made all the blood drain from hers. Dark centers that had been swollen with arousal shrank to pinpoints. Her body went still as stone, though limp enough that he had to tighten his grip to hold her upright.

She was white. Utterly white. Her lips, her cheeks.

It froze him to the bone.

"Christ, Hannah. What the devil is wrong?"

Her eyes remained open, but she was gone. Just ... gone.

Bloody hell, had she been poisoned? The very thought sent a blaze of panic through him. He didn't think. He stooped to retrieve his coat and wrapped it around her, then bent and lifted her into his arms. She said nothing. Moved not at all. Stared vacantly ahead.

"God Almighty, love." He scarcely knew what he said as he ran with her through the rain. "Stay with me, do you hear?" He kissed her cool cheek. Breathed her rain-on-roses scent. "We'll get you back to the castle. We'll find you a physician. Everything will be all right."

He whispered the reassurance over and over—perhaps for himself more than her. But the urgency inside him was screaming. And his heart was thundering a warning. Something was wrong. He must discover what it was then battle it with everything he had.

Because this woman was his.

His to carry. His to kiss. His to keep. And whatever the cost, he would see her safe.

Chapter Nine

*"Your kiss changes nothing, Bainbridge. You are, however,
welcome to try again. One never knows when practice may
turn the tide toward improvement."*

—LADY DOROTHEA PENWORTH to Malcolm Charles Bainbridge,
Earl Bainbridge, in a letter challenging said gentleman to
develop latent talents.

SIX-AND-A-HALF FEET OF MASS AND MUSCLE STOOD BETWEEN
Jonas and his woman. And if Sebastian Reaver hadn't brought
his equally large cousin, the Earl of Tannenbrook, to help
contain the "bloody mad wolf," Jonas would even now be
holding her.

Or tearing her brother apart to find out what sort of plant

Holstoke had fed her. It was the only explanation, he'd decided. He hadn't smelled liquor upon her breath, but her bizarre behavior had suggested intoxication. Then, she'd collapsed.

His heart was still pounding, though not from the exertion of carrying her up the hill to Grimsgate. He'd shouted for Holstoke the moment Nash had opened the door. The earl had appeared moments later, grim and nearly as pale as Hannah. He'd tried to take her from Jonas's arms, but Jonas had threatened to cut his hands off at the wrists. Confusingly, the earl had given him a look of sympathy before nodding and leading him upstairs to her bedchamber. Holstoke had sent Nash to fetch his wife, and while Jonas sat on the bed with Hannah in his arms, the earl had quietly asked what happened.

Jonas had explained as briefly as possible, sparing the more intimate details, and demanded to know what Holstoke had given her.

"Nothing," the earl had insisted, his brow furrowing. "She resists taking anything that might be considered an intoxicant. Strong drink. Laudanum. I had to coax her to try valerian tea, despite the severity of her discomfort."

Jonas had recalled seeing evidence of her monthly pain the first time they met. It had gnawed at him in the most peculiar way. He remembered demanding she explain what was wrong, feeling a bewildering concern for a woman he didn't know. He should have let it alone—she'd been embarrassed when she'd realized he suspected the cause of her discomfort. But from the beginning, he'd been unable to distance himself from her. Unable to think of her as faceless and nameless, the way he did with most people.

There was the problem. Nobody else compared. Her beauty. Her grace. The stillness and the niggling sense that entire worlds existed beneath her pristine surface. She'd intrigued him from the first and, despite his best efforts, his preoccupation hadn't abated.

Which was why it had taken two giants—Reaver and

Tannenbrook—to wrestle him away from her and out into the corridor.

Now, they stood shoulder to shoulder, one black-haired and the other dark blond, both rough-hewn and outsized and wearing matching sympathetic expressions. If hitting them hadn't been a sure path to unconsciousness, he'd be tempted to try it.

Through the bedchamber door, he heard Lady Holstoke arguing with her husband. "This is her decision, Phineas. She understands the risks, and they are hers to take."

"She is not ready. I told you—"

"If we continue treating her as fragile, she will never heal."

Alarm pealed down Jonas's spine. God Almighty, she *was* ill. She'd sworn she wasn't, but this could only mean—

An enormous hand landed hard in the center of his chest. "Calm yourself, Hawthorn," Reaver ordered.

Jonas hadn't realized he'd charged the door again. This was driving him mad. He needed to see her. He wanted answers. "Let me through," he growled.

Tannenbrook shook his head. "We ken you're out of your head, man. But we cannot let ye pass."

Reaver nodded his agreement. "Trust Holstoke. He's been caring for his sister a long time. He'll let no harm come to her."

A small, quiet maid appeared in the corridor carrying a stack of linens. He recognized her as Hannah's lady's maid. She bobbed a curtsy and handed him a towel. "For you, sir." Her accent was faintly French.

He took the towel, realizing he was still soaked from the rain. He'd left his hat on the road, his coat around Hannah. The two giants parted to allow the maid to slip into the room. He strained to see through the opening then cursed when the door closed.

"If you don't let me in, I'm going to hurt you," he warned the giants. "I don't want to. But I will."

"Dry off," Reaver advised. "Calm down."

Just as Jonas planned his attack on Reaver's knee and Tannenbrook's throat, the door opened. It was the maid.

"Mr. Hawthorn? Miss Gray would like to speak with you."

The giants parted.

Jonas swallowed. God, his heart was going to beat him to death. He nodded and ran the towel over his face. Then, he followed the little maid into the chamber.

Hannah sat in a chair staring out an open window. She was still wrapped in his coat. Her hands clutched the wool as though someone might try to steal the thing.

"Jonas," murmured Lady Holstoke, drawing his attention by tugging his sleeve. Brown eyes that normally danced were solemn as she gazed up at him. "Gently, hmm?"

He didn't know what that meant. Gently? What the devil was wrong with Hannah?

"She has recovered," the petite countess answered before he could ask. "She will explain." She glanced at her husband, who did not seem pleased. "We will leave you two alone, now." Her tone was firm, as though finishing an argument. She then shooed the maid out, grasped her husband's hand, and tugged him from the room. The door closed softly.

Barely daring to breathe, he drifted toward her. "Hannah." His voice was coarse gravel. "What happened?"

That moonlight gaze fell from the window to her hands. "I wish I could tell you."

"Try. I need to know what's wrong."

For a long while, she didn't speak.

He wandered closer, careful not to startle her. "Did I cause this?"

"No. You are not the cause."

"Are you ill?"

Her lips pressed together. "In a ... manner of speaking. But I am attempting to get better."

He moved closer, unable to bear the distance. Then, he crouched at her knees. Breathed against the need to demand answers. Feeling his way, he decided to use one of his old tricks—distraction. "Do you like my coat, love?"

Her fingers tightened, and a little smile curled the corners of rosebud lips. "Yes. It is warm and smells like you."

He chuckled. "It should. I wear it often. Probably more than is sensible, given the heat."

"It has a great many pockets," she observed. "I can see why you would find that useful."

He let silence fill the space between them while he soaked in every detail of her—the damp, black hair, now plaited over one shoulder. The soft, creamy skin of her throat and the soft, petal pink of her lips. Her color had returned, though she still trembled.

"I am sorry I frightened you, Jonas," she whispered to his coat. "That was not my intention."

A surge of remembered panic nearly knocked him on his backside. He'd never felt that. Not even during battle. "I shouldn't have kissed you. I lost my head ..." He blew out a breath and ran a hand through his damp hair. "You'd obviously taken some kind of herb or—"

"No."

"—poison to be talking such nonsense, to kiss me like you did—"

"I was not intoxicated in the slightest." Her eyes, downcast since he'd entered the room, lifted to his shoulders. "I meant every word."

Had she but breathed upon him, he'd have fallen backward. How could it be true? She'd bloody well asked about his horse then proposed marriage. "Perhaps you're still a bit—"

Suddenly, she grasped his hand where it propped on his knee. Her fingers were cool and slender. They gripped him with surprising strength. "I am perfectly lucid. Phineas would not have left me alone with you otherwise."

True enough. Her brother's pattern was too protective. He stroked her fingers with his thumb and frowned. "But that would mean you intended to—"

"Yes."

"That makes no sense."

"Do you want me?"

God, she knocked the air from his chest. He couldn't inhale, let alone answer.

Her hand squeezed his until her knuckles went white. "Do you?"

"Bloody hell," he breathed, his voice worn to a thread. "Yes. I want you."

She shuddered, her shoulders heaving. Trembling. Then, she raised those extraordinary eyes to his. "I shall be yours," she said, locking his heart in a vise. "But I have c-conditions."

In his head, he wondered what her demands might be, of course. But no other part of him gave a damn. She could ask him to ride naked through a beehive covered in jam and chicken feathers, and he'd agree to it, fool that he was. Still, he would hear her out. "What are they?" he asked.

She swallowed, her eyes revealing nervousness. Turmoil. But also courage. "You must marry me. Soon. Straight away, in fact."

He examined her closely, trying to decide what the rush was about. "Now?" He gave her a grin. "It's already full dark."

"Tomorrow would be fine."

"Tomorrow."

"Yes." That proud little chin rose. "I wish to be your wife. Very, very soon."

He rubbed his jaw and tried to persuade his cock to calm the hell down. "Understood. What else?"

"I should like for there to be rules when we ... when we lie ... together."

"What sort of rules?"

"I shall explain after the wedding."

"Beg your pardon?"

"You heard me."

"There are to be rules governing how I make love to you, but I'm not to know until after the wedding."

"You have it."

"Afraid not, love. Give me one. I deserve that much."

Her breathing quickened. A small flush appeared in her cheeks. "Very well. Whilst I have no objection to your touch, I would prefer to remain clothed during our ... whilst we are ... engaged in ... intimacies."

He frowned at the odd request. "Why?"

She blew out a breath, her shoulders slumping. "This is the reason I wanted to wait to tell you. Now, you'll think me strange, and you won't wish to marry me."

If she suspected how eager he was to pick her up, put her on the back of his hired horse, and ride the few miles to Scotland, those soft cheeks of hers would be scarlet rather than pink. "It is an odd request, you must admit. But so long as I may touch you as I please, I suppose it is not too much to ask."

Her eyes fell to where their hands clasped and twined. "I loved kissing you, Jonas," she whispered. "Much more than I anticipated."

Tomorrow couldn't come soon enough, by God. But since she was confessing her desires, he asked for more. "Tell me another condition."

At first, he didn't think she would acquiesce. Her chin turned stubborn, those pale eyes narrowing. Then, she wetted her lips and nodded. "I want children. You must provide them."

"Well, children are often a consequence of—"

"No. Not a consequence. You must apply yourself fully to the task." She was frowning in a way that grasped his ballocks and twisted them up tight—as though she suspected he might be a laggard in his husbandly duty and was quite vexed about it.

He suppressed his grin with all his might. In the end, he had to cover a cough to disguise it. "You are demanding my—"

"Your seed. Yes, I am."

Whatever blood might have been freely roaming in his body rushed to deliver her order. His head swam. Another sleepless night loomed as a near certainty.

"I have studied this in some detail," she continued. "Regularity is the key. Multiple attempts per week would be ideal, though I shall certainly make allowances for any difficulties that arise. Not all males share similar ... drives."

He covered another, deeper cough and cleared his throat. "Mmm. And, if greater frequency is required? Conceiving a babe can be an uncertain business, you know. Might take months. Are you willing to accommodate my 'drives'? So long as I'm applying myself, of course."

"Of course."

"Of course," he agreed, his hand settling over his mouth as though deep in thought. "And I may touch you however I please."

"Yes. So long as I am clothed."

"Well, some parts of you cannot be clothed. For conceiving purposes."

She clicked her tongue. "I am hardly ignorant, Jonas."

"No, of course not." He pretended to think. "Would *I* need to be clothed?"

Her eyes flared wide. She blinked and glanced at his chest, her cheeks firing hotter. "I–I think I should prefer you weren't, actually." Her desire appeared to confuse her. "You are very handsome."

"I'm delighted you think so, love."

"I mean your whole body, not merely your face."

He nodded. "It pleases me that I might please you."

"Oh, you do. Very much."

"Good. Now, are there any other conditions I should know about?" When she hesitated, he cajoled, "Come now, I haven't balked at anything so far."

Warming to her subject, she nodded. "You must permit me to purchase a proper home for our family."

His gut hardened and went cold. "No," he said softly.

"Our children need a safe—"

"I will provide our home, Hannah. Me."

She frowned. Glanced down at his coat then back up at him. "But—"

"I'll be your husband. You must trust that I will provide for you. Can you do that?"

Glaring at him with apparent pique, she shifted her hand and slid their fingers together. "Yes. But my funds will be at your disposal."

He inclined his head as though he accepted her offer. He didn't. "Is that the last of your conditions?"

Her fingers tightened where they laced with his. "Eugenia says I am not being fair to you," she said quietly. "It is true. I am not."

"What's unfair?"

Jaw tightening, she blew out a breath. "Asking you to marry me without telling you ..." She shook her head. "I am not normal, Jonas. Perhaps you already suspected it. Perhaps not. I promise I will do everything in my power to improve, to be a good wife to you. But at first, I may need you to do certain things. Things to prevent more episodes as I had today."

"Such as?"

"I may ask you to ... cover your eyes. Particularly whilst we ..."

His shock must have been apparent because she brought her free hand up to her mouth.

"Drat and blast. I shouldn't have told you," she mumbled through her fingers. Dismay crinkled her brow. Distress shook her shoulders.

He stroked her hand with his thumb. "You surprised me, that's all." The need to understand was grinding his insides. But she plainly did not want to tell him what was wrong until the vows had been spoken and they were permanently bound together—which meant it was bad.

And if it involved her keeping her clothes on and him covering his eyes, she was either disfigured or had visible signs of an illness. Neither of which changed his mind, of course. He didn't give a damn except that he would die to keep her from hurting. She'd admitted to an illness "in a manner of speaking." Perhaps she was recovering from a childhood ailment. Or perhaps she wouldn't recover at all.

What if she died? What if he married her, planted children in her belly, had two or three years, and then she was gone? It would fit the godforsaken pattern of his life, to be sure.

"At least tell me this," he rasped, scarcely able to get the words out. "Are you dying? Is that the source of the urgency?"

Soft, tentative fingers touched his jaw, bringing his eyes up to lock with hers. "No, I'm not dying. No more than anyone else, at any rate. Barring unforeseen misfortune, we shall have a long life together, Jonas Hawthorn."

As far as he knew, she'd never lied to him. And he saw no evidence that she did now.

Relief nearly sent him rolling onto his backside. Instead, he hung his head forward then lifted her fingers to his lips. Kissed them over and over. "Promise you'll tell me everything once we marry," he said when his heart settled into a normal rhythm.

"Yes. I promise."

"Promise we may revise your conditions as needed."

She hesitated. Then, "I promise."

He lost a small piece of his control and made his final demand. "Promise I may have you, Hannah Gray. That I may keep you."

She paled a bit. Squeezed his hand so hard, her nails formed grooves in his flesh. Thick, dark lashes fluttered oddly. Then, she swallowed. Leaned forward. Brushed his mouth with rosebud lips and whispered, soft as snowfall, "I promise."

Chapter Ten

"Marriage? My dear Bainbridge, you are mad to suggest it."

—LADY DOROTHEA PENWORTH to Malcolm Charles Bainbridge, Earl Bainbridge, in a letter mentioning marriage for the first time.

THEY HAD CROSSED THE RIVER TWEED AN HOUR AFTER sunrise. Wisps of mist still swirled on the banks. Sun glinted off the windowpanes of the little stone tollhouse on the north end of the bridge.

Viola had chattered away with her own recollections, filling Hannah's ears with tales about the funny Scottish tailor in the very white waistcoat who had performed Lord and Lady Tannenbrook's marriage at the same tollhouse years earlier. "How determined I was," Viola sighed. "He is grateful now, but at the time, my James was more than a trifle vexed with me."

Too nervous to speak, Hannah had listened as the coach she rode in—one of four carrying far too many of Lady Wallingham's guests—had traveled north from Grimsgate to Coldstream.

"It may not have been the wedding a lady dreams of," Viola had continued, her voice fond and wistful. "No church or rector. No flowers or music. Not even any family present. But our marriage hasn't suffered a jot for all the haste and simplicity of its start. No, the life we built together is what matters. And that has been wondrous."

More than a dozen people—Lord and Lady Wallingham, the dowager Lady Wallingham, Phineas and Eugenia, Viola and Lord Tannenbrook, Colin and Sarah Lacey, Reaver and Augusta, Maureen and Dunston—crowded inside the tiny room in the Coldstream Toll House to witness Hannah's marriage to Jonas.

He'd worn a steel-gray coat borrowed from Lord Wallingham. She'd worn her favorite pink gauze gown with the puffed sleeves and white rosettes. Phineas had given her a bouquet he'd selected himself—lily of the valley, deep-pink roses, and fragrant sprigs of lavender. Eugenia had decorated her hair with pearls, white rosebuds, and silk ribbon. When she'd drawn back to admire her handiwork, she'd beamed her Eugenia smile then hugged Hannah fiercely, whispering, "Never doubt you are strong, dearest. Today is proof. Brave and beautiful and strong."

Hannah had scarcely dared breathe while a bespectacled Scottish "parson" performed the ceremony. In part, it had been Jonas. His handsomeness had fairly melted her bones. Several times—particularly when he'd gazed down at her with flashing eyes and spoken his vows—she'd felt her head lifting away. But she'd used the trick of digging one of the flower stems into her palm, which had kept her feet on the ground.

Afterward, they'd all returned to Grimsgate for the wedding breakfast, a feast that began with thyme-seasoned, ham-dotted omelets and ended with a spiced cake topped with sliced peaches and sugared flowers. Now, Hannah gazed across the drawing room at Jonas—her husband. Tall and strong and capable. She examined his shoulders, his backside. She imagined having the freedom to touch him as she pleased.

His lips. His hair. His chest.

He was surrounded by other gentlemen, all of whom appeared to be giving him advice. He drank tea and wore his usual wry expression. But she could see his impatience building.

It sent a queer thrill through her belly.

He wanted her. Perhaps even as much as she wanted him, which was a very great deal, indeed.

Their kiss had stunned every part of her—from her lips to the tips of her hair. She'd found it explosive. Maddening. She'd never experienced anything as heated or sweet. She'd never imagined such desire existed.

If he hadn't pulled back, if he hadn't asked her to look at him ... well, it didn't matter now. Now, they were married.

She glanced down at her ring—the one Jonas had seemingly pulled from nowhere. He hadn't had time to purchase it, certainly. Nonetheless, it was extraordinary. The band was gold, the setting silver. In the center was a crescent-shaped series of pearls, a glowing moon set in polished silver. Within its embrace was the darkest sapphire she'd ever seen, faceted and shimmering blue. Surrounding the celestial duet were five tiny, star-like diamonds. Delicate, whimsical, and beautiful, the ring was an entire sky upon her hand. Merely looking at it made her smile.

"Hmmph. After he locates my trunk, you must insist he visit a tailor, my dear." Lady Wallingham came to stand beside her, examining Jonas through her quizzing glass. "His is a form best suited to properly fitted coats."

Hannah's heart swelled with unaccustomed heat. "He is most handsome."

"Yes. Proficient, too, if I don't miss my guess. Once you've tested the extent of his skills, I suspect you'll be jealous of his time. Only natural. Still, I cannot allow him to leave Grimsgate without first completing his task. Apologies in advance."

Hannah hadn't the faintest notion of what the old woman was on about, so she studied her new husband and listened with half an ear.

"I suggest pacing yourself, my dear. With a man like this, you'd be surprised how swiftly gluttony becomes a habit. Before you know it, you're spending your precious free hours outside the bedchamber finding new ways to please him—rearranging his desk to better suit a left-handed man. Wearing green because he mentioned it flatters your eyes. Secretly purchasing sandalwood soaps that remind you of his scent when he must be away. Desperate, foolish things only a desperately besotted girl would do. That is no way to manage a husband."

Too busy admiring Jonas's backside to pay much attention, it took Hannah a moment to digest the old woman's ramblings. "Left-handed?" she murmured in confusion, but Lady Wallingham and her purple plumes had already drifted away toward her son and daughter-in-law.

Lady Berne approached with all five Huxley daughters. The group of brown-haired ladies circled her, offering their felicitations and advice.

"Have you asked him about his favorite dish, dear?" asked Lady Berne. She pressed a hand to her ample bosom when Hannah shook her head. "You must ascertain this at once. Also, his least favorite dish. These tools work best together. Oh, and ask whether cats cause him to sneeze. Do you like cats?"

"Never mind that, Mama," Eugenia said. "The proper

question is: Can she persuade him to move to Dorsetshire? Weymouth is lovely, you know. Do you recall the Martin-Mace property I mentioned?" Eugenia sniffed and raised a brow. "Still for sale."

"What would a Bow Street runner do in Weymouth?" asked Annabelle. "Chase down windblown hats for a fee?"

"I can think of worse occupations," Eugenia replied.

Annabelle snorted. "Not many." She nodded toward her husband, the broad-shouldered Lord Robert Conrad, who stood with his cane propped beside his boot, listening to the other gentlemen give Jonas advice. Lord Robert frowned as though he'd heard a lot of rubbish but hadn't decided whether to intervene. "Asking a Bow Street man to leave London would be like asking Robert to abandon Rivermore Abbey. How would he provide for a wife and children?"

"Perhaps he could become a consultant," Jane suggested. "An investigator for hire." She pushed her spectacles until they brushed the fringe of hair covering her forehead. "Maureen, weren't you telling me Dunston regularly employs such men?"

Maureen nodded, nibbling her lower lip. "From time to time. Little projects here and there."

Kate, two years younger than Hannah and Eugenia, rolled her eyes in classic Huxley fashion. "*Little* projects. I doubt the Home Secretary regards them as 'little.'"

Jane continued, "My point is, he might work anywhere, given proper connections. And, with recommendations from Dunston, Holstoke, Blackmore, and Wallingham, not to mention Mr. Reaver, Atherbourne, and Tannenbrook, surely there will be 'little projects' aplenty."

"A clever suggestion, Jane," approved Lady Berne. "Now, then, about meal planning."

Kate groaned. "Not this again, Mama."

"It has worked on your father longer than you've been alive, Katherine Ann Huxley."

Hannah frowned. She recalled Eugenia laughing about this

once. Her mother liked to serve Lord Berne's least favorite dishes when she was vexed with him, and his favorites when she was pleased. Eugenia preferred a more direct approach— when she was displeased with Phineas, she told him so.

"Have you read *Pride and Prejudice*, dear?" Jane asked. "I should be glad to lend you a copy. Superb wit and insights into the complexities between men and—"

Kate spun in place in her customary theatrical way. "It should be a play, Jane. Perhaps you could write it."

"It has already been written. Just because you haven't the patience to read a novel does not mean—"

"Let us not argue," Maureen begged. "This is Hannah's day." She smiled sweetly. "We are so very happy for you, dearest."

She opened her mouth to thank them, only to be regaled by further arguments between Jane and Kate about whether Sir Walter Scott's earlier works were better than his more recent efforts. After performing a dramatic reading of *Macbeth* during her last season, Kate had grown enchanted with Scottish adventures, and she'd demanded Jane send her copies of every Scottish story she had. Sir Walter's more recent works had not been set in Scotland, and so had been deemed "worthless and tedious."

Annabelle and Maureen continued offering advice on selecting a house with proper piping and purchasing a new range for one's kitchen. Both recommended Nottinghamshire as an ideal location, close to Lord and Lady Berne as well as Annabelle and Robert. Eugenia continued insisting Dorsetshire had a superior climate to Nottinghamshire, and that Hannah must certainly settle there, as she would miss the sea far too much.

Hannah grew dizzy after another quarter-hour of advice on cookery, Scottish history, fictional men with large fortunes, the "barren, ice-shrouded moors" of Nottinghamshire winters, and the importance of an organized larder in proper meal planning. So, she begged their pardon and left the group to

find tea—and perhaps a bit of peace in which she might gather
the strength she would need for the night to come.

"A PLEASANT HOME BEGINS WITH A PLEASED WIFE, MR.
Hawthorn." Lord Berne raised his cup of tea as though to toast
his own wisdom. Hazel eyes twinkled. "Please her well."

The other men surrounding Jonas chuckled and murmured
their agreement.

"Aye," said Reaver, clapping a giant hand on Jonas's
shoulder. "You'll find it serves ye, most days. Though, I've
found a little disagreement now and then to be a fine bit of
pepper for the sauce, eh?"

More laughter and knowing smirks.

"As soon as you've settled into a house, give her a room of
her own," advised Lucien Wyatt, Viscount Atherbourne. The
black-haired lord was another escapee from a painting—this
one depicting a fallen angel or a dark, mythical god.

Many of the men agreed to his point—the tall, golden-
haired Duke of Blackmore; the duke's brother, Lord Colin;
Lord Wallingham; Lord Berne; Holstoke.

"Wives adore having a sanctuary for their pursuits,"
Atherbourne continued. "Mine is a painter. The finest
portraitist I know."

Tannenbrook nodded agreement. "No doubt of it. She is
exceptional." The blond giant warmed with affection. "My
Viola has taken up the harp again. She turned one of the
parlors into a music room and is teaching our daughters to
play." His smile took on the glow of a besotted male. "Their
laughter is all the music I require."

Dunston grinned and ran a hand over his bright-gold
waistcoat. "I've turned the kitchens over to Maureen entirely.

My only complaint is that I must triple my exercise to keep from overburdening my mount."

"I've placed all of Steadwick Hall in Julia's hands," remarked Lord Wallingham. "No man's home is so well ordered, I assure you. She rearranged the spices last week, first by name then by color. Remarkable woman."

"Whenever she's with child," added Lord Colin, "Sarah produces quilts at a prodigious rate. Half of my music room is presently stacked with them."

"Jane and I share two libraries," offered Blackmore. "She prefers the old library, and I find I do agree. Whenever I wonder where she's gone, it is the first place I search." The man's patrician features relaxed. Softened. "It is her favorite reading spot." The duke pulled out his watch then glanced across the room toward his wife.

"Harrison, put that thing away," ordered Dunston as though he'd said it to Blackmore a thousand times.

"Eugenia has two hat workshops," remarked Holstoke. "She hasn't said why she needs two, precisely. But it causes her to glow like a lantern. Sufficient reason to give her ten more, in my estimation."

All this talk of houses and rooms and glowing wives chafed Jonas's neck like the cravat Wallingham's valet had wrapped too tightly. Bloody hell, he was choking.

It was also possible that he wanted to bed his wife. More than possible. He'd been careful not to look at her too much since they'd returned to Grimsgate.

But he felt her in his skin. He wanted her with every breath. He'd waited too damn long.

When could they leave, he wondered. Was now too soon?

"Another half-hour at most," said a deep, quiet voice beside him. It was Lord Robert Conrad, a dark-haired man with a cane—some sort of accident in his youth, or so Jonas had heard. "Wait for Lady Wallingham to declare it is time to play battledore and shuttlecock. Should be coming shortly."

Jonas's mouth quirked. "Attended that many of her parties, have you?"

Conrad nodded then eyed Jonas with a penetrating gaze. "You were a soldier."

Jonas took a drink of cold tea before answering. "Aye. Thirty-Ninth Regiment of Foot."

"Dorsetshire?"

He nodded.

"Is that where you're from?"

He gave the other man his usual grin and his usual reply. "I'm from lots of places."

Conrad, a quiet, stolid sort, appeared to accept his answer. "Were you sent to the Continent?"

Jonas preferred not to discuss the wars. Nothing good came of remembering. But, he'd learned it was best to satisfy curiosity and move on. "Aye," he replied. "Spain and Portugal. Then, Canada for a year or so."

Conrad gestured toward Atherbourne. "He was at Waterloo. My grandfather fought at Belle Isle. Never leaves a man, once he's seen what other men are capable of. What we're all capable of becoming."

Damn and blast, this was the last thing he wished to discuss on his wedding day. "I survived," he said, ignoring the rattling hollow to take another drink. "All that matters, really."

"Annabelle tells me you and Hannah haven't yet decided where you might settle."

His neck itched at the question. "We haven't discussed it." There was a lot they hadn't discussed, and one of the topics burned in his chest. She owed him answers, and he meant to have them.

"My wife favors Nottinghamshire, of course," Conrad continued. "She is fond of Hannah and would enjoy having her live nearby." The blue-eyed son of a marquis leveled a stare upon Jonas that reminded him of his commanders in the army—hard, steady, and deeply rooted. "A place you and

Hannah have in common might suit best. Dorsetshire, perhaps?"

Lady Wallingham's trumpeting voice intruded. "Come, come, everyone. Let us journey to the south lawn for a rousing contest of battledore and shuttlecock." She turned to her son. "Charles, fetch Bain at once. He must learn to master the shuttlecock if he hopes to hold his head high with Rutherford's boy."

Conrad angled closer, leaning upon his cane. "Now's your chance, Hawthorn," he muttered, nodding toward the windowed corner where an ethereal woman in pink gauze sat alone. "Appears your bride could use some company."

Dear God. His bride. She was his. His.

He'd spent the past twelve hours starving for this moment.

Conrad's hand patted his shoulder. "Go on, then," the man murmured as though he could read Jonas's thoughts. "She's yours now. Take good care of her."

Jonas's heart nearly knocked his ribcage loose. She was so beautiful, his gut ached with the tension of holding still.

The other men slapped his shoulders and shot him amused glances as they passed by. Meanwhile, he wondered what in bloody hell he'd done.

He wasn't a husband, for Christ's sake. At best, he could offer her his name, which meant nothing. No family. No connections. No fortune. Just him—Jonas Bartholomew Hawthorn—on his knees before a Snow Queen. Little wonder she'd taken so long to decide she'd have him.

Her delicate shoulders shuddered on a breath. Ice-green eyes gazed out the window. Soft, white hands lay folded upon pink gauze skirts.

He gathered his senses. Made his way forward through the emptied room. When he came before her, he lowered into a crouch.

She sighed and swallowed. After a hesitation, she lifted her eyes to his. "Jonas," she whispered.

"Hullo, love," he whispered back. "Would you come with me?"

She blinked, looking both poised and nervous at once. "Y-yes."

He held out his hand. She slid hers into his grasp. And together, they walked from the drawing room, a husband who should not have been a husband and a wife who shouldn't have married him.

They found their way to his chamber. Neither spoke as they traversed the grand gallery to the grand staircase and down the long corridor.

It was only once he led her inside the room with the brown velvet and blue silk that he thought of asking whether she wanted her maid. Or a bath. Or any of the dozen other questions a considerate husband should ask.

He ran a hand over his face. At least Wallingham's valet had shaved his damned whiskers. He wouldn't mark up her skin.

Squeezing his eyes closed, he tried to rein in wild visions of Hannah wearing signs of his whiskers on her white throat, her white breasts, her white thighs.

"Jonas," she said with a tremble and a squeeze. "I don't wish to—to talk just yet. Not on this day. Is that all right?"

He stilled. "You promised you would explain."

Her gaze fell to the blue carpet. "I know. But, for now, I'd rather kiss you again. And ... touch you."

And just like that, he was in her thrall.

Chapter Eleven

"Frankly, had I known what awaited me,
I might have suggested marriage sooner."

—DOROTHEA BAINBRIDGE, COUNTESS BAINBRIDGE, to Malcolm
Charles Bainbridge, Earl Bainbridge, in a letter acknowledging that
some men's talents are unusual and some men's wives are fortunate.

HER SKIN PULSED WITH EVERY POUNDING BEAT OF HER HEART.
She'd tried to gather enough courage to tell him everything.
But she'd found it impossible.

Merely standing here with him now, in his chamber,
holding his hand and staring at his well-worn boots made her
belly quake.

Suddenly, he released her. Paced to the other side of the

bed. Began tugging at his ... cravat? Yes. He was trying to loosen what appeared to be a lovely Osbaldeston knot.

"Very well," he said, his voice low and rough. "Let me loosen this damnable noose."

She took a deep breath and followed him, circling around to reach for his hands. "Allow me," she murmured. His fingers dropped away, and she went to work unraveling the mess he'd made. "The problem is the starch, you see," she explained. "It makes everything stiff and a bit sticky." She felt his throat ripple on a swallow. "Apply too much force, and the tightness will work against you."

"God Almighty," he rasped.

As she often did when she was concentrating, she pressed her tongue against her lower lip. "Almost there." One tug. Another. A pluck and a long sigh. And, at last, the cloth came free. "You see?" She grinned up at him, triumphant.

His eyes—oh, heavens, his eyes were afire. Silvery and ravenous. They devoured her with lust. Need. Possession.

Her head began to float. Recede.

No! No, no, no.

She grasped his neckcloth and yanked him closer.

He grunted.

She wrapped the white, starchy linen around her hands tightly. Tighter and tighter. Forcing it to bind her fingers together to the point of pain. Then, she tugged him down to her, rose up on her toes, and breathed his name against his lips. "Jonas."

"Bloody hell."

"I must close my eyes, now." She did so, needing the darkness. "Then, I should very much like you to kiss me."

"Mmm."

"Afterward, I want to touch you. Naked. To be clear, I should like for you to be naked, not me. If you don't mind."

"You are killing me, love."

"When you touch me, you must move slowly. I—I startle

easily. Soon, I hope that we needn't be so cautious."

"I hope the same."

"Eugenia was frank in her explanations. Frightfully so."

"Was she?"

"Yes. I know what to expect. I am not ignorant."

"Good. That is good."

"One day, I shall be an excellent lover, Jonas. You shan't regret the necessity of performing your husbandly duty."

"A relief, I assure you."

"I shall apply myself with great diligence."

"Diligence. Aye."

"Am I choking you?"

"No, though perhaps we should sit. May I hold you, love?"

She squeezed her eyes shut tighter and braced herself. Then, she nodded.

Strong hands slid slowly along her hips, trailing firmly across her buttocks and up to her waist. He grasped her there, his fingers digging in just a bit. She liked it. Strength. Pressure that spoke of tension. He backed up several steps, pulling her with him. Then, she felt him lowering to sit on the bed. He drew her forward until she sensed their faces were aligned. His breath fell upon her forehead, her cheeks. Its rhythm was fast.

"You mentioned kissing, did you not?" His voice held a teasing note as he brushed his lips against hers.

She felt a flush of heat rising everywhere—breasts, thighs, cheeks—as she nodded. "Please."

"Such politeness." He chuckled, the sound warm and resonant. "Shall I remove my coat?"

"Yes." Her mouth went dry. She wanted to open her eyes. To look at him. The frustration ate at her. "Can you do so while you kiss me?"

"I think you'll find I have unusual capabilities in that regard." His mouth took hers. His tongue, slick and strong and flavored with spiced peach and strong tea, became an explorer.

Her head began spinning, but only in the most delicious

way. She moaned against his lips, gripped his neckcloth harder and pulled him deeper. Heavens, she was starving for him.

Vaguely, she felt his hands leave her. His shoulders shifting. Then, his hands returned, curving around her lower back and pulling her deeper into his embrace. His teeth tingled her lower lip. His fingers wrapped around her nape. His thumbs controlled her jaw. Caressed her cheeks.

Gently, slowly, with sweet strokes of his tongue and his lips, he brought their kiss to a conclusion. Withdrew from her.

She wanted him back. She wanted to growl her protest. Instead, she grunted and dug her fingertips into his shoulders. "Jonas." Her voice was hoarse. Breathless. "Why did you—"

"First, I kiss you. Then, I unclothe myself. Wasn't that the command, love?"

Her skin felt tight. Her breasts swelled against her stays. "I want to see you."

"Then, open those beautiful eyes."

How she wished she could. "I cannot," she whispered.

He fell silent for long seconds. His hands gripped her waist. Explored her hair and her jaw. His fingers traced her lips. "I'm going to take your hair down," he rasped. Immediately, his fingers began plucking at her pins. She felt him remove pearls and ribbon and rosebuds. She heard him gasp when her curls came down.

"By God, you are exquisite," he breathed.

Her heart raced as his hands skimmed down along her throat, gently along the upper curves of her breasts, then down lightly—so lightly—across her straining nipples. She gasped at the sensations. The need they stoked. The weakness in her thighs and knees.

"I—I want to see you," she repeated. "Touch you."

"Let go of the neckcloth. There's no need for a leash. You have me firmly in your power, Snow Queen."

She didn't know what that meant, but he was right—he couldn't very well disrobe if she refused to loosen her hold.

With effort, she released first one end then, reluctantly, the other. "I didn't hurt you, did I?" Her voice sounded small.

"No." He jerked the linen free, his movements rougher than before. "Hold steady." His motions shook the bed. She heard a wad of cloth plop onto the carpet. "Now, then. Take those pristine hands and put them on me before I bloody well expire."

"I want to see you," she said again.

"God, Hannah. Open your eyes."

"I—I need you to cover yours first."

Silence.

"Please, Jonas. This is the only way."

Several heartbeats passed before she felt him leaning, reaching for something. Then, he sat up and a moment later, said, "There. Covered."

When she finally gathered enough courage, she opened her eyes. Oh, heavens. Her hand reached for him of its own volition. She didn't think, didn't hesitate. His muscles leapt as she felt him with fascinated fingers—thick, lean, hard. Dark hair. Heated skin.

He reached for her. She gasped and flinched away, despite her determination not to. He withdrew, clenching his fists beside his hips, panting and frowning.

As her heart settled, she resumed her explorations. "How lovely you are," she murmured, unable to help herself.

"I prefer handsome. Deific also works. Herculean."

"When you were injured, much of you was covered in b-bandages. I knew you were strong because of your arms." She traced the swells of his forearms, played with the hair along his wrists. Then, she slid higher, sweeping over biceps, pausing over the scar left by a poisoner's arrow. This, she circled and circled with her fingertip. "You were beautiful then. More so now that you've healed. So strong, Jonas Hawthorn. I want to pull you inside me. I want your strength to become mine and mine to be yours."

With a long, low growl, he leaned back on his hands and

lifted his hips up as though reseating himself. His head fell
back on his strong, naked neck as his chest worked like a
bellows. The muscles in his shoulders and flat belly rippled.
The white linen of his neckcloth shone starkly against his skin
and hair.

He'd blindfolded himself. And he was obviously keeping his
hands virtually bound. For her. Given the state of the veins
along his chest and neck, this was generating significant distress.

She granted herself a moment to look. To savor the sight of
him. Behind the fall of his breeches, the source of his distress
was visible. Intimidating. It swelled against the cloth, a
massive stalk thrusting upward to demand its due.

Her heart fluttered. Her thighs squeezed against an ache.

"I think we should join now, Jonas."

"Bloody, bleeding hell."

"I shall loosen your fall. Stay as you are."

She sank down between his splayed knees. First, she
permitted herself a slow, gliding stroke of his thighs.
Swallowing against a dry throat, she marveled at the thickness,
the hardness there. Her palms swept upward. The buttons
were easy, if a bit tight with all the strain. Then, his naked
member was in her hand.

She'd never seen or felt anything like it. Soft as satin. Hard
as stone. Swollen and veined. Hot and flushed. She'd viewed
drawings in some of Phineas's scientific texts, but the subjects
had to have been much smaller men.

Jonas's member, by contrast, was alarmingly long and
much, much thicker than she'd been led to believe possible.
Hannah frowned as she recalled Lady Wallingham's reference
to "girth." Was there such a thing as too much girth? This
could be a problem.

Hannah nibbled her lower lip as she ran her hands over his
length, enjoying the sensation of silken skin, pulsing veins, and
the small bead of fluid emerging from the head. Beneath, still
tucked inside his breeches were his ballocks, tight and full.

He was certainly ready for her. Was she ready for him?

The aching heat in her lower belly was similar to what Eugenia had described. Her breasts felt full, her nipples tight and sensitive.

Perhaps she was ready.

A queer sensation struck her chest—a squeeze, a flip, a pang. It was all three at once. "Jonas?" She stood. Ran her hands over his chest. Caressed his hard, straining neck. "I shall straddle you now."

His skin was fiery along his cheeks. "Let me touch you," he growled. "Fuck. I need it. I will fucking beg if that's what you want."

She'd heard the word before, of course. It was vulgar—a sign of his crumbling control. Other signs were his fists wadding the velvet coverlet and his hips subtly thrusting.

He needed her. She was his wife. She must give him comfort. Ease.

She clasped his right wrist and brought his hand up to her breast. While he groaned and squeezed and pleasurably caressed her, she gathered her skirts higher, bunching them at her waist. She started by placing one knee upon the mattress beside his hip. Then she held onto his shoulders and climbed atop his thighs the way a man might mount his horse. It felt strange, but not bad.

While Jonas's right hand pleasured her nipple through the layers of her gown and stays, his left moved to clutch her bare thigh. She didn't want him exploring too much, so she kissed him and drew his hand between their bodies. Then, as she'd dreamt of doing nearly every night since Jonas Hawthorn had first entered the drawing room at Holstoke House, she laced her fingers with his and drew his fingertips to her center.

He groaned into her mouth. "You are so wet, love. God Almighty." Lightly, he traced her folds with his fingertips, swirling and testing, pressing and pulsing. "I need inside you."

She ran her fingers over his blindfold in a dappling motion.

Kissed his lips—the ones she hadn't been able to resist. "Yes. I need you, too."

His right arm circled her waist. Lifted her high against him. His left hand positioned his member at her opening.

He paused. Strain shook his whole body. "All right, love?" he rasped.

Around her heart, heat and light burst and expanded. He'd halted at the furthest point of desire to ensure she was well. She kissed him again, caressing his jaw and his neck. "Yes," she whispered in his ear. "Now, Jonas."

Breeching her maidenhead was a painful sting, but she noticed the stretching more. He was very big, and the pain of the unaccustomed intrusion stole her breath. He groaned, long and deep, as he sank inside her.

"Sweet, bloody Christ. I'm going to come." He sounded amusingly alarmed, as though he'd never had such a problem before.

She smiled, though he couldn't see. Kissed him. Ran her tongue along his lower lip. Began to move, despite the discomfort of having him inside her.

"Does it hurt?"

"You are very big."

He grunted and thrust deeper.

"It feels hot. Burns a little."

He thrust deeper.

The thought occurred to her that he hadn't actually put himself fully inside her yet. She moved her hips experimentally. "How much more of you is there, precisely?"

"I'm not going to ... make it," he panted. "This is bloody disgraceful."

She frowned. "Am I doing it wrong? You must tell me so that I may improve."

"So wet. God, so wet and tight and mine." His hand came back and touched her directly upon the little knot that held limitless pleasure.

She gasped as the sensations began to coalesce and expand. He sank deeper.

"Oh! That—that is ... it aches a bit, but ... I like that, Jonas."

Deeper.

She groaned. "Hmmm. Yes. What is that you ...?"

Deeper. A hard thrust upward.

She gasped. Dug her nails into his shoulders. "Oh, sweet heaven."

Another. And another. And another.

His hand stayed and pleasured. His other hand braced her waist and controlled their movements. Set a rhythm that started slow then gained momentum.

Soon, she caught it, too. This feverish pace, this grinding of him against the deepest part of her. This beauty. The beauty of them together. Of his surrender and hers.

And, as she gazed upon her blindfolded man, felt him filling her past the point of comfort, past the point where there was even a breath for anyone other than him, she gathered up every drop of pleasure he gave her, threw back her head.

And rode.

It felt like flying.

Wave after wave, crashing like Primvale's waters after a storm. Shifting entire shorelines and long-embedded stones with its force. She took the pounding thrust of his hips, all pain a distant memory. Rippling, cascading, rolling waves of ecstasy burst through her body. She gasped and moaned and reveled in the power of the pleasure he gave her.

Finally, she held him and reveled in *his* pleasure.

Perhaps that most of all. Because she'd given him this. For all she'd taken from him, for all the distress and difficulty he'd suffered before—and all that might still come—she took his seed inside her, heard his deep roar of completion, and savored the knowledge that in this one thing, she could be a normal wife.

She could take him. Ease him. Pleasure him.

And in this way, he would always be hers.

Chapter Twelve

"On the contrary, lending you my assistance is an act of generosity. If one man helps a slightly less clever man rebuke the Prime Minister, is that termed 'interference'? I think not."

—DOROTHEA BAINBRIDGE, COUNTESS BAINBRIDGE, to Malcolm Charles Bainbridge, Earl Bainbridge, in a letter protesting erroneous definitions and abrupt departures.

JONAS LEFT THE ONLY COACHING INN IN ALNWICK WITH LITTLE hope and abundant frustration. But, then, frustration appeared to be his lot. The innkeeper at the White Swan hadn't recognized his sketch of the thief, offering only the advice that Jonas "inquire at the public house, sir, where thieves are more likely to be found than in a fine establishment such as mine."

The pompous innkeeper had been insulted, of all things. Perhaps Jonas had been a trifle short with him, but after the past three days, his patience was more battered than his boots. He collected his hired horse and walked the short distance to the ramshackle public house around the corner from the inn.

Inside, the smell of wood smoke and fish mingled with the scent of beer and the grime of local villagers who spent their few farthings in ramshackle public houses.

It wasn't a "fine establishment," but it felt familiar. Jonas had spent his life in places like this. During the hot part of the day, it had customers, but not many. Alnwick might be a market town, but it was small and remote.

After requesting a pint, he spoke to the tall, thick-armed man behind the bar. "Looking for this man." He unfolded the sketch, sliding it across the wood. "Have you seen him in the past fortnight or so?"

The barkeeper squinted at the sketch. Started to shake his head. Then paused. "Mayhap. Looks a mite familiar." He glanced up. "Bit like you. He your kin?"

Bloody hell, it was the same response he'd had again and again. "No," he replied, plucking another sketch he'd completed the day before from his pocket. "What of her?"

It was a likeness of Elly Allen, the missing maid.

When the barkeeper's eyes widened, a prickle lit upon Jonas's nape.

"Aye, indeed. She was here three days past. No, four. Load of haddock arrived shortly before she left. Bad lot. Sat in the sun too long. Went foul."

"Was she with anyone else?"

"Aye, a man. Not him, mind." He tapped the thief's sketch. "Lighter hair. Rough sort."

It was the first hint of a trail since the maid had disappeared, and he chased it eagerly. "Did either of them say anything? Ask for a direction, or mention where they might be heading?"

The big man scratched his chin and shook his head. "Not as I recall. Though, I did think it a mite peculiar when he asked about the tides."

Another prickle along Jonas's nape. "Tides, eh?"

"Nearest port of any size is Blyth. Naught but fishermen betwixt here and there. This fellow mistook my haddock for cod."

"Didn't strike you as a seafaring sort, then."

The man grunted and shook his head.

"Anything else you recall?"

"He weren't from Northumberland, that much is certain. Kept whingin' about the winds during that wee sprinkle a few days past." The big man scoffed. "I've had bigger gales come out of me arse."

Jonas chuckled. "Could you place his accent?" In his experience, the men who tended the bar typically developed an ear for it—the better to distinguish locals from travelers and charge accordingly.

"Yorkshire, mayhap. Kept on about needin' to addle some brass, or somewhat. Fellow I knew from Yorkshire used to say that when he was pockets to let."

Jonas thanked the man and started to finish his beer when he felt a presence behind him. A curvaceous shadow fell across his arm.

"Bloody hell," he muttered. "For the last time, I don't need your help."

A slender arm in red velvet reached past his elbow to pluck his sketch of the maid. "Is this her?" asked his disobedient wife. "Miss Allen?"

He turned. God, she stole the air from his chest. Wine-red velvet hugged her soft bosom and slender waist. It fell in folds to form her skirt. It made his heart pound like a furious drum. Or, rather, she did. The velvet was incidental. "Go back to Grimsgate, Hannah."

Her chin tilted upward. "I wish to help."

"There is nothing you can do." And many things she could do to make it harder. Distracting him, for one. Increasing his frustration, for another.

"I have an excellent mind, I'll have you know."

"That is not in question."

"If you will set aside your manly obstinacy, you'll see it is far better to make proper use of the resources at your disposal."

At the moment, his body had a single use for her. But even that had proven unsatisfying. And he was damned if he knew what to do about it. She still hadn't told him a thing. Not one bloody thing. She'd kissed him and fucked him and taken his cock and his seed. All without letting him touch her properly. Without letting him see her properly.

Without letting him inside.

He'd thought that having her would be enough. But he didn't have her. And what he did have wasn't nearly enough.

"Go back to the castle," he gritted, finishing the last of his beer and retrieving his sketches. "Or must I escort you?"

Those pale eyes flashed a defiant glint. Her pert, red velvet hat might as well be a crown. "Let me help."

He shoved away from the bar and made for the door. She followed, as he'd known she would. Outside, the glare of late-day sun made the sandstone buildings glow gold. "You'll help me most by enjoying the party with your friends."

"They might be your friends, too, if you'd let them."

As he reached the horses—hers was a pristine white mare with a gleaming sidesaddle, while his was a hired old gelding with a sparse mane and poor stamina—he offered to help her mount. She sniffed and nodded, turning her back to him to position one boot in the stirrup.

He drew close. Eyed the bare skin between her collar and her hair. Smelled roses and his woman. His body reacted predictably. But he ignored it, gripping her waist and lifting her easily onto her saddle.

She settled her skirts and retrieved her riding cane. "Thank you, Jonas."

His answer was to mount his horse and start north, knowing she would follow.

"I fail to understand why you refuse my assistance."

"Because I want you to remain at the castle."

"You've said as much, but that is silly." They rode in silence as they passed the White Swan and made their way along the small streets of Alnwick. "Do you play chess?"

He frowned. "What has that to do with anything?"

"I play chess. I am an excellent player."

"Congratulations."

"Phineas and I play every evening. He is the only opponent who consistently defeats me. He is brilliant. But make no mistake, I am very, very good."

"Fascinating. I have a fondness for sketching." Perhaps he was being a boor. But devil take it, she had defied his express orders at every turn. Further, she was distracting him from chasing the thief's trail—and he needed to complete this job.

He had a wife now. She wanted babes. He couldn't afford to fail. These three thoughts drove him with urgent force.

"Chess requires one to anticipate an opponent's moves and countermoves. To plan. To maneuver. To trap," she continued, ignoring his sarcasm. "All skills which, I daresay, might prove useful whilst pursuing a thief." She sniffed. "If one is not blinded by one's pigheadedness, that is."

He tried to sigh away his frustration and focus on the dusty road to Grimsgate. "Odd. I thought you liked me better blinded, princess."

That bought him several miles of silence. She didn't speak again until he pointed to a small path through a clump of trees and mentioned they should water the horses. And then, all she said was, "Very well."

He was a disaster as a husband. He knew it. She clearly knew it. And, if he didn't find Lady Wallingham's trunk, they'd be living in rented rooms in London, and he'd be back at Bow Street, chasing petty thieves for pittances.

She wanted to help, but he needed to focus on his task. At the moment, it was all that mattered. Finish the job. Collect the reward.

He led her to a shaded spot along a small brook. He'd stopped there while traveling to Grimsgate. It was a lovely, peaceful place. The brook wound amidst a copse of willows, and as the evening sun slanted golden fingers through the leaves, light played upon her black hair, white skin, and little red hat.

His breath caught in his chest, hands tightening upon his reins.

Beautiful. The most beautiful thing he'd ever seen.

He forced himself to dismount, leading his horse to the water's edge before turning to help her down. But she'd already dismounted on her own. Now, as her horse drank, she gazed up at the willow canopy and closed her eyes.

Her gloved hands folded at her waist. Her throat craned like a swan's. Her shoulders were slim. Graceful.

He knew every line by heart.

"I love the way the wind sounds," she said. "Music played in whispers."

He turned his back, needing distance. Needing to stop wanting her so damn much.

"Do you regret our marriage, Jonas?"

His gut hardened. Went cold. "Do you?"

A pause. "No. Although, I do wish you would let me assist you in your investigation."

He released a half-chuckle. Removed his hat and ran a hand through his hair. "I had that impression."

"You permitted Dunston to help you."

"He followed me. It wasn't my choice. Appears to be a common pattern of late."

She went silent for a moment. "You seem ... discontented with me."

He hung his head and rubbed his nape. "I must finish this task. If you'll stay where you belong, everything will be fine."

"But I wish to make you happy."

He closed his eyes tight. His hat's brim bent inside his fist. He heard a rustle, a whisper of velvet. Breathed roses and a hint of rain.

"Tell me what I am doing wrong," she said. "Should I not have asked you to ... this morning? I thought because you were ... so hard ... that it would ease you if I—"

"Stop." If he thought about that morning, he was going to lift her skirts and fuck her against the tree. "Nothing is wrong. Let's just return to the castle."

"I wanted to take you in my mouth." She whispered her confession. "Would you like that better?"

"Bloody hell." He felt her moving closer. Warmth. Softness.

"I am a swift learner, Jonas. You will see." Her hand, tentative as a butterfly, touched his arm. Stroked down to his wrist. "Tell me what pleases you most, and I shall seek to master it."

"Devil take it, woman," he growled, jerking his arm away. "You're my wife, not my whore."

He knew the moment he said it, he'd regret that loss of control forever. He felt her withdraw, watched her shadow go motionless beside his. Choking on his own unforgivable words, he couldn't look at her. Didn't want to see the pain there.

Sinking into a crouch, he threw his hat across the glade with a vicious snap. It landed in the water. Drifted downstream. With both hands, he scraped his hair, his fingertips digging into his scalp.

"God, Hannah." He breathed deep. Covered his face. Blew a gust into his cupped hands. "I'm so bloody sorry."

"Wh—why would you say such a thing to me?"

"Because I am an idiot." He dropped his hands. Braced his elbows on his knees. "A frustrated, foolish, maddened idiot."

"Frustrated. Because of me?"

He wanted to deny it. But he didn't have any masks left. Not even one to spare her feelings. "Yes."

"I don't understand. What have I done except try to be a good wife to you?"

He stood. Turned. Faced the woman he'd married but couldn't have. "You lied to me," he said softly.

A confused crinkle appeared. "I wouldn't—I didn't—"

"You said you would tell me everything once we were married. You've told me nothing. Given me nothing. Most especially yourself."

The confusion deepened, her eyes darting around him instead of remaining still. Her mouth worked. Her head shook. "We—we have—"

"Aye. We have. But I'm not allowed to look upon your body. Or touch your skin. Or see your eyes when you come for me. Every time I draw close to your boundaries, you stop me. That's not lovemaking. That's procreation. We shouldn't have boundaries between us, Hannah. And you won't even tell me why they exist."

She went whiter. Swallowed. Stared at him as though he'd burned her house to the ground. "I'm not ready to tell you."

"You don't trust me."

"I do. I do trust you."

"Then tell me the truth."

She looked stricken. "You will hate it. I will hate that you know. That you see me differently."

He didn't have an answer for her because he didn't know what she was hiding.

A breeze came up. Her hand settled over her belly. She shuddered. Gasped a breath. "All right," she whispered finally. "I will tell you."

He held himself still. Forced his muscles not to carry him toward her.

Her hands twisted together. Her shoulders shook. "I—I was four or five. I'm not certain which. It was winter. We lived in

Bath, my mother and I. Papa was ill. He brought me a doll each time he visited. I had dozens by the time he ..." Her mouth trembled into a tiny, grieving smile. "He was kind. His eyes were like mine." She swallowed. "Mama would often take me up the hill in the park to the confectioner's. She did so on the day she died."

Cold started low in his spine. Traveled upward as she spoke. But he disciplined himself to stand still. To listen.

"We were returning from the shop. There was frost on the steps. I thought everything had been frozen by fairies. It sparkled and ..." She shook her head. Looked down at her hands. A wince of grief flickered across her face. "Her neck was broken, I think. Her eyes were open. She was reaching for me when she fell."

Cold sank deeper. Deeper and deeper.

"H-he pushed her. I'd gone down the hill first. A fairy riding a horse, I imagined. I was there, at the bottom, when she landed."

Bloody hell.

"He took me."

"Who?"

She shook her head. "I don't like to say his name."

Cold was roiling now. Building. Burning. "Please tell me."

"He said it was to save my life."

"Who, Hannah?"

Squeezing her eyes shut, she released a tiny gasp. Her hands formed claws over her midsection. Then, she opened her eyes.

And sweet Christ, he wished she hadn't.

"His name was Horatio Syder."

"No. Ah, God. No." Something was crushing his chest. Grinding his bones. Burning him alive.

"He took me—"

"No."

"He h-hurt me—"

"No!" His roar hurt his own ears. But he was dying. He

couldn't bear it.

"Kept me. For a very long time."

The ward. She was the ward Dunston had told him about. A delicate, pale-eyed little girl in the hands of a butcher.

"I survived, Jonas. I am here, and he is gone."

He needed to move. Started prowling in circuits through the glade while visions of how that monster must have hurt her gouged deep, tore him open. Odd, guttural noises were rumbling out of his chest.

"Jonas." She ventured closer, cautious and light. "I—I must tell you everything."

He shook his head. Pressed his palms to his temples, needing the visions to stop.

"You must know, and I cannot do this a second time."

Bracing himself against a tree, he slammed the trunk with his fist. Once. Twice. Again.

"Please." She stood closer, now. Snowfall and roses. "Listen."

His hand was bleeding. It dropped to his side. His head dropped forward. He couldn't get enough air.

"It was not the pain," she rasped. "Everyone assumes so. They believe the beatings and c-cuttings were the worst thing. But that is not true."

Beatings and cuttings. The butcher had taken a knife to her soft, white flesh. Jonas slammed his fist into the tree several more times, shaking branches and splitting skin.

She continued calmly, as though his guts weren't being torn to pieces. "He loved me. That was the worst part. He was a madman, of course, and his love was ... twisted up, somehow. Obsessive. To him, I was a beloved daughter. His punishments were to instruct. To protect. He required that I call him Papa. After a time, he even convinced himself that he and my mother had been ... affectionate." Her voice faded to a thread. "He hired tutors and housekeepers to care for me. He kept me hidden from the one who ordered my death. He taught me to play chess."

He rested his forehead against his arm and struggled to breathe. "God Almighty, love."

"In some ways, he played a father with me, I suppose. I learnt a great deal from him. He was building an empire, you see. He wished to share it with me once Lady Holstoke had been dealt with. His lessons were ... quite thorough."

"How long?" His question ground like a millstone inside his chest.

"Ten years."

"Was there no one—"

"No. Anybody who tried to help me was killed. Or worse. A housekeeper, Mrs. Lisle, intervened once. She stopped him. Grasped his w-walking stick as he was ..." Hannah shook her head. Panted. "Mrs. Lisle was gone by the next morning. He presented her hands to me as a gift."

He was going to retch. He felt his gorge rising. Panted and swallowed. Sweat sprang up on his neck.

"He believed he was doing right," she continued, swaying near him, her gown too red and her skin too white. "The way he looked upon me." She drew a shuddering breath. "It was ... possession. Love transformed into a dark fever. And in my head, those things are a tangle."

"That is not love. It's demonic." He rubbed his fingers over his eyes. "God, it's anything but love."

"I know. Even then, I knew. Because my papa's love was gentle. He would never have hurt me. But S-Syder took everything else away until all I had was ... him. Just him and his love and the pain."

"Did he ..." Bloody hell, he was terrified to ask. Needed to know. Didn't want to know. Jonas had seen many things during his years of hunting in the darkest corridors of London. Young girls were treated no better—and sometimes worse—than animals. "Did he ever touch you ... as a man touches a woman?"

A puzzled frown crinkled her brow. "No. Dunston asked me a similar question several years ago. It was never ... Syder did not regard me in such a way. My sense is that he had those feelings for Lady Holstoke."

"Lydia Brand."

"Yes. She wanted me dead. He warned me about her over and over. Gave me a miniature so I would recognize her, should she ever find me. He even taught me to fire a pistol. He often spoke of her with both fear and peculiar longing."

He sagged against the tree as a wave of relief hit him. His wife had been a virgin upon their marriage. He knew that. But there were many things a depraved butcher could do to a girl without taking her maidenhead.

The things she'd already told him about were damage enough.

"So, when you ask me to cover my eyes, it is—"

"It is not our intimacies which cause me distress. I—I adore touching you, Jonas. Kissing you. The pleasure of it is"—she drew a shivering breath—"transcendent."

Further relief surged, driving away some of the burning cold.

"When you look upon me, I can see your heart." She stared at her twisting hands. "It burns me alive."

The implication sickened him. "Do not say I remind you of him."

Pale eyes finally lifted to meet his. "Love reminds me of him. Love. Even my brother's affection is sometimes difficult to bear. Phineas has always been very careful with me. I have lately asked him to dispense with his caution."

"Why?"

"For the same reason I married you." After hesitating a moment, she moved into him. Her hand fluttered upward. Settled softly upon his chest. "If I cannot bear to be loved fully, then I am Syder's prisoner forever."

This time, he was the one shuddering. Shaking. "I need to hold you."

She slipped into his arms. Laid her cheek upon his chest. Wrapped her arms around his waist. Sighed. "Nothing will ever hurt you again," he vowed. "I will bloody well kill anyone who tries. I wish I could kill the man who did. Over and over. Every day for the next thousand years." She nodded against him. Snuggled into his arms. Breathed into his old wool coat. "I survived," she repeated. "I am here. He is gone."

But the damage remained. She didn't have to say it. He knew. Her coldness hadn't been coldness but armor. She hadn't rejected him out of disdain but out of fear. "Let me take you back to Grimsgate," he said, needing to surround her with stone walls and protective allies.

"First, you must hold me properly."

"I am."

"No. You are treating me like wet paper."

He blinked. Realized she was right. The hand he'd used to strike the tree throbbed, but that wasn't why his palms hovered along her back, lightly skimming red velvet. The rage of the last hour howled inside him, rattling its cage like a crazed beast.

"Hold me tighter, Jonas."

"I cannot."

"Touch me."

His lungs ached as he held his breath. Tried to control the rage, slow his heart, relax his muscles.

"Please." Her hands clawed into his coat. "Please do not do this."

"We must go. It will be dark soon."

"Jonas."

Slowly, gently, he withdrew. Her hands clung to his coat. Her eyes remained on his face, though he kept his own gaze lowered. "Let me take you where you will be safe."

Her arms fell away. She fell silent.

And for the rest of the ride to the castle, not another word passed between them. Only the sound of wind and horses. The thick scent of the sea. And the sun sinking behind distant Northumberland hills.

Chapter Thirteen

"Every room feels empty without you."

—Dorothea Bainbridge, Countess Bainbridge, to Malcolm
Charles Bainbridge, Earl Bainbridge, in a letter written at midnight
by the light of the moon.

Long after midnight had come and gone, sleep drifted
like a loosened skiff beyond Hannah's grasp. She'd waited for
Jonas to say something. Take her in his arms. Kiss her. Instead,
he'd stripped down to his breeches and advised her to sleep, as
she'd had a difficult day.

She hadn't slept, of course. Memories churned up by their
conversation had bothered her at first. But they were ancient
cobwebs. She'd been sweeping them away for years.

This feeling—her anger at Jonas's reaction—was a thorny thicket she hadn't anticipated. Newer, sharper tools would be necessary.

So, as soon as she sensed he was asleep, she'd put on her dressing gown and left their bedchamber. The gallery had been bright blue with moonlight streaming through the windows. She'd trailed her fingers lightly along the glass as she wandered its length.

Now, she did the same to the windows in the drawing room. The sills were painted silvery white by night's brush. She liked the room this way. Empty. Quiet. Dark.

Distantly, she heard tapping. Not rhythmic, but erratic. Almost playful. It started faintly and acquired a snuffling accompaniment. Soon, a warm, wet tongue stroked her hand and a low whine sounded. She smiled.

"Good evening, Humphrey." She stroked his smooth head and played with his long ears. "You should be sleeping. Silly boy."

He sat and leaned into her, his solid weight a comfort.

"Hmmph. There you are," said Lady Wallingham from the shadows near the doorway. "I should have known. Like most males, you never miss an opportunity for petting."

The old woman held a cup of tea and wore a white gown with a lace cap. Her white hair shone blue as she crossed toward them.

"It is late, my lady," Hannah said softly. "Trouble sleeping?"

The old woman sat in her favorite chair near the fireplace then took a sip of tea before answering. "A consequence of age, I'm afraid. I expect the clockwork must fail as readily as the rest. Nature spares no one." The old woman sniffed and gestured to Hannah's bosom. "And no part. Consider yourself warned."

Hannah's lips quirked. "May I sit with you?"

"Mmm." The dowager waved an imperious finger toward the nearest chair.

Humphrey followed and lay at her feet—or, more rightly, upon her feet.

"What has you rattling about this old castle at all hours, dear girl? You should be upstairs enjoying the benefits of a proficient husband."

Sighing, Hannah shook her head then let it fall against the chair's wing. Perhaps it was the darkness. The quiet. The fact that they were both in their dressing gowns. Or perhaps her despair simply wanted out. But her confession escaped before she could stifle it. "I fear I have much to learn in becoming a proficient wife."

"Heavens, girl." Lady Wallingham's cup clinked. "Have you tried bedding him?"

Hannah was accustomed to plain speaking—Eugenia was her best friend, after all. So, rather than taking offense, she considered the point. "Yes."

"And?"

Hannah met the old woman's eyes, which gleamed sharply in the moonlight. "I believe he is dissatisfied."

A frown. "Are you completing the act?"

Hannah nodded, grateful for the darkness.

"Then there is no chance he is dissatisfied." She sipped her tea and returned her cup to the saucer as though she discussed such intimate subjects every day. "Men are simple creatures."

"Our marriage is no simple thing, my lady. How I wish it were."

"Nonsense."

"I am damaged. Scarred."

The old woman snorted. "Do you suppose he is not?"

Hannah blinked. Went oddly numb. Then hurt with a flooding ache as she realized she had supposed that very thing. In fact, she hadn't contemplated Jonas's scars. She'd been too concerned with her own.

"The man went to war when he was sixteen."

"H-he did?"

"How much do you know about your husband?"

Apparently, not as much as she'd thought. "I ... didn't know about that part."

"Yes, well. I have excellent sources. When one hires a Bow Street man, one is well advised to inspect the merchandise, as it were."

"Sixteen. A boy, really."

"Hmmph. I doubt he was ever a boy. Too clever. He would have realized quickly which direction the river runs in this life."

She must ask him about his upbringing. Now that she thought about it, she must ask him a great many questions.

"No, what you sense in Mr. Hawthorn is not dissatisfaction, my dear. It is loneliness."

The dowager's arrow shot straight and true, piercing Hannah's heart between one breath and the next. Loneliness. Oh, heavens. She should have seen, should have recognized the same pain she'd often felt. How had she missed it?

"The remedy for such a condition is similar to the remedy for dissatisfaction. With one crucial difference."

"Yes?"

"Bedding him remains essential, of course. As I said, simple creatures." She gestured toward Humphrey, who had begun to snore. "Rather like hounds. Keep him well fed and ensure he understands it is in his interest to please you, and all will be well." She held up a finger. "You, however, did not marry a hound."

Hannah frowned her confusion. "No, I—"

"You married a wolf. Wolves do not take to domestication the same way hounds do. They require careful handling. The solitary ones most of all."

"Solitary." Hannah blew out a breath. Ached inside as she considered his resistance to friendship, his deliberate masking of his true character. "Yes. That is it precisely. What must I do?"

"Lure him into an attachment."

"We are married. Our attachment is permanent."

"No, girl. You have his name. But that is merely a leash, for his instinct compels him to escape entanglements. Make yourself essential to him. First, offer a bounty he cannot obtain elsewhere. Near-nakedness is a fine start."

Hannah's eyebrows shot up. "Near?"

"Indeed. Wear something provocative and easily discarded. Men enjoy having a small task to do before they're granted their prize."

"I'm not certain I—"

"After he's grown accustomed to your offerings, you must earn his trust and guard it fiercely. A wolf is not so easily won as a hound, but his loyalty, once yours, will attach him to your side more surely than any tether."

Trust is the soil. Love is the bloom. Eugenia's words echoed in her head, reminding her that, indeed, trust must be cultivated. Hannah didn't know how she might build trust between them. Assisting him with his investigation, perhaps? Thus far, he'd resisted her overtures in that quarter, but she must persuade him to accept her help if she wished to spend time in his company. It was not as though they'd been playing a lot of battledore and shuttlecock with Lady Wallingham's guests. Jonas chafed at such frivolities.

Hannah hesitated, eyeing the old woman across from her. "My lady, I do see the wisdom in your advice."

"Of course you do."

"But my own difficulties have resulted in great strain between us."

"Then, what are you doing here?"

Hannah frowned. Hadn't she just explained? The strain wouldn't let her sleep.

"Hmmph. You should be upstairs, girl. Near nakedness is wholly ineffective without proximity."

Nakedness was the problem—she didn't want him to see

what her past had done to her. She hated the very thought of his pity.

"Oh, do stop with the tragic sighs. The devil already came for you, and you survived to tell the tale of his death. Seducing your husband requires a mere fraction of the fortitude you've already proven to possess." The old woman leaned forward in her chair, spearing Hannah with a commanding glare. "Go upstairs. Offer yourself to him. Do not accept a denial any more than you accepted defeat at the hands of that demon." Her voice lowered, growing resonant in the dark. "If you want your wolf, make him yours."

The idea of it—seducing Jonas, letting him see her—was terrifying. But Lady Wallingham was right. Hannah must be strong. She must not let the fear triumph. She'd already come too far. Before she lost her nerve, she pushed to her feet and, stepping carefully over Humphrey, started out of the room. Just as she reached the door, a strange inkling made her pause. She glanced back.

The woman everyone called a dragon sat in her chair, white and small, creased and fragile. She gazed distantly out the window, green eyes glowing blue in the moonlight. Alone. So very alone.

"Go on, now, girl," the dragon said softly. "You've better things to do than keep an old woman company."

Something in Hannah wanted to stay, to ask how she knew so much about a man like Jonas—how she knew his pain was loneliness. But she sensed the dowager wished to be left in solitude, so she simply thanked her and bid her goodnight before rushing back toward the gallery.

This time, her toes scarcely touched stone as she dashed toward the grand staircase. Her heart pounded. Her breath came short and fast. Heat flashed through her, mingling with trepidation.

As she traveled the corridor, she began unplaiting her hair. As she opened the door to their bedchamber, she began untying her dressing gown. As she closed it behind her, she began unraveling the knot at her center—the one that feared his reaction.

Moonlight streamed through the window, landing on his naked back. His muscles looked deeper with the shadows. Stronger.

Quickly, she went to the dressing room and flung open her trunk. Tossing silks and linens and muslins aside, she came to the garment she'd been seeking. A peignoir. Silver silk and white lace.

Shaking, she discarded her dressing gown and slippers and nightdress and shift. She closed her eyes. Breathed. Remembered what Lady Wallingham had told her.

Then, she slid the peignoir over her body, letting it skim down past her hips and thighs. Barely a whisper, it caressed her skin as beautifully as his hands.

How she longed for his hands. For him.

Entering the bedchamber, she slowly moved toward the bed. His breaths were steady, his skin paled by the moon. He lay on his front, his head turned toward the bedside table, away from the window.

She remembered watching him when he'd been injured and feverish. Then, she'd only dared touch him while he slept. She'd found his body fascinating. Beautiful. She'd struggled to cool his fever, ease his pain.

Her heart had nearly died at the thought that he might not survive.

Now, she had him. Here. Close. In her bed. But she must make him hers. And for that, she must be strong.

She drew a breath and sat upon the bed, her hip beside his. She traced the lines of his beautiful mouth. She bent and kissed his dark brows and his square jaw. She ran a hand across his shoulders, caressing skin and muscle and bone.

That's when she felt them—scars. Small. Barely noticeable. Except they were not from an arrow. There were dozens of little puckers and lines. Immediately, she spread both hands over him, exploring her husband's back as she hadn't done before. Then, unable to help herself, she kissed them. Each one. Stroked them with her hands. Touched him with a new understanding.

He'd been wounded. Long ago, he'd been wounded. And these scars were now part of him.

He groaned. Ground his hips against the mattress. Sighed and turned his head. "Hannah?" His voice was roughened with sleep. "What are you doing, love?"

She smiled softly. "Touching you."

His hand raked over his face. "You should be sleeping."

"I cannot sleep until you see me."

He blinked. Turned on his side. Shoved up to sit on the bed. Silvery eyes dropped to her bosom and widened. "Bloody hell, woman."

She stood. Released a shuddering sigh. "I must show you now. I am afraid, but what I fear stands between me and what I desire most." She began inching her skirt higher, drawing up silk and lace above her knees. "Fear has had its last victory over me."

She raised the peignoir onto her thighs. Swallowed. Let the membrane of fear pass through her, a wave that nearly stole her breath. Then, she raised her chin, held his eyes, and drew the gown up to her waist.

His hand stretched out while hard, gray eyes burned her skin. Shaking, his fingertips lightly traced the thin, white scars from her knees to her hips. A muscle flexed and flickered in his jaw. He swallowed and warmed her skin with his palm. A deep, agonized groan sounded in his chest.

As though he'd been the one who was cut.

She pulled the peignoir off her shoulders and let it fall away.

And stood naked for him.

Chest heaving on rough breaths, he shoved to his feet.

Prowled a circle around her body. He viewed her lower back. Her buttocks. Her thighs. She felt his eyes upon her. Felt his pain as he traced the old, raised scars with his fingers. Then, his forehead landed upon her shoulder, his breath warm and hair cool against her neck.

Grinding, anguished sounds emerged from his throat—the sounds of an animal gravely wounded.

She turned in his arms. Needed to hold him. Slid her arms around him and pulled him against her, skin to skin.

"It is over," she whispered against his neck, kissing his jaw and clutching his hair. "It is over now. He can never hurt me again."

Jonas's arms tightened around her waist. Seized her hard against him.

"I want you to touch me," she murmured, stroking and stroking and stroking his neck and his face and his shoulders. "I want you inside."

"God, Hannah." His hands came up to thread through her hair. He gathered up her curls and held them to his face. Breathed her in.

"Do you ... want me?" She was terrified to ask. Terrified of his answer. "Do you want me still?"

"Yes," he rasped, his lips finding her cheek, her forehead. He cupped her face and kissed her mouth. "I want you so much, it's killing me."

Her sigh was nearly a sob as a warm rush of relief flooded in to replace the tension she'd been holding at bay.

His hand shook as he stroked her hair. "I'd do anything to spare you pain, love. If I could have taken it for you—"

"My scars are part of me. Just as yours are part of you." She braced herself and took his jaw between her hands. Then, she captured his gaze and gave him the truth. "I am not fragile. I am strong. I need you to believe that. I need you to make love to me as if you know that."

His eyes flashed silver. Went brilliant and hot. His lips parted as he mouthed her name.

Then, she stood on her toes. Held his eyes. Brought him down to murmur against his mouth, "Take me." She ran the backs of her fingers over his cheek. "Make me yours, Jonas Bartholomew Hawthorn. Always."

Chapter Fourteen

"My amenability to seduction has nothing whatever to do with acquiring new gowns. I've only said that new gowns improve a husband's odds of finding his wife in good spirits. And a wife employs the levers at her disposal."

—DOROTHEA BAINBRIDGE, COUNTESS BAINBRIDGE, to Malcolm Charles Bainbridge, Earl Bainbridge, in a letter explaining the necessity of marital congress and generous allowances in maintaining domestic order.

SHE WORE NOTHING BUT MOONLIGHT. CURVES HE'D ONLY ever seen covered by gowns wove a sinuous spell. Made his head spin and his cock harder than the stone in St.

Cuthbert's Cave. Nipples he'd only ever touched through cloth were hard, too. They were pink. Dark, dusky pink jewels on sweet, snowy breasts.

He'd laid her out on the bed. Now, he stood beside her, looking his fill.

He wanted to look forever. But there was too much touching to do.

Running a hand through his hair, he considered his options. He needed to keep control. It had never been a problem before her, but it was bloody well a problem now.

Nothing was as beautiful to him as his wife. The curve of her waist, nipped in just so from slender hips. The flat of her belly, velvety as a peach. The thatch of black curls between her thighs, a dark glade for a thirsty man.

"Jonas?" Snowfall inflamed him. Made his heart pound and his muscles ache.

He paced away from her. Tried to breathe against the everlasting need. To take her. Hard and deep. Long and rough. No boundaries. No stopping.

What he needed was a strategy. A way to make certain she was with him at every step. That he did nothing to cause her fear or pain.

He turned. Paced back to her.

She looked confused. "Jonas?"

"I am going to describe what I intend to do." He absorbed the shock of her beauty again. By God, she made his head swim. "Before I do it."

"Oh."

He swallowed and nodded. It was a good idea. She didn't want him to regard her as fragile, but he'd just been awakened from a dead sleep to be shown the vicious, horrific truth of what she'd endured. She would simply have to accept this compromise.

She sighed and wriggled deeper into the mattress, sending his body into a fever. "Very well. If you must."

"I must."

"Shall we begin now, or ...?"

"Yes." He stared at her breasts, wondering how they tasted. He stared at the enchanted black glade between her scarred thighs, wondering the same thing.

"Jonas."

He should probably keep his breeches on. Better control that way.

"Perhaps you should kiss me."

"I shall remove my breeches now."

"Good. I'd like that."

If she was naked, he should be naked. It made sense. He quickly dispensed with them, hopping on one foot as his other foot caught.

Rosebud lips curved in a mischievous smile. Her fingers drifted to her mouth. "It appears your desire remains unaffected."

He glanced down before tossing the breeches aside. "Aye."

"This makes me very happy."

"I'm going to lie beside you now."

She nodded, scooting toward the center of the bed to make room.

"I've changed my mind."

Moonlit eyes shadowed with disappointment. "Y-you have?"

"Aye." He dropped to his knees. "I am going to take hold of your legs and move you toward me."

She blinked. "Oh. For what purpose?"

"So I can taste you."

Thick lashes fluttered. Soft lips parted. "Oh, my."

He reached for her knees. Turned her sideways and pulled her toward him. Positioned her precisely where he wanted her, with her backside at the edge and her legs propped on his shoulders. He was glad to be on his knees, for her scent had him in his cups as surely as a bottle of Wallingham's cognac. Roses. Rain. Sea storms and sweet woman.

He spread her thighs wider. Savored the beauty of his

woman. "I'm going to kiss you here, love." He ran a finger along her inner thigh. Lightly. Just a breath, really. He used his other hand—the one still sore from his battle with the tree—to dip into her folds, spreading the honey he found there to her pleasure center. Then, he sank a finger inside her drenched sheath. "And here." He added another. "I'm going to taste you and make you come for me."

She moaned his name. Her sheath clenched upon his fingers. Rippled and demanded more.

He kissed the edge of one of her longest scars first. White and thin, it started on her outer thigh and stopped above her knee. Then, he moved to her inner thigh, where the demon hadn't ventured. Where the soft, white flesh was as pristine as fresh snowfall. He kissed her there, tasting rosewater and salt. Tasting his woman.

The black-thatched glade waited, however, and he gave her what she presently begged of him—a deeper stroke of his fingers. He repositioned them to test a theory. Repositioned again. Received a panting, "Oh, my heavens, Jonas. What is ... that is ... oh, my heavens."

And his grin grew. He bent his head to her. Pleasured her with firm strokes of his tongue. Drove her higher and higher. Used every damned thing he'd ever learned to draw out her sweet, pulsing bud and make it sing. Make Hannah understand how beautiful she was to him.

He licked and savored. Pressured and stroked.

And tasted. God, how he wanted to drown in her.

She clawed his hair. Squeezed his fingers until they ached. Arched her back and chanted his name.

After he'd brought her to completion once, he decided to do it again. So, as he'd promised, he withdrew his fingers and replaced them with his tongue. Forced her body to accept the pleasure he gave as its due.

He didn't want to let her go. He didn't want to pull away. But his own body was making hard demands.

On the heels of her second climax, he repositioned her again, lifting her slender hips deeper onto the bed and rising to his feet.

"I'm going to suckle your breasts, now, Hannah."

"Jonas," she panted, her eyes glowing, her arms lying limp and sprawled beside her shoulders. "I—I don't know if I can—"

"You can," he assured her. "I'll show you."

He lay down beside his wife. Stroked her cheek and her midnight hair. Kissed her throat and pulled her into him.

She gasped as she felt the enormity of his arousal. "Oh, heavens. Come inside me. Please. You must be so—"

God, she was soft. And her nipples were hard. "I'm going to touch you." He stroked his hand over her right breast. Squeezed her nipple and drew it out. Felt her belly ripple. Heard her snowfall voice thread with arousal. Moaning. Surprised. Not understanding how much more pleasure he could give her. He took her in his mouth—velvety and ripe as peaches.

Her thigh came up, her legs wrapping around his hips as she demanded.

He cupped her breast from beneath and suckled deep. Plumped and squeezed and nibbled and feasted. Then, he moved to her left breast.

That one seemed to please her even more. Her fingers dug at his nape. Pulled at his hair. Made him smile against her skin. Her third climax came just as he drew his teeth across the sensitized tip.

Her sweet cries of ecstasy soothed him. Made something chaotic inside him still. He eased her down from her peak with kisses upon her sweet mouth. Caresses of her tongue with his.

"I'm going to fuck you now," he said, all his control gone. He shouldn't use such words with her. But his mind wasn't talking. His body was.

She nodded, her cheeks flushing, her breasts ripe and swollen. "Yes," she rasped.

"It will be deep and fast."

She moaned. Her neck arched as she squeezed her eyes closed for a brief moment. When she opened them again, they were alight. They devoured him. "Yes," she growled. "Yes, yes. Yes."

He spread her thighs wider. Took her beneath him fully. And slid deep into his wife without stopping. Without boundaries. Without anything between them but moonlight and lust.

She gripped him hard—her sheath, her arms, her fingers. Held him fast as he began his rhythm. He buried his face in her neck. Kissed her skin and breathed roses. His hips were acting on their own, hammering away faster and faster. His cock was inside a silken, tight furnace. It wanted to explode. Everything was brighter than it should have been. Her skin. Her eyes. The glow inside his chest.

He knew nothing, felt nothing but her.

Her legs locked around him. Her arms tightened and her lips moved beside his ear.

Then, he heard it. His name.

He wanted to see her. Needed it.

So, he looked. Found palest green.

Something flashed there. A flutter. An oddity.

She gritted her teeth. Grasped his face between her hands with a ferocity he didn't know she had. "Keep me with you," she demanded, panting and kissing him. "Keep me here."

He didn't know what she meant. His body was thrusting, driving them both toward a precipice. She reached for his hand. Dragged it to her cheek. Took his thumb into her mouth. Suckled hard and nipped before releasing him.

"Keep me with you," she repeated.

"What do you need?"

She pulled his hand to her breast. Took his thumb and finger and squeezed her own nipple—much harder than he would have done. With a gasp, she arched upward as though he'd given her another peak. She was almost there; he felt it coming. Rippling around him. But when she looked into his eyes, it was with desperation.

"Please," she sobbed. "Keep me here."

He gave her what she asked, and in return, she gave him herself. Even as he pounded into her, felt his own peak cresting like a rogue wave, she didn't look away.

She held him. Took him. Loved him.

And let him love her.

Let him inside.

Inside moonlight and midnight and roses and rain. Inside her heart, which glowed so brightly, he felt blinded. But he wasn't. He saw her.

And, God, how he loved her.

"Hannah," he panted, desperate to have more. He touched his forehead to hers. Kept her with him.

A look of wonder that was almost pain crossed her face. "I am here, Jonas," she said as her body began to seize up with her climax, to demand he give her his in return. "Oh, sweet heaven, I am here."

And when the pleasure surged and exploded inside him, he surrendered gladly, all the while repeating the one thing he knew to be true: "You are mine, love. Only mine."

SHE AWAKENED TO MOONLIGHT AND A SILKEN BREEZE KISSING her bare body. Her eyes opened. She shifted in bed, her inner thighs sore and protesting. Remembered pleasure made her smile.

Then, she saw him. He was sitting by the window, bare shoulders painted silver, sketchbook in hand. He stared at her. Tilted his head.

"You are bloody exquisite, do you know that?"

Her smile deepened. Her breath caught. "Are you sketching me, husband?"

"I am."

She swallowed. Looked down at her hips and thighs. Thin scars shone whiter in the moonlight—lines and lines and lines. Evenly spaced. Precise. Older scars were longer, extending down nearly to her knees in some places.

"What did you mean when you asked me to keep you here?"

His question made her heart twist. Her eyes fluttered. She covered her mouth with the backs of her fingers. Then, her eyes found his. "I don't know why it happens," she whispered.

His frown was dark. Intense. "What happens, love?"

"Something frightens me and I ... go away. Behind my eyes, I am far away. Floating. Often, I cannot remember ..." She couldn't hold his gaze any longer, so she focused on his shoulder and the open window. "I cannot remember anything of the time I am away. I simply disappear. The episodes are less frequent than they once were. I've learned to fight them. Strong sensation helps. But sometimes, I fear I may leave and never return."

"After our kiss. That was—"

"Yes."

"I frightened you."

"No. You carried me." She sighed. "None of this is your doing. I am not normal, Jonas."

He went silent for a long while. Finally, in a roughened voice, he repeated, "You are exquisite. Every single part. Inside and out."

Her heart swelled. Quickened. "You make me feel beautiful."

"Only because you are."

"Do you remember the day we met in the drawing room at Holstoke House?"

A sensual smile curled the corners of his mouth. Silvery

eyes burned a path from her breasts to her hips. "I could see your shape through your gown. A haughty Snow Queen whose beauty set me afire."

"You wouldn't let me hide," she murmured. "I tried not to want you. But there you were, close enough to kiss. Kneeling at my feet. Seeing me as both desirable and ... normal. Speaking to me as if I were strong enough to accept your challenge."

He ran a hand over his jaw and set his sketchbook aside. "I was too bloody fascinated to be polite."

"I didn't need politeness. I needed to be shaken. Tempted. I just didn't realize it."

He pushed to his feet. Wandered to the bed, his face shadowed, his hardness flagrant. "Do I tempt you?"

"Endlessly."

Muscles in his shoulders flexed as he drew a deeper breath. "Tell me what I must do." His hands tightened into fists then released. "I never want you to ... disappear because of something I've done."

She reached out for him.

He hesitated before taking her hand in his.

"Touch me," she said, her heart in her throat. "Please, Jonas."

He sat on the bed, his expression hidden by the darkness. "If I ever hurt you—"

"Never. You never will." She drew his hand between her breasts, flattened his palm over her heart. "I know it here. You mustn't allow my scars to come between us. Do you understand? Promise me."

He shook his head.

"With you, I mustn't be fragile," she insisted. "Promise you will always challenge me to be stronger. Promise you will always touch me without boundaries."

A low, deep groan emerged from his chest. In the next moment, he slipped his arms beneath her back and neck. Lifted her to his mouth. Kissed her until she was clinging to him, moaning for him.

Her back met the mattress again, but this time, he flattened her, weighted her. Inflamed her.

She loved everything about lying beneath his lean, hard body. His mouth upon hers, his chest pressuring her breasts and chafing her nipples, his thighs wedging between hers so that she lay open and vulnerable to him.

She welcomed him. Needed his thick hardness filling her again.

"Jonas," she whispered against his mouth. "I want you so much." It wasn't merely his body or his hands that she longed for. What she wanted most was the connection they'd shared earlier, the transcendent moment when she'd felt herself merging with him. She tried pulling back long enough to see his eyes. But, oddly, he avoided her gaze.

Instead, he kissed her throat, his breath hot. Then, he suckled her breasts, his whiskery jaw chafing her skin in a way that made her writhe.

"More," she panted. "I need more of you."

He growled against her, his hands holding her still, cupping beneath her breast to position her for his mouth.

She worked her hips lower, trying to tempt him into sliding that thick, hard stalk inside her. How empty she felt without him. Threading her hands through his hair, she once again attempted to draw him up so she could see his beautiful, silvery eyes.

Once again, his gaze slid away.

She frowned, frustrated and growing hotter, needier by the moment. "Jonas."

His shoulders heaved on rough breaths.

She tried cupping his jaw.

He clasped her wrist and tugged her hand away. Then, in a flash, he shifted and flipped her onto her belly. Drew her hips up beneath him so that his hardness became an intimate caress against her backside.

She moaned into the pillow as the new position introduced

new sensations—his lips against her nape, the hair of his chest against her back, the thrill of his hands gripping her hips and digging in as though he couldn't stop himself. Heat and hardness surrounded her while one of his hands slid between the mattress and her belly.

Slid down to where she was wet for him. Stroked hard and sure against swollen flesh.

His mouth suckled at her neck. His teeth scraped and his tongue soothed.

She'd wanted connection. He gave her raw pleasure.

"J-Jonas. Let me ..."

He pulled her up onto her knees, his strength a massive force. "No boundaries," he growled in her ear. "Tell me you still want it. Even when I take you this way."

Good heavens. Was he testing her? She felt his arm bracing her hips, pulling her back into him. He leaned upon his other arm, holding himself above her. Waiting. Waiting for her to shrink away.

He'd be waiting a long while. She adored his strength. His hardness. The primitive lust she sensed in him. She would have preferred being able to see his eyes, but if he liked her in this position, she'd happily oblige.

"I want it," she purred. "I want you."

His forehead touched her shoulder. His breaths were hot and harsh. Between one and the next, his blunt, thick member found her opening. Pressed inside.

She was still a bit tender from their earlier lovemaking, and he felt bigger at this reverse angle. But heavens, how her body rejoiced at being filled again. She tightened and groaned his name.

"Relax, love," he panted. "Let me ... ah, God. Let me inside."

She struggled to do as he asked, relaxing her muscles and focusing on the feel of him inside her. Stretching. Pressuring.

Long, slow thrusts carried him deeper each passing second. His hand came up to play with her nipples, stoking yet more heat where they were joined. His mouth suckled her neck and his tongue traced her ear. "Feel me there," he rasped. "We'll take this slow. You'll like how it builds." He nipped her earlobe. "I'll like knowing how deep I've been, how you'll still feel me tomorrow."

It was precisely as he described—slow, methodical, a fire built upon smoldering coals. His hardness slid out on long strokes until he nearly left her. Then back inside, so deep the pressure became an ache.

His hand remained busy, caressing her breasts and belly, sliding down between her thighs to tease her swollen bud, to test how strongly he stretched her.

The cadence of his possession was controlled yet relentless. It didn't quicken or slow, just claimed like waves claiming a shore.

"That's it, love." His palm cupped her belly while his fingers caressed her mound. Then, he used the base of his palm to add yet more pressure. "Feel me?"

She was gasping, fighting for air. The heat and stretch and pressure were all one thing. They expanded and swelled. Stroked and filled. Became a burgeoning storm of heat and light. Rolling. Rolling. Rolling.

Bursting open and releasing. Releasing. Releasing.

Seizing upon him with gasps and sobs.

She clawed into the mattress. Groaned his name into the pillow. Tightened around him over and over as pleasure and her husband held her in an explosive grip.

Only then did his tempo increase. Pounding. Pounding. Pounding.

And she took his release inside her, warm and complete.

Replete. Her husband, fully claimed. As their bodies sank together onto the bed, he remained joined with her, his strong arms drawing her back against him, crossing her belly and shoulders.

He kissed her neck and her cheek. Held her tightly.

She tried to turn her head. Wanted to see his eyes and feel their connection.

Instead, he held her in place. Held himself inside her, still semi-hard. "Sleep now, love," he murmured, kissing her ear.

Indeed, she felt a lovely lethargy pulling at her. He'd rolled them so that they both faced the window, and the cooling breeze came up to dance across their joined bodies. And, as sleep came to claim her, she ran her hands over his, touched him wherever she could, and murmured a stray thought that made no sense and perfect sense, all at once.

"Don't leave me alone," she said, her words slurred with drowsiness. "I need you here with me."

His only reply was to nuzzle her hair, lay a kiss softer than a breeze upon her cheek, and hold her close as moonlight was swallowed by the darkening sky.

Chapter Fifteen

"Meredith Huxley has suggested I serve your favorite foods whenever you please me. But if I serve peach tarts at every meal, we will soon need a coach with stouter wheels. And a bed with stouter boards."

—DOROTHEA BAINBRIDGE, THE MARCHIONESS OF WALLINGHAM, to Malcolm Charles Bainbridge, the Marquess of Wallingham, in a letter expressing appreciation for men of strong appetites.

SEATED BESIDE HIS WIFE AT GRIMSGATE'S TWENTY-FOOT DINING table the following morning, Jonas discovered his hunger was stronger than ever. Not for food—his appetite remained consistent in that quarter. No, this hunger was for ... her.

As he gazed upon her cheek, her neck, the white muslin modestly gathered along her collarbone and tucked into her bodice, he licked his lips and debated whether to haul her upstairs immediately or wait another quarter-hour for her to finish breakfast.

He was inclined toward the former.

Soft, pink color bloomed in her cheeks as she took a bite of brioche. She swallowed and sighed. Set her fork beside her plate. Took a delicate a sip of tea.

He watched her breasts rise and fall, the rhythm quickening as she replaced her cup and tucked her hand beneath the table. Her lips parted. Her tongue darted out to trace the lower one.

Then, he felt it. Her hand. His thigh. God Almighty.

Her eyes fluttered upward. Found his. Burned his skin and hardened him mercilessly. Bound him to her inexorably.

He pulled his gaze away but claimed her bare hand. Guided it to where his hunger centered.

A slow, sensuous smile curled her lips.

Bloody hell. He was going to catch fire, right there at a dragon's table.

"... must purchase a new copy of *Waverley*, for Kate refuses to return the one I lent her."

Jonas swallowed his lust and returned his wife's hand to her lap as the Duke and Duchess of Blackmore entered the room. The pair joined Robert and Annabelle Conrad and Lord and Lady Holstoke on the opposite side of the table.

"We have three additional copies at home, Jane." Blackmore glared at a footman whose gloved hand brushed the duchess's sleeve while pouring her coffee. "Is that not sufficient?"

"What if I wish to lend another? Then, I shall be left with only two."

The duke, whose rigid posture could hoist a mainsail, retorted, "Should that occur, I will happily buy you a new copy for your collection."

She sniffed and adjusted her spectacles then went about adding a spoonful of cream to her coffee. As she stirred, her husband watched her hands as a cat might eye a bright, elusive bird—with hunger and fascination.

Watching the interplay, Jonas felt an odd kinship with the man. They were nothing alike, of course. The golden-haired duke had been born to privilege and carried himself as though the whole of English propriety rested upon his rigid shoulders. But this—the near-worshipful regard—felt too damned familiar.

Apart from that single similarity, however, he felt as out of place as a street stray amongst prized hunting hounds. Conrad and Holstoke discussed drainage schemes and fruit tree cultivation. Blackmore attempted to persuade his wife that two libraries were sufficient for their needs. Lady Holstoke and Annabelle Conrad gossiped about Clarissa Meadows's flirtation with someone named Andrew Farrington, who preferred ladies with dark hair.

He shifted in his chair and drank his coffee and wondered what in bloody hell he was doing there. Then, his wife delicately cleared her throat.

"Jonas," she said softly.

"Aye?"

"Do you intend to finish that?"

He glanced down. She was eyeing his half-eaten brioche. Her lashes fluttered. She looked both longing and hopeful.

Chuckling, he leaned close. "I believe there's more on the sideboard, love. Wouldn't you rather have a fresh one of your own?"

She licked her lips. Lit with a blush that fired him hot. "I like finishing what you've started."

He fought the lust that held him in thrall. "Everything I have is yours. Take whatever you desire."

With a mischievous smile, she did just that.

He downed the remainder of his coffee in a single gulp. As

he replaced his cup, he noticed Lady Holstoke shooting them a speculative glance from across the table.

She appeared approving. "Hannah, Phineas and I went riding along the beach earlier. Positively splendid. We'd hoped we might see you there. Did you miss your morning ride?"

Hannah gave her sister-in-law a secretive smile. "No. I rode. It was most invigorating." Then, calmly, she sank her teeth into his brioche.

Dear, holy God. She was killing him. He shifted in his chair, trying in vain to convince his erection to subside. In desperation, he poured himself some tea and downed the half-warm stuff in two swallows.

"Ah, yes," said Lady Holstoke. "Morning rides are delightful. I'm sure Mr. Hawthorn would agree."

He glared and poured more tea.

"How is your investigation coming along, Mr. Hawthorn?" she inquired.

He opened his mouth to answer, but his wife interjected, "It would be going better if he would permit me to help."

He shifted his glare to her. "I don't need help."

That small, stubborn chin went up. "Perhaps, but why not take it when it is offered?"

Sighing, he drummed his fingers on the table. "I'm headed back to Alnwick today. You should stay here and enjoy the party."

"Rubbish," she said pertly. "I will go with you."

"No, you will not."

She arched a black brow. "We shall see."

Hoping for support from someone sensible, he made the mistake of turning to Lady Holstoke. Eugenia Brand looked upon them with sparkling fascination. She was beaming like a proud mother. "Well, the weather is quite fine today. I should think your blue habit would be perfect for a jaunt to Alnwick, dearest. Wear the hat with the white feathers."

Damn and blast. He was being besieged from all sides.

Just then, a loud clatter sounded out in the corridor, like a tray dropping on stone. A slurred, masculine voice intruded, insisting, "I am a Bainbridge, for God's sake. I am always invited."

Jonas heard Nash speaking too quietly to make out words. A moment later, a short, large-chinned, dark-haired young man stumbled through the open doorway. The man's face was unshaven, his eyes red and his cheeks redder. His waistcoat was misbuttoned and his cravat askew.

Nash followed, trying valiantly to retrieve the stray sot. "Her ladyship's instructions were explicit, Mr. Bainbridge," the butler said sternly. "I must insist you leave, or I will be forced to see it so." He gestured to two large footmen.

The drunkard yanked his arm from their grasp and collided with the table. The rattling china and sloshing liquids caused several feminine gasps, and three of the men at the table stood, moving to position themselves between Bainbridge and their wives. Holstoke went first. Then, the duke. Then, Conrad.

Jonas kept his seat, eyeing the man's weak frame and thickening belly. He drank his tea and waited.

"Where is Wallingham?" the drunkard demanded. "My allowance is no toy to be withheld for his amusement. I was his heir, damn his eyes. The least he could do is meet his obligations."

Bainbridge's arms flailed as he evaded Nash, the footmen, and the three protective aristocrats attempting to drive him away from the women.

Jonas kept the intruder in his sights, setting his cup on the table and leaning back in his chair. He waited. Watched.

Something about the man seemed familiar. It made his neck itch. The chin, perhaps? If he was Wallingham's cousin, that would explain the similarity. Large chins featured prominently in the portraits of Bainbridge men throughout the castle.

Bainbridge staggered toward the sideboard, knocked a tray of tiny cakes onto the floor, and turned resentful red eyes on Nash. "You and Wallingham are the same. Forever doing her bidding. Like dogs, you are. Afraid of a scolding from a bloody female."

Nash closed in. Bainbridge shoved sideways. Toward Hannah, whose shoulders tensed and shuddered as he veered too close.

In an instant, Jonas was on his feet, twisting the man's arm to the point of breaking. He slammed the miserable sot facedown onto the table. The man's weight flattened a stray brioche.

"Being drunk was not your mistake," he muttered in the sot's ear, applying pressure to ensure he was listening. "Coming here was not your mistake. Disobeying her ladyship and her ladyship's butler was not your mistake."

The man whimpered piteously.

"Shall I tell you your mistake, Bainbridge?"

Another whinging moan.

"You were careless. Round my wife, I don't tolerate careless."

Wallingham entered a moment later. Ordinarily, the man had a calm, distinguished air about him. But he also had his mother's eyes—and, occasionally, her fire. He took in the scene, blazing with controlled fury and giving Jonas an approving nod. "My thanks, Hawthorn. Unfortunately, my cousin never learnt the value of circumspection, despite Mother's countless efforts." He nodded to the two footmen, who moved in to retrieve Bainbridge, hauling him away. Wallingham inclined his head. "Please accept my deepest apologies. Rest assured, Cecil Bainbridge shan't trouble us again."

Wallingham spoke briefly with Holstoke, Conrad, and Blackmore before leaving the room. Meanwhile, Jonas crouched down beside Hannah's chair and covered her hands with his. "Everything all right, love?"

She nodded, her eyes holding his. She looked steady. She looked like she wanted to kiss him. "Yes. He startled me, that's all."

"I would never let him touch you."

"I know." She cupped his cheek. Bent forward and kissed him. Sighed. "Proficiency is most ... reassuring," she whispered.

He didn't know what she meant, precisely, but he would accept her affection no matter the cause.

"Now, I must go upstairs and change into my riding habit."

"Hannah—"

"I am going with you, Jonas Hawthorn. That is that."

"Bloody hell."

"While I am gone, you should consider the value of accepting assistance which costs you nothing and may benefit you immeasurably." She patted his jaw. "I believe Dunston is in the garden."

He blinked as she rose gracefully from her seat. For a moment, she stood above him and he gazed up at her like a moonstruck hound at a Snow Queen's feet. Perhaps this was where he belonged, mongrel that he was.

But then, she gazed down with an adoring light, bending at the waist to kiss him again with her lips on his mouth, her hands on his face, and her breath coming fast.

He might be at her feet, but she was in thrall, too. It should comfort him. It didn't.

A short while later, he found himself in the garden, ambling toward the fountain as he considered her point about accepting help. He hadn't much time left to complete his investigation before Lady Wallingham lost patience and offered the reward to someone else.

Still, it chafed that his wife thought he needed assistance to finish a job. He'd worked with other men before—Drayton had been helpful upon occasion. But he worked better alone. He always had.

He wandered past a hedge and listened to the fountain, wondering how he might persuade Hannah to stay where she belonged.

"Perhaps Hawthorn will settle this. Hawthorn!" It was Dunston, standing with several other men on the opposite side of the fountain near a pair of urns. "Brown Bess or Baker rifle, my good man?"

He approached the group—Dunston, Atherbourne, Reaver, and Rutherford—with suspicion. Dunston might prefer knives, but he knew guns better than most. There was little reason to ask Jonas his opinion unless Hannah or Lady Dunston had put him up to it. "Depends," he called as he neared the men. "Would you prefer to kill your target or wound him?"

"Never fire unless you mean to kill, I've always said." Dunston's grin was wide.

"Well, if you're close enough, you can kill a man with either weapon. Past seventy yards, however, you'll find the Brown Bess useful only as a prop for aiming your Baker rifle."

Dunston clapped Reaver's shoulder. "You see? I did not lose twelve guineas to an amateur."

Reaver grunted, glowering first at Hawthorn then at Dunston. "It was a fool's wager. A bottle of brandy for each of you. Bloody, bleeding hell. 'Tis a wonder you didn't mistake your own backsides for targets."

"I'm telling you, Holstoke couldn't have made that shot, and he's the finest archer I know."

Jonas rubbed his jaw. "Still sore about that, eh?"

"Curious. You never did say how you acquired such skills."

Ordinarily, he preferred to avoid direct answers to such questions. There was little advantage to be had from trading confidences. A man only did so when he wished to cultivate friendship. He didn't need friendship. He needed to tip things in his favor, come out on the winning side of having nothing and having enough. None of these men could understand his desperation.

Yet, he hesitated to brush Dunston's question aside, instead eyeing each of the men in turn. They were wealthy, to be sure. But their privileged positions hadn't come without cost.

Atherbourne was the sort of handsome that made women stare and swoon. He had a lovely wife, four children, a title, and a rich estate in Derbyshire. But Conrad had mentioned he'd been at Waterloo. That was one of the few battles Jonas had missed. Later, when he'd heard reports from infantrymen who had been there, he was thankful to have been thousands of miles away.

Reaver was a canny sort. The giant was the only one of the group who'd come up rough, as Jonas had. He hadn't discovered his connection to Tannenbrook until after he'd built the most successful gaming club in London using nothing but fists and sweat and shrewdness. After meeting him the previous year, Jonas had come to admire the man's unyielding ambition. He, too, had a wife. He, too, had an estate in Derbyshire, though he and his wife preferred their home in London. With a brood of five boys who all seemed destined to take on their father's proportions, Jonas could see how more than one house would be sensible.

Rutherford was harder to decipher. Benedict Chatham appeared to have everything a man could want. He was a marquess with old bloodlines and a thriving estate. Jonas had heard the quantity of coal beneath his lands would keep Newcastle's ports busy for the next hundred years. Meanwhile, the turquoise-eyed lord appeared as contented as a cat after gallon of cream and an hour's stroking. He and his unusually tall, redheaded wife had two sons and a daughter. Like Atherbourne and Dunston, fortune appeared to have smiled upon him.

But Jonas happened to know that before his marriage, Benedict Chatham's fortunes hadn't been so brilliant. In fact, he'd been at the edge of killing himself with drink. Reaver had explained it late one night when Jonas had stopped by his club to obtain information for a job. He'd lamented that his sources weren't what they'd once been. Then, he'd explained how he'd once had the future Marquess of Rutherford working alongside him ferreting secrets. "Had to cut him loose," he'd lamented. "Bloody shame. He was first-rate. But the stubborn sod was walking death. Needed a boot to the arse, that much is certain."

Then, there was Dunston, the man who'd lived two lives, one of silk waistcoats, the other of violence. He'd told Jonas once that he still occasionally felt the disorienting sensation of walking in two worlds—one light and one dark. Five children, a pretty wife with a sweet smile, an expansive estate, a grand title. And the earl, while nauseatingly happy, nevertheless bore scars from his time as a hunter of ghosts and demons.

Against his will, Jonas had come to know Dunston over the past year. He actually liked the man.

So, now, with Hannah's words echoing in his ears and four men staring at him expectantly, he rolled his shoulders and opened a door he probably should leave closed. "I learned archery as a lad. My father trained me."

"He was an archer?"

"A gamekeeper. For a time, at any rate."

"Then, you must know how to hunt." Dunston smiled. "For game other than thieves, I mean."

"Aye."

Dunston's smile broadened into a grin. "Splendid, indeed. My annual hunt is in November. Fairfield Park. You must come, old chap. We shall test your aim past seventy yards." He gestured toward Reaver. "His oldest boy, Ash, is a veritable prodigy. Took down a stag last year at four-hundred yards. Natural talent like that cries out for tutoring."

For a while, the other men bantered about hunting and shooting, including him in the conversation as though Jonas were a bloody peer. He rolled his shoulders again and wondered at Dunston's invitation. Wondered if Hannah was the reason for their friendliness. But, then, Dunston had made such overtures before.

Now that he thought about it, Dunston had been

attempting to befriend him for over a year, buying him dinner at Reaver's. Drinking pints with him at the Black Bull. Making drunken archery wagers and recommending him for jobs.

So far, he hadn't asked anything in return.

Hannah's admonition about accepting help surfaced again. He didn't want to. Lady Wallingham had told him to be discreet, not to involve her guests overmuch. But he had only a week remaining before she withdrew her offer and called upon Drayton. So, perhaps he could ask. Just this once. Just to see this job through so he could stop picturing Hannah being forced to live in empty, rented rooms with an alley view.

He cleared his throat. "At the moment, a thief is my quarry," he said as the gentlemen debated the challenge of pheasant over duck. "He's proving elusive."

Reaver crossed massive arms. "What do you have so far?"

Jonas outlined his findings, explaining about the missing maid and the slipper in the cave and what the man in Alnwick had told him.

"Any idea what the trunk contains?" asked Atherbourne, dark eyes thoughtful. "It seems that would tell us what the thief is truly after, which might help in identifying him."

"No," Jonas answered. "Lady Wallingham refuses to speak about the trunk's contents, and nobody else seems to know."

"Have you asked her son?" inquired Reaver. "Wallingham knows the dragon best."

Jonas nodded. "First thing. He didn't know about the contents. Only said she's had problems keeping lady's maids through the years and wondered if one of them might have stolen the trunk out of spite. I looked into it. Her last three lady's maids are all happily employed elsewhere."

"You say she kept the trunk in her dressing room," said Rutherford. "Rather personal, then. Keeping it close to hand implies either extreme value or extreme sentiment. Perhaps both." The marquess tilted his head to an assessing angle. "I could make inquiries if you like. Discreetly, of course."

Jonas bit down on his instinctive resistance and nodded. "I'd appreciate it, my lord."

Rutherford's smile turned wry. "Consider it done. And dispense with the 'my lord.' Rutherford will do. Or Ben, if you're feeling cheeky."

"He must like you, Hawthorn," commented Atherbourne. "He bristles when I call him Ben, and I've known the scoundrel since Eton."

"I was Chatham then," Rutherford retorted lazily. "Had to give that title over when Jameson was born. Now, I am Ben to my friends."

Jonas sensed tension between the two men but couldn't quite decipher the cause.

"Hmm. You say the man with the maid asked about tides?" Dunston asked.

Jonas nodded. "What are you thinking?"

"Occurs to me the thief has a fondness for caves."

"Aye. But there aren't many round here. St. Cuthbert's is the closest one of any size."

Dunston's gaze took on a sharpened gleam. "If you're inland, perhaps."

Jonas shook his head as he took his meaning. "In Dorsetshire, I might agree sea caves are logical. But the beaches here are flatter. Fewer cliffs. Fewer caves."

"They do exist, however." The cold, flinty voice sounded behind him. Holstoke strode across the lawn, wearing his usual inscrutable expression. "Northeast of Alnwick. Remote. Accessible when the tide is out. Less so when it is high. A good place to avoid being seen by anybody other than the gulls."

Reaver grunted his agreement. "We need to determine whether the maid was working with the thief or merely his victim. If she's truly been taken against her will, she's in danger."

"Count on the latter," said Dunston. "She didn't seem the scheming sort when Hawthorn questioned her. More impressionable, I'd say."

The giant's heavy brows drew together. "I'll find answers. Perhaps a bit of pressure upon the male servants, a bit of coin to those who may know more than they're sayin'. We don't want the lass sufferin' unduly for falling prey to a thief's charms."

Atherbourne asked, "You say you have sketches of them?" At Jonas's nod, he offered, "I could ask Victoria to copy them for you. The hunt might go faster with several sets."

Jonas pulled the sketches from his pocket and handed them to the viscount. "My thanks."

"Come, Hawthorn," said Holstoke. "Wallingham has a map in the library. I'll show you where the caves are located. I believe they've been used for smuggling from time to time."

As he thanked the gentlemen and followed his brother-in-law back into the castle, Jonas fought the urge to rush back and tell them he'd handle the investigation on his own. Letting other men do his job made his skin writhe. The feeling reminded him of the time when he was a boy and a group of lads had torn open the door to the privy while he was relieving himself—just as a group of girls had wandered by.

He supposed this was better, but he still felt like he had his breeches down around his knees.

The feeling didn't ease when he entered the library, noting the grandeur of the twenty-foot ceiling and dark, towering shelves. He could never give Hannah something like this.

He watched Holstoke pull a large, leather-bound book from one of the lower shelves and lay it out on an ornate table.

He'd be asking his wife to leave a castle as grand as this one, to forgo enormous libraries and elaborate gardens. Even if he collected his reward from Lady Wallingham, they would always live within lesser means than she'd enjoyed as Holstoke's sister.

Nevertheless, if he wanted to provide an acceptable home for his wife—a home with servants and fine horses and a pianoforte and velvet upholstery—then he must find the bloody trunk.

"Here we are," Holstoke murmured, smoothing a page with his palm and tapping it with his finger. "Caves do exist along the water round Lindisfarne, as well. But given the man you mentioned was spotted in Alnwick, I'd wager these are more likely."

Jonas wandered closer. Eyed the location. Committed the map to memory. "More than one in the same area, then?"

"Indeed. But this one seems the likeliest." He tapped the smaller of two coves. "Deeper than the rest. I studied the area's geology before Eugenia and I ventured to a nearby beach." The earl's black brows drew together. "She'd been disappointed by the shortage of intact seashells round Grimsgate. She likes to collect them for decoration."

Jonas grinned. He'd long found Holstoke's relationship with his petite, plainspoken wife amusing. From the beginning, Eugenia had appeared to enrapture the chilly, inscrutable lord against his will. Evidently, Holstoke continued to be both fascinated and occasionally bewildered by his charmingly impertinent wife.

An odd tickle of familiarity danced along his skin. His smile faded.

Holstoke raised his head. Pale eyes assessed him. "Hannah appears quite content. I am gratified to see it." He paused, seemingly gathering his thoughts. "For seven years, it has been my sacred duty to protect her from all harm. However, I may have carried my duty too far by warning you away from her. At least, that is what Eugenia tells me." Holstoke's mouth quirked. "She does not mince words." He cleared his throat and elevated his chin to an angle Jonas recognized—it was a mirror of Hannah's. "I do trust you'll take excellent care of my sister, Hawthorn."

Jonas acknowledged the peace offering with a nod. "You may be assured of it."

Straightening, Holstoke clasped his hands at his back. "We never discussed her dowry."

Cold seeped into his skin, writhed like worms. In his mind, flashes emerged of a beautiful woman's gray eyes going from dancing to dull to vacant to gone. Visions of her gowns turning into haggard rags, her laughter to hopelessness, taunted him.

"A dowry isn't necessary," he said finally.

Holstoke frowned. "I am happy to offer it. I wish her to be well provided for."

"She will be." His voice was harsh. Cold. "I am her husband, and I shall provide."

"And if something should happen to you? What then? A dowry offers a widow security."

"I will take care of my wife, Holstoke." He didn't know why it mattered that he win this argument. Pride, he supposed. Before Hannah, he hadn't given a damn what anyone thought of him. In fact, he'd enjoyed being underestimated. He was tempted to tell Holstoke the truth. But he wanted to finish this damned job first.

Holstoke shook his head, a puzzled frown forming. "Very well. I suppose a dowry is a bit unnecessary, given the size of her fortune."

Jonas frowned. *Fortune?*

"Eugenia would also likely take me to task for insufficiently crediting Hannah's business acumen." Holstoke smiled. "She really is quite remarkable, you know." His gaze turned thoughtful. "My mother wanted her dead. Hunted her for years, all for a doll my father had given his daughter. I doubt he even knew what it was. He was quite ill by then. As we later discovered, the doll had once belonged to my mother. It concealed a fortune in jewels. I asked Hannah what she would like to do, and she decided to sell them. Over the past five years, she took that fortune and doubled it. Investments, primarily. She has a talent for speculation. Treats the whole thing as a game of chess." He smiled again, his love for his sister glowing brightly. "She used her fortune to establish schools for girls, two outside London and one near Bath. They are orphanages, really, though she has no liking for the term. She prefers to call them sanctuaries for girls who have no family, no way to care for themselves. Each school trains the girls in a craft they may use to gain employment when they are of age. She also pays the tuition for girls of insufficient means to attend Lord and Lady Colin's school in Devonshire. Her friend, Biddy, is one. Hannah never told her." Holstoke closed the cover on the book of maps. "Extraordinary."

Yes. She was. And nothing Holstoke had described came as a surprise to Jonas. The intelligence, the generosity, the courage. Courage most of all. "She is the most beautiful thing on this earth," he murmured, his voice tight.

Holstoke's gaze sharpened upon him. Examined him like a new breed of plant. Tilting his head, the earl nodded as though confirming a suspicion. "You will tell me if you ever need anything."

Jonas frowned.

"I am confident in your ability to care for her. That is not in question." Holstoke's shoulders squared. "But you are now a member of my family, Hawthorn. Family helps family. That is what Eugenia says, at any rate." A small smile tugged. "She also insists I should like you."

Chuckling, Jonas replied, "Good God, man. Let us not get carried away."

Chapter Sixteen

"This is not to imply your stores of cleverness are but dust-ridden shelves. No, surely not. However, in perilous circumstances, one benefits from an overflowing larder. You would be well served to have a woman of my resources at your side."

—Dorothea Bainbridge, The Marchioness of Wallingham, to Malcolm Charles Bainbridge, the Marquess of Wallingham, in a letter arguing the benefits of a resourceful wife in one's parliamentary battles.

Jonas hadn't said a word in four miles. But, then, she'd followed him against his express wishes and multiple attempts at husbandly commands.

As Hannah had informed him of her intention to accompany him to the caves Phineas had pointed out on Lord Wallingham's map, he'd interrupted her with numerous denials. While her arguments had been sound, his had been marked by obstinacy and increasing signs of frustration.

"I shall bring a pistol," she'd assured him. "I am an excellent shot."

"Likely you'd end up shooting me. Just stay here." He'd been growly and fierce—more than usual.

"There is nothing for me to do here except play garden chess with Mr. Farrington. I wish to be helpful, and I cannot do that unless—"

"Farrington?"

"Yes. Lady Rutherford's cousin. You haven't met him yet. An exuberant player. Boyish, really. Splendidly good-humored."

Jonas had turned his back and paced away. "Played with him before, have you?"

"Indeed, a day or two before our wedding. He is the most charming fellow. Charlotte did warn me, but I must say, I found him far more delightful than expect—"

"Stay. Here." The order had been explicit, growled in a menacing tone he rarely used with her.

That tone had resumed when she'd caught up with him on the road to Alnwick.

"Bloody hell, woman. Go back," he'd barked. "Go! Or I'll put you over my horse and haul you back myself."

"I shall only follow you again."

"Not if I enlist your brother to keep you where you belong."

"Phineas already tried. And I am here." She'd raised a brow to imply the conclusion was obvious. "Think of the hours wasted retracing our steps. The tides are sensitive to timing, are they not?"

He'd ground his teeth. Speared her with a glare. Then continued south.

His mood hadn't improved over the past hour. In fact, it had grown gradually stormier, descending into resentful, manly silence.

Now, as she enjoyed the steady gait of her mare and the expansive beauty of Northumberland's coastline, she eyed her husband with puzzlement. "What is your plan, if we should find the thief hiding in one of these caves?"

"Take him down. Retrieve the trunk." His eyes remained fixed upon the road ahead.

She tried again. "Phineas offered to come along. Don't you think it might have been wise to—"

"I don't need his help. I don't need yours, either."

Releasing an exasperated breath, she took another tack. "In Dorsetshire, caves such as these are commonplace. They were used often for smuggling, and—"

"I know about Dorsetshire."

She blinked. "Oh? I recall your stay there being rather short-lived. You departed with some haste, if I remember correctly."

"I left because you wouldn't bloody well look at me. Or speak to me. Or acknowledge my existence."

"I wanted you to stay."

"You never said so. Just treated me like I wasn't there."

"I was frightened. What lies between us is ... very strong."

His jaw flexed. He went silent.

After another mile, she asked, "How do you know about the caves in Dorsetshire?"

At first, she thought he might not answer. Then, in a low, grudging voice, he said, "I spent a couple of years in Poole. Worked the docks."

Frowning, she examined her husband. "Why did you never say?"

He shrugged. "Left when I was sixteen."

"And before that?"

Finally, he glanced at her. His gaze was wary. "London."

"Did you work the docks there, too?"

His shoulders rolled. "Aye. A bit."

"And before that?"

A long pause. "Norwich."

"Is that where you were born?"

"Thereabouts."

"Jonas. I am asking where you were born."

He gritted his teeth. Glared straight ahead. "North of Sandringham. Round the Wash."

She tried to remember that this was about gaining his trust. Thus far, she had been abysmally unsuccessful. But, as in chess, neither victory nor defeat could be declared until the game had been played through. "I've told you all the worst things about me, you know."

He ran a hand down his face. "Hannah ..."

"I am only asking for information. A simple thing to grant your wife, I daresay."

After another half-mile, he finally relented. "I was born on a rich man's land. My father was his gamekeeper."

"And your mother?"

He rubbed his nape. "She taught me to draw. Taught me to look for beauty. To see it, no matter where I was."

"She sounds lovely."

"She was."

"What was her name?"

His eyes softened. Saddened. "Grace."

"And your father?"

The hardness returned. He looked away. "Jacob."

"He was a gamekeeper."

"Aye."

"And you were born on the land that he managed?"

"A cottage, there."

"What happened?"

He sighed. "Hannah, must we discuss this now—"

"We have another half-hour of riding ahead of us, by my count. Seems an ideal time to me."

His jaw flexed. "Very well. My father was a gamekeeper for a baron. Lord Hibbard. Bingham Park was his hunting property. When I was seven, Hibbard invited his nob friends to a hunt. One of them discovered my mother tending her garden. Tried to have his way with her. I was there. Had a knife, as I was cleaning up after breakfast. I threatened to stab him with it if he didn't leave. He laughed. Just bloody laughed." He ran a hand over his face again. "My father returned and saw what the man was trying. Struck him. Told him he'd kill him if he saw him again." He went quiet for a time then continued, "Later that evening, Lord Hibbard dismissed my father without a reference. We were tossed out of the cottage, forced from our home in the middle of the night."

Hannah didn't know what to say. How frightened he must have been. Seven years old, valiantly protecting his mother. She could picture it. Understood how it felt to be ripped from everything familiar all at once.

"We made our way to Norwich. My father found work there. Without a reference, it was trying, but we managed. I worked some. Then, my mother fell ill. She went quickly. Matter of days."

Her heart hurt for him. She, too, had lost her mother. "I am sorry, Jonas."

He nodded. "My father was ... inconsolable. Her death changed him. He became ..." He sighed. "I don't know. Fanciful. Unreliable. He drifted about. Dragged me with him. Told me wild tales about how I would be a grand man one day. Spent every farthing we had collecting books from the circulating library. Made me read them. Every one. We were bloody starving, and all he could think about was how his boy would be a grand man one day. Educated and wealthy. Absolute rot. He'd gone mad." His face hardened. "Death was a mercy, by the end."

"How did you survive?"

"I worked. That is how it's done, princess."

"Jonas. Look at me, please."

It took a moment, but he did as she asked. His eyes were filled with fiery resentment. "I am sorry that this happened," she said. "I am sorry for what you endured. It is dreadful. But you survived. Scarred but strong."

"Right. I survive. That is my lot. To watch others die while I live."

"Jonas—"

"Leave me be."

"But I—"

He rode ahead, ending the conversation.

An hour later, they left the road for a path to the small slice of golden beach tucked inside high cliffs of weathered rock. Waves roared onto the rocky stretch beyond the cliffs, drowning out the sound of wind.

When they reached the beach, Jonas dismounted and came to lift her down. It was the first time he'd touched her since breakfast, and she went dizzy and weak as her body brushed against his. But his face was as hard as the cliffs that now surrounded them, striated by water and time.

"Tide's coming in," he said, scanning the area with a narrowed gaze. "We'd best hurry." He turned a glower upon her. "Stay close. Do as I tell you and don't bloody hesitate. Understand?"

She didn't care for his harsh tone but nodded anyway.

He led the way around the interior of the cove. Though the beach was strewn with rocks and driftwood and seaweed, his steps were swift and sure. She clambered to catch up, reminding herself he'd likely spent his boyhood exploring such ground. She'd worn sturdy boots, but the wet sand and slick, sporadic rocks made for uncertain footing. Her skirts were well suited to riding but less so to beach rambles. By contrast, his legs were much longer. And, he was propelled by annoyance at present.

She followed him through a narrow gap between the high cliffs and towering stacks.

"I said stay close," he growled, glaring at her over his shoulder.

She lifted her skirts higher and blew out a breath. "You're in a devilish temper, Jonas Hawthorn."

"You should have stayed at Grimsgate."

"I cannot help you at Grimsgate."

"No, just play bloody garden chess with bloody *boyish* men."

She frowned. "Why does that displease you?"

"It doesn't."

Stepping carefully from one seaweed-laden rock to another, she snorted. "It sounds very much as if it does."

"This is a daft conversation."

"I could teach you to play if that is your objection. Chess is really quite enjoyable once you—oh!"

He halted so abruptly she collided with his back. His hand reached back to her hip, sliding around her waist to stabilize her against his body. She clutched his coat and peeked around his shoulder. They'd passed through the crevice into a second, smaller cove. This one was heavily shadowed with less sand and more rock. Along the shore-side cliffs, inside a recess surrounded by boulders, water had carved a deep, black cave.

The opening was wide but shorter than Jonas. Everywhere around them, the rocks were dark and wet.

He grasped her hand, his gaze as predatory as she'd ever seen it. "Stay quiet. Stay close." With his free hand, he reached inside his coat, withdrawing a pistol.

The dashed man had brought a gun when he'd forbidden her the same liberty. "Jonas," she hissed. "I thought you said—"

"Shh. Quiet and close."

All his attention focused upon the small, black cave. His eyes flickered to the top of the cliffs, the three access points leading into the cove, the rising tide. "Come."

He held her hand and tugged her with him, edging around the interior curve with the sea to their right and the cliffs to their left. Soon, they picked their way to the small alcove surrounding the cave's mouth. When they passed between a boulder and the cliff, Jonas stopped and pushed her back against the rock.

"Stay here," he warned softly, sparing her an intimidating glare. "Anything happens, run for the horses. Ride to Alnwick. Do not wait for me. Understand?"

"Jonas—"

"Do you understand?"

Her breathing quickened along with her heart as every part of the civilized mask he normally wore fell away. She clutched his hand, feeling her head try to lift and float. Biting down on the impulse, she instead rose up on her toes and kissed him. "Be careful," she whispered.

Wolfish, silvery eyes narrowed upon her with naked hunger. With a last squeeze of her hand, he released her to edge into the cave's opening.

She closed her eyes briefly, digging her fingers against the rock to either side of her. *Must stay,* she chanted to herself. *Must stay, must stay, must stay.* She focused on the waves, loud and crashing and rhythmic. Above, sea birds swooped and sang. Beneath her boots, wet rock smelled of fish.

She was here. She must stay with him. He needed her.

Shaking as seconds turned into minutes, she dug fingers against rock. Breathed. Let the fear rise but pictured it leaving like smoke through a chimney.

He would be fine. She would be fine. Everything would be fine.

"Hannah."

Her eyes flew open as she jolted. Blinking, she found him frowning at her from a crouched position in the cave's opening. "J-Jonas?"

"You were expecting someone else?"

She swallowed. "I was worried. You took a long time."

He nodded toward the cave's interior. "I found the trunk. It's inside a fair distance."

She started to enter, but he stopped her.

"I should like to see," she protested.

"No reason to go in. I only came out to tell you what I'd found. I'll carry the trunk myself."

"I shall help."

"No need."

"I'd prefer to go with you."

He released a breath. "It is dark and close. They left a lantern, but—"

She slipped past him, ignoring his curses. He was right—the cave was small at the opening, though bigger inside. And quite dark once she moved ten yards deeper. But she'd never feared dark places. The solid rock and quiet dripping soothed her.

"Have I suddenly lost the ability to speak English?" he asked through gritted teeth. "Because I'd swear I told you to follow my commands."

"Oh, you did," she reassured him, tracing fingers along old, carved dates gouged into the cave's ceiling. "Look here, Jonas. Sixteen ninety-three. Do you suppose it was actually inscribed in sixteen ninety-three? Or is this merely a lark some boys carved a few months ago?"

With his head lowered to avoid braining himself, Jonas grunted a noncommittal response and, after pulling a flint and knife from his pocket, bent to light the lantern he'd set upon the ground. The glow only emphasized the darkness, casting odd shadows upon the greenish black of the cave's interior.

She wandered deeper, fascinated by odd sea creatures clinging to wet surfaces. "Why would they bring the trunk here?"

"It's a good hiding place. When the tide is up, nobody can get in."

"Or out," she murmured, shivering. "Is that how you knew they wouldn't be here?"

He went quiet.

She glanced back at him. "I am not daft, Jonas. The tide is rising, and only a fool would willingly trap himself inside a cave for hours. Secure hiding place or no."

"When given the choice, I'll not take chances with your safety. Ever."

She glanced at his hands—lean and strong and capable. One was still a bit swollen from when he'd struck the tree. He'd hurt himself for her. Nearly died for her. He'd married her because she'd asked. Agreed to her terms. Brought her unimaginable pleasure.

And what had she done for him? Apart from insisting he take a wife made of wet paper. The damp chill of the cave seeped past the blue velvet of her habit. It swallowed her skin.

"I shall help you carry the trunk," she murmured. In this, at least, she might be of some use to him.

He released an exasperated. "Do as you like."

She followed him deeper into the cave, which ballooned inside so that Jonas was able to walk upright. The sandy floor was wet and littered with the sea's leavings near the entrance, but as they walked, the ground inclined upward, becoming dry sand then drier rock. Finally, they followed a branch to the right.

And there it was.

A black trunk with brown trimmings. It wasn't especially large—perhaps thirty inches long and twenty high, the same size of trunk Hannah often used for her slippers and reticules. She glanced around the space, noting a blanket folded near a small pack. She skirted around Jonas to investigate the pack.

"Don't bother," he said. "I already searched it. Nothing but a map of Alnwick and a flask of whisky."

She glanced over her shoulder, examining her husband carefully. He'd set the lantern on a long shelf of rock beside the trunk. Now, he was grasping the handle of the trunk itself and testing the weight. Before she could say anything, he heaved the thing up and onto his shoulder.

"Good heavens, Jonas. I said I would help. Is it heavy?"

He gave her a grin—the first one in hours. It made her heart flutter. "Light as lamb's fleece. I reckon you could carry it while I carry you." He glanced behind him. "But, in the interest of time, why don't you carry the lantern, instead?"

Swallowing the knowledge of her utter uselessness, she nodded and retrieved the lantern. "Ready?"

"Lead on, princess."

Every time he called her princess, it felt like a bit of sand had entered her boot—by now, she was forming blisters. Nevertheless, she'd been enough of a nuisance to him today, so she ignored her irritation and started back toward the cave's entrance.

"Does this mean your task is finished?" she asked.

"Half of it. The other half is finding the thief. Her ladyship would like a chat with him. So would I, to be fair. There's also the matter of the missing maid."

She sidestepped a wet, crawling creature before asking her next question. "Did you look inside the trunk? What if it's empty?"

"I did. And it's not. Though, it's still possible the thief took everything of value and left the rest. Another reason to run him to ground."

She frowned. "What is inside?"

"Miscellany. Pile of letters. A gown or two. Slippers. An old tin of soap. The whole thing smells of sandalwood."

A flush prickled her skin. "Sandalwood?"

"Aye. Something about that tickle your fancy, princess? Perhaps your boyishly charming gent stinks of the stuff."

She halted.

He grunted.

She spun.

He frowned.

"Why do you insist on calling me 'princess'?"

He adjusted the trunk on his shoulder, glancing at the cave's ceiling. "Let's discuss this after we've reached the—"

"Every time you say it, you sound vexed, as though I've slighted you."

"The tide is coming in. We need to leave."

A cold, sick feeling rose in her stomach. She watched his face, saw the resentment there—at least, she thought it was resentment. What did she really know about her husband? "Y-you don't like me very much, do you?"

"What the devil? You sat astride me only this morning. Shouted my name with some conviction. That was you, yes? I didn't mistake that."

She shook her head. "Wanting and liking are not the same."

"This rubbish conversation is going to get us trapped in here."

She went colder. Her eyes fell away from his. Out of long practice, she gathered her composure, letting numbness buffer the pain. "Please do not call me princess. You say it to mock me, and I do not deserve it."

"Noted," he snapped. "Now, shall we find our way to daylight before the sea adds us to her collection of refuse?"

She inclined her head and resumed walking toward the entrance. As she reached the last ten yards, she heard the roar of wind and waves tangling. Rock being battered. Close. So much closer than before. Her stomach swooped as seawater dragged at her feet.

Jonas lagged behind, having stopped to reposition the trunk. When she saw how close the tide was, how it filled the little cove, she lost her breath.

"J-Jonas," she whispered. She glanced back.

He held the trunk by one handle, bracing it across his upper back. Stooped and cursing, he trudged through ankle-deep water.

She rushed forward. The lantern swung, golden light dancing oddly with reflected sunlight from the cave's entrance. "Hurry, Jonas," she managed, her voice thin but louder than before.

He glanced up. "Bloody hell. Wait."

"We must hurry," she called, sloshing the last few feet as the surf surged toward them.

"Hannah. Wait for me to—"

"Must hurry." She reached the ring of sunlight, her heart pounding.

Just as a burst of exploded rock showered over her head.

And a loud crack echoed above booming waves.

And pain seared her right thigh.

And a wolf howled her name.

Picked her up with one arm.

And hauled her back into darkness.

Chapter Seventeen

"I take exception to your use of the word 'disaster.'
It is not as though the Prime Minister has never heard
such vulgarities before."

—DOROTHEA BAINBRIDGE, THE MARCHIONESS OF WALLINGHAM,
to Malcolm Charles Bainbridge, the Marquess of Wallingham, in a
letter of non-apology for a disastrous wifely intervention.

HE'D ONLY FELT RAGE THIS EXPLOSIVE TWICE BEFORE. THE
first time was when a prostitute who looked too much like
Hannah had been savagely beaten to death and left for him to
find—a signpost of the poisoner's intention to kill her. The
second time had been when she'd told him about Horatio
Syder.

Now, she was his to protect. Yet, he'd allowed her to come here, knowing the possibility of danger. He'd counted on his own ability to keep her safe. He'd been a fool.

Pure, thundering fury—at himself, at the shooter—powered his sprint with both Hannah and the trunk in his grasp.

The shot had to have come from high ground. The cliffs on the land side, likely. Hannah had been startled, but he didn't think she'd been hit. She was keeping up with him. She hadn't gone slack or cried out or even dropped the lantern.

Remarkable woman.

He ran for the chamber at the farthest reach of the cave. They'd be relatively safe there while the tide was up—while he decided how to kick his own blasted arse for not turning around and hauling her back to Grimsgate.

He released her and set down the trunk. "Set the lantern there." He nodded to a shelf of rock and pulled his pistol, checking the powder. "We may be here a while."

She did as he asked, light wavering as her hand shook. "Do—do you think he will attempt to attack us in here?"

"Doubtful." He positioned himself at the turn that led into the chamber. "If he does, he's a dead man." Urgent rage pounded inside him, drowning everything but the need to kill. "Probably a dead man anyway."

Definitely a dead man anyway.

He sensed Hannah moving behind him. Heard the swish of her skirts, her panting breaths. But he kept his eyes fixed upon the tunnel. If that piece of shite came anywhere near her, Jonas would tear his throat out.

"The tide should recede in an hour or two," she observed, her voice perplexingly calm. "Enough for us to leave, at any rate. An additional pistol would be a boon, indeed."

"If I'd thought it necessary for you to bring a gun, I wouldn't have let you follow me into the cave."

"A miscalculation, then." She sniffed. "I've similarly underestimated my opponent before. Phineas likes to lure me to my demise with a pretense of weakness. His brilliance is that I rarely see it for what it is until he has me cornered." When she next spoke, her voice came from the back of the chamber. "Often, he grants me small victories. His queen or a rook." She paused. "Those are important pieces in chess."

She had the tone of a governess patiently instructing a fractious boy. Despite his tension, he replied, "If you know his tactic, why not develop a counter?"

"Oh, I have. Many times. That is what makes him brilliant. Always ahead of me, my brother." Another pause. "I've learnt a great deal from him."

He heard a click. Turned. She held a pistol. Was loading a pistol.

Bloody hell, she'd brought a pistol.

Calmly, she tucked her powder flask into a hidden pocket between the folds of her skirt. Pale green eyes came up to meet his. A small smile curved her lips. "I am an excellent shot."

A thousand curses filled his head. He clenched his jaw to keep them in. He knew she was a good shot—Reaver and Dunston had told him she'd been the one to shoot Lydia Brand when the previous Lady Holstoke had taken her and Dunston's wife hostage. In the midst of a vicious assault, a girl of sixteen had picked up a gun and shot the woman who'd killed her mother, poisoned her father, and hunted her for over a decade.

His beautiful wife knew how to fire a pistol. She knew how to put a bullet between the eyes of a murderer. But she shouldn't bloody well have to. It was his job to keep her safe. His.

He turned back to the tunnel, listening for signs that the shooter had followed them. All he heard was the roar of waves filling the cave's opening. The roaring echo grew louder, giving him chills. After a few minutes, the noise's pitch changed. Quickly, he moved to the trunk, threw open the lid, and found what he'd been looking for. He lit the candle and set it beside the lantern then picked up the lantern. "Stay here," he told

Hannah. "This time, for God's sake, do as you're told. And don't shoot me when I return."

Then, he traveled down the cave's long shaft until seawater lapped at his boots. Glancing around, he noted signs of a waterline roughly four feet further in. They were nearly at high tide. Over the next hour, the water would peak and begin receding. Within two, they'd be making their way back to Grimsgate—provided he could kill the shooter quickly.

He returned to the chamber to find Hannah sitting calmly upon the blanket, her pistol in her lap and the thief's map in her hands.

Blowing out the candle, he laid his pistol on the shelf and placed the lantern near her shoulder. Then, he sat beside her. Released a breath. "I should have taken you back to Grimsgate. Locked you in our chamber with Reaver and Tannenbrook outside the door. Waited until tomorrow to come here." He ran a hand through his hair. "Bloody stupid."

She glanced up, blinking slowly. "Nonsense. Your thinking was sound. Near high tide, the thief would not be in the cave, yet it would still be accessible. You knew that. Had you returned me to Grimsgate, I would have followed you again. You also knew that. And I watched you survey the surrounding cliffs. No one was about when we ventured down to the beach. Even so, you exercised caution."

Her placid recitation struck him as odd. He examined her closely. Was she paler than before? Difficult to tell in the low light. "You should be inside the castle right now, not trapped in a cave with an ill-tempered hound." He huffed a chuckle at his own expense and rubbed his eyes. "Perhaps you should have married the boyish charmer, love. Little chance of being shot while playing garden chess."

"I didn't want him."

God, he was an idiot. A jealous, mad idiot.

The way she'd spoken about Farrington that morning had lit his fuse to a bewildering degree. He'd pictured them

together, laughing, charming one another, sharing witty
conversation and peach tarts. Playing bloody garden chess.

His eyes found hers. "Why did you choose me?"

She looked at his chin then lowered her gaze to her lap.
"Many reasons," she murmured. "Most I cannot explain in
words. We are connected. That is all I know."

Watching her, he noted her skin appeared whiter. It might
have been the light, but he didn't think so. "Hannah."

Her eyes fluttered closed.

"Hannah." His voice went sharp as her arms seemed to
slacken. He gathered her close, alarmed by her listless posture.
"Love, what is it? What's wrong?"

She shook her head. Blinked slowly. Her hand fluttered to
his chest. Her head lolled onto his shoulder. "Nothing. A bit
drowsy is all. May I rest here awhile?"

He plucked up her pistol and the map and placed them on
the shelf beside the lantern. Then, he plucked up his wife to
place her on his lap.

His arm came away wet.

He frowned. Had she been sitting in a puddle? Unlikely.
The chamber was dry.

He glanced down at his sleeve. The liquid was warm. Dark.
Red.

Holy God. She was bleeding. His wife was bleeding.

"Hannah." His voice cracked on her name. Panic surged.
"Ah, God. Hannah. Where are you injured, love?"

She clung to his neck. Buried her face against his collar.
"Right leg. I'll be fine. Just a bit of blood."

Frantically, he dragged her skirt up to see a red-soaked
strip of muslin tied around her thigh. She'd used a piece of her
petticoat to bandage the wound, but it had bled through,
soaking her skirt. "God Almighty."

"The bullet must have ricocheted," she said, her voice soft,
her hand stroking his jaw.

He untied the soaked cloth and gently angled her leg to

view the long furrow in her upper thigh. "A graze," he rasped. "But a deep one. Why didn't you tell me?"

"All I am is a distraction. I–I thought you needed my help, but you don't. I didn't wish to make things worse. I am fine."

"You are not bloody fine," he snapped, his head spinning, his pulse racing. "I need to get you out of here. I need to–"

"Shh. Jonas." She kissed a spot below his ear, her thumb running over and over his jaw. "Injuries are far from new to me. Remember?"

He shook his head, hating the reminder.

"This will bleed. Then it will heal."

He held her tighter. Stroked her back. Her neck. Her shoulders and arms. He grabbed hold of the blanket. Ripped at it with his teeth and tore a long strip off one end. Swiftly, he tied the cloth around her leg, cinching it tightly to slow the bleeding.

She didn't so much as wince.

"I know it hurts, love," he whispered, rocking her in his arms, stroking her back. "I'm so damned sorry."

"Pain is nothing, Jonas." She stroked his cheek. "You mustn't fret."

He reached for the leather pack and retrieved the flask of whisky. "Here. Drink."

"I don't want to–"

"Drink," he barked.

She took the flask. Took a swallow. Coughed.

"Another."

She drank again.

They repeated the process until he was satisfied she'd had enough to dull the pain. Then, he took the flask from her limp fingers, drank a bit himself, and tucked the flask away. "Once the tide's low enough, I'll take care of the shooter. Then, I'll come back for you and bring you to the surgeon in Alnwick."

"Mmm." She nuzzled her nose against his throat. "You smell lovely, Jonas. Have I ever told you?"

He rubbed his eyes. An hour. Less, perhaps. Only an hour. She would be fine. "No, love. Tell me."

"It's unlike anything else. I cannot explain. You smell like ... pleasure."

"You're injured. This is no time for seduction."

She giggled. "It is always time for seduction. I want you to *want* to be near me."

Ridiculous thing to say. She was woven into his fabric. Without her, he unraveled. "Then, you have your wish."

"Not merely for lustful reasons. We must be bound together. *Attached.*"

The absurd statement, combined with his body's predictable reactions, deepened his frown. "Trust me, it's best if I retain use of my hands."

She sighed, her breath warm against his skin. "Lady Wallingham says you are a solitary wolf. But I wish for you to stay with me. Always."

Her words had begun to slur at the edges. His little Snow Queen was a wee bit sotted. Despite the crushing pressure in his chest, he kept his words light. "Good thing you married me, eh?"

"Oh, yes. A very good thing. I will do whatever I must to ensure your happiness, Jonas Hawthorn. Whatever I must."

"When your wound is healed and we've a proper bed, I'll hold you to your word."

"I want to bear your children. I want to serve your favorite dish for supper. What is your favorite?"

Puzzling at the odd question, he nevertheless answered, "Honey."

"Honey is not a dish."

"If I lay you down on a table, it is."

A snort. Then, a giggle. "I meant food, silly."

"Peaches, then."

"I adore peaches."

"As do I."

A pause. "You still are not talking about food, are you?"

"No." He shifted her in his lap. "Now you know why."

She moaned. Kissed his neck. "You make me weak."

"That's the blood loss. And the whisky."

"No. It's you. Only you."

They sat in silence for a while, her head lolling on this shoulder, her grasp of his neck slipping. His muscles flickered and fought against the impulse to crush her body into his. To kill the one who had hurt her. He forced them to wait. Because that was all he could do.

"Jonas?"

"Aye."

"Why would a thief go to so much bother to steal Lady Wallingham's slippers?"

"I don't know, love."

"Her slippers wouldn't fit a gentleman."

He chuckled. "I doubt it's the slippers, precisely. Although some gentlemen do rather fancy them."

"You said there were letters." She paused. "Perhaps he sought to blackmail her. Or perhaps—"

Needing a distraction, he stretched sideways to snag the edge of the trunk, dragging it close. "Let's have a look." He dug past a gown and two pairs of slippers. "Here we are." He handed her a pile of letters that had once been folded and wrapped with twine but were now loose.

She set to reading while he continued digging through the dowager's belongings.

"Oh, my. Jonas. These are ..." She shuffled through several more pages, turning them over and covering her lips with her fingers. "They are love letters."

"Hmm." He tipped the trunk to see if he'd missed anything. He heard something slide and thud. "Any information worthy of blackmail?" he asked.

"Nothing obvious so far. It seems only a correspondence between her and her husband." She raised the paper to her nose. "Sandalwood," she murmured.

His fingers brushed something metal. He pulled out a small case, hinged on one side, oval in shape, filigreed and flat. He opened the cover.

And the itch along his nape sparked into a full-body chill.

"Is that a miniature?" Hannah tilted her head against his chest to view the likeness, painted on ivory.

"Aye," he rasped. "Bloody, bleeding hell."

"He looks a bit like you." She tilted her head in a different direction. "And Lord Atherbourne." Another direction. "But more like Lord Wallingham. The chin, I think. Is this ... do you suppose this is Lord Wallingham's father? I've never seen a portrait of him."

"'Tis the thief. Or, at least, it matches the man Miss Allen described. Perhaps she viewed this portrait while trying on her ladyship's slippers and took a fancy to him."

"Mmm. I certainly see why she would."

He glared down at his tipsy wife. "Do you, now?"

"He is very handsome."

He snapped the cover closed and dropped the miniature back into the trunk.

She peered up at him, pale eyes softened by drink but nonetheless thoughtful. "Still, she would have to be either part of the conspiracy or daft beyond measure to describe the man in Lady Wallingham's miniature as the thief. I suspect she sought to mislead you and that the man she was with in Alnwick is her true partner."

"Perhaps." He battled his irritation over her admiration for the man in the miniature. "Regardless, I must confront Lady Wallingham when we return to Grimsgate. She is hiding something. I showed her my sketch of the thief, and she claimed no recognition." He waved to the trunk. "An obvious lie."

Hannah gave him the letters to return to the trunk. "Perhaps she is not concealing the truth so much as ... her grief." Her hand came up to stroke his jaw then slid down over his heart. "These are her memories, Jonas. Her memories of him."

He rolled his shoulders, ignoring the twisting pang her words produced. "Regardless, I cannot finish this job until I know everything."

Hannah snuggled deeper into his arms. He kissed her head, inhaling rosewater and his sweet woman. Then, as she nodded off, he began planning his attack upon the shooter.

By the time the tide receded enough to implement his plan, he had envisioned the scenario a dozen times. He stripped down to only his breeches, wrapped Hannah in the blanket and woke her long enough to give instructions. Then, he kissed her long and deep to stop her protests and lit the candle for her before taking the lantern and making his way back to the waterline.

He set the lantern on the ground twenty yards from the cave entrance. Then, he waded in as water pushed and pulled with the receding tide. As a youth, swimming had been a near-daily ritual. The water's chill was an old friend—rising past his hips, rolling on a wave over his shoulders as he crouched and half-waded, half-swam toward the opening. Just before he dove beneath the water, he scanned the cove for signs of the shooter. Nothing. But, then, the shooter would be complacent, for the tide was still high.

Filling his lungs, he submerged and pushed on, feeling his way past the cave's entrance and then immediately turning right. A wave struck, driving his shoulder against rock. He ignored the bruising pain of it, the burning starting in his chest. Reaching for the gap between the boulder and the cliff face, he slipped inside as waves churned and swirled, pulling him in three directions at once.

He needed air, but he had to go farther into the cove first. Needed to emerge where the shooter would not expect to see him. Propelling himself along the rocks beneath the water, he dug and pulled himself along, fighting the battering surges, until he felt sand. Then, beside a solid wall of rock, he finally dared lift his face above the surface.

Gasping as air replaced burning deprivation, he shook seawater from his eyes and turned to where he thought the shooter must have perched. There, high on a cliff with a fair sight of the cave entrance, sat a man. Blond. Ugly. Rough. A long gun lay across his lap. He was eating something, his hand jerking as he tore off a bite. Then, he swilled from a flask. Wiped his mouth.

Oblivious. Perfect.

Jonas grinned. Planned. Then, with another deep breath, he went back beneath the water and found his way to the second cove. To the beach. Then the trail.

And, finally, to the man who had harmed the only thing on this bloody earth he loved.

He stalked him first. Snaked through high grass and found the angle he wanted. Waited for the blond head to turn.

The man tossed away whatever dried meat he'd been chewing. He uncapped his flask. And when he tipped his head back, Jonas struck.

Arm across the throat. Squeeze. Control the thrashing.

The man clawed and kicked. His rifle launched from his legs and landed in the grass.

He was strong. Thick about the shoulders. But Jonas had leverage, the element of surprise. Rage that wanted release.

He held tighter. Squeezing. Squeezing. And just at the end, a moment before the man went limp, he whispered, "Sleep now. Dream of the pain to come."

Chapter Eighteen

"If chins were fortunes, the Bainbridge men
would be kings, my darling."

—Dorothea Bainbridge, The Marchioness of Wallingham,
to Malcolm Charles Bainbridge, the Marquess of Wallingham, in a
letter of amused reflections on the birth of their son.

Hannah awakened with a remembrance of warmth.
The warmth of her husband's arms. The softness of his
whispers against her ear. The heat of sunlight upon her damp
skirts.

He'd entered the cave like a primitive beast, naked and
wet, a savage look upon his face. She'd asked what happened,
noting the ruddy bruises forming on his shoulder. He hadn't

answered, merely donning his shirt, wrapping her in his coat,
and carrying her out to the cove without a word. Then, he'd
retrieved the trunk and, together, they'd made their way back
to the horses. She'd noted he'd acquired a rifle somewhere
along the way, as well as an additional load—a man, by the
looks of it, either unconscious or dead. She hadn't asked
which. He'd draped the man over her saddle and covered him
with the blanket that was still soaked with her blood.

He'd lifted her onto his horse, mounted behind her, and
handed her the flask of whisky.

"Drink," he'd growled.

It seemed single syllables were all he could manage.

He'd taken her to a surgeon in Alnwick, only a mile or two
away. Then, he'd threatened to "carve a gash five times deeper"
into the surgeon's flesh if the man did anything to hurt her.

As the surgeon cleaned and stitched and bandaged her
wound, Jonas had held her hand, his jaw flickering and his eyes
burning.

She did not enjoy being touched by anyone other than him,
so the process had been an ordeal. But she'd not wanted to
cause her husband distress, either, so she'd closed her eyes and
breathed.

Breathed.

Breathed.

That hadn't dissolved the queasy membrane of fear. So, at
last, she'd reached for Jonas. He'd stroked her hair and told her
how strong she was.

She'd opened her eyes to find her husband's gaze, silvery
and strong, fierce and protective. There was no insouciant
humor. No cynical grin. No ready quip.

He was as raw as she'd ever seen him.

Then, the surgeon had begun the stitching, and the pain
had made her flinch. Jonas's eyes had shifted to her wound. For
a moment, she'd glimpsed anguish. Fear. The beautiful silver
had turned bleak. Then cold. Then stony. Then remote.

He'd continued holding her hand, but his grip had loosened and he'd abandoned the soothing stroke of her hair.

She'd spoken his name, hoping he would look at her again. Not her wound but *her*. He hadn't. Soon, whisky had clouded her head; laudanum had weighted her eyes. She'd faded into sleep still wanting him to come back to her.

Now, hours later, she awakened in their bed at Grimsgate, feeling his absence as an encompassing chill. Someone small emerged from the dressing room.

"Oh, mistress," Claudette cried softly, rushing to her side. "Let me help."

Without thinking, Hannah had instantly thrown aside her blankets and started to rise. Claudette held out her hands, waiting for Hannah to take them. Hannah did, but only to squeeze her maid's fingers and give her a grateful smile. "I should be obliged for tea. Laudanum leaves me with a dreadful thirst."

"Of course. I have a tray just there." She nodded toward the small table near the window. "Are you in pain? Shall I fetch more laudanum?"

"No. I must speak to my husband. Help me dress?"

Claudette hesitated, a frown of concern creasing her brow. "Certainly, I will. We must take care, though. Your wound is fresh."

"I am fine," she assured. "First tea. Then a lovely frock. Pink, I think. Then I must find Mr. Hawthorn. It is most urgent that I speak with him."

Nodding, Claudette smiled with warm reassurance. "Straight away, mistress."

Hannah's head spun as she sat up on the edge of the bed. But she must carry on. She must find Jonas. She must rise and dress and speak to her husband.

Because she'd felt him leave her. She'd watched him shut away the pain and fear inside a wall of indifference.

She knew what it looked like. She'd done it to him.

But she could not allow it. That fortress might keep out those who would harm him, but it locked in the loneliness. She'd fought for seven years to tear down her own walls, and she refused to let him build a new one in the center of their marriage.

Claudette served her tea, helped her wash, brushed and pinned her hair, and helped her dress. The long-sleeved gown she'd chosen was simple silk velvet with few adornments. But its color was extraordinary—the rosy blush of a ripened peach. Hannah smiled as she imagined tempting him, kissing him, loving him in this gown.

Her maid's light humming soothed her as she fastened a delicate pearl necklace and secured a set of shell combs in her hair. Hannah reached for Claudette's fingers as the maid tidied wisps of her hair. She pressed the girl's hand and met her eyes in the mirror. "Thank you." She held the maid's lovely blue eyes. "Thank you for always taking such excellent care of me."

Claudette's smile beamed. "It is my honor, Mrs. Hawthorn. My honor, indeed."

Mrs. Hawthorn. She was his wife. The knowledge filled her. Warmed her. Made her glow. She took a deep breath. "Let us go and find my husband, hmm?"

According to Mr. Nash, Jonas had requested a meeting with Lady Wallingham immediately upon their arrival, or so Claudette had reported. The house party guests, including Eugenia and Phineas, had all accepted an invitation from Lord and Lady Rutherford to visit Chatwick Hall and had been gone for hours. Consequently, the corridor and, indeed, the entire castle seemed empty and hushed.

Hannah's leg pained her, though not as much as before. Still, she accepted Claudette's help as they descended the staircase and entered the gallery.

"Heavens," Hannah exclaimed seeing rain sheeting the gallery's windows. "When did the downpour begin?"

"Would you like me to fetch your shawl? It will only take a moment."

"No, I ..." She watched water snaking down the glass. Her leg throbbed. A queasy sensation struck. She halted. Braced a hand on the window's casing. "Perhaps. Yes, I think so. Thank you, Claudette."

It was an odd memory, she thought as the maid hurried away. Rain on glass. Pain along her thighs and hips. A man stroking her hair as though he loved her.

But he hadn't. He'd hurt her over and over, tried to destroy her, all while fashioning her into something different. Distorted. Wrong.

His darkness had nearly swallowed her. Then, he'd gone. And she'd been free—except that she hadn't. She'd had to fight and fight and fight. She'd had to push and push and push. She'd had to heal.

She was still healing. Because of love. Colin and Sarah Lacey had made her feel safe for the first time. Maureen had reminded her what it meant to be cared for as a mother cares for a child. Lord Dunston and Mr. Reaver had offered their protection with no expectations. Phineas had given her a home and a family and a place to belong. Eugenia had tirelessly battered Hannah's fortress of indifference until she'd given in and let herself love her. Then, Eugenia had taught her to understand her own strength.

And, finally, there was Jonas. Her wolf. Who had wanted her, challenged her, placed his body and his strength between her and danger, purely on instinct.

But he was scarred, just as she was. *I survive. That is my lot. To watch others die while I live.*

Hannah had lost her family once. Then, she'd endured the bad time. But she'd rebuilt a new family from the best people she could find. She would help Jonas do the same. She would help him discover his own strength, and she would be tireless about it. Like Eugenia, she would accept no less than his unconditional surrender.

Because she loved him. His cleverness pretending to be

charm. His fight pretending to be carelessness. His heart pretending to be unattached.

A grin curved her lips. She traced rain's path down the glass and considered how very relentless she would be. Her husband didn't understand. She'd fought this battle. She knew every move. And she had a singular advantage—he wanted her.

The thought was satisfying.

Just then, she saw a flicker out of the corner of her eye. Thinking it was Claudette, she glanced down the length of the gallery toward the stairs.

But it wasn't Claudette. It was a man, wearing a dripping hat and dark coat, slipping through one of the glass doors from the garden. Handsome—a lean, square jaw like Jonas's, dark eyes like Atherbourne's, a proud nose and long chin like Wallingham's. He turned toward her.

He must have seen her eyes widen, her breath halt.

Oh, God.

She backed away, but he'd already started forward. Her heart pounded. Ears pounded. Everything felt slow. Her leg was sore and weak from her injury and all the exertions of the day. She stumbled backward as he reached her and gripped her arms.

Skin crawled. Old membranes of fear blended with new swells of imminent danger, sending her head spinning. Her lungs panting. Her mind floating away, a yard behind her eyes. Then upward.

He was clutching her, his fingers digging into her arms. "... won't hurt you unless I must. Now, stay quiet, beauty."

Her head wanted to float. Escape. He held her against him. Had a knife. Knives were bad. His pressed against her ribs.

Syder had never cut her ribs. He'd always worked upon her thighs. He'd always known how deep he could go before the wounds became fatal.

Her mind floated higher.

He shook her. Demanded. A place to hide.

Cold soaked her. Rain slithered down the window.

A reflection flashed there amidst water and glass. White shawl. Blue eyes. Filled with horror.

Claudette. Her sweet maid with the soft hands.

Hannah could not let her become prey, too. She must stay. She must fight. Before he noticed Claudette standing behind him clutching a shawl.

The man was shaking her hard enough to bruise. "Move. What the devil is wrong with you?"

She forced herself down, down, down. Forward into her eyes. She willed herself to move and speak. "I—I know a place where you can hide. A cellar. No one ever goes there. I'll take you."

He spun her, grasping her upper arm painfully tight, then pressed his blade harder against her side. "I don't wish to cut you, beauty, but I will. Make a sound, try to summon help, and I will."

An hour earlier

JONAS DRAGGED THE MISERABLE PIECE OF SHITE BEHIND HIM like a bag of horse leavings. He rammed the man's head into the drawing room door. The man groaned.

The sound was bloody satisfying.

He hauled him twenty feet to where the dragon sat sipping her tea. Tossed the wretch aside. Set the trunk down beside him. Gave her a low bow. "Your trunk and your thief, milady."

With an imperious sniff, she arched a brow and set aside her tea and lorgnette. "This is, indeed, my trunk." Her fingers waved dismissively toward the bag of horse leavings. "But that is not my thief."

Jonas glared. "He took a shot at my wife."

Her eyes sharpened into brilliant emeralds. "Well, kill him if you must. I shan't gainsay you. But he is not the man who stole from me."

Behind him, the drawing room door slammed closed with a crack. "You're right, Mother. He is not." Wallingham strode into the room, hauling Cecil Bainbridge in much the same way one might haul a reluctant hound—by the collar. The marquess shoved his slovenly, drunken cousin into a chair and came toward Jonas with a dark glower. He pulled a sheet of paper from inside his coat and unfolded it, holding it up for both Jonas and Lady Wallingham to see. It was Jonas's sketch, though copied by a finer hand than his.

Wallingham looked furious. He dangled the sketch in front of his mother, who turned her cheek. "When Lady Atherbourne completed her first copy, Atherbourne showed it to me. He's rather admiring of his wife's talents. Imagine my astonishment when the face so closely resembled my father's that it might as well be his ghost."

"Oh, do cease with the dramatics, Charles," the dragon chided. "Your father had sharper cheekbones and a higher brow. Additionally, his lips were more defined. This man may be handsome, but he is not your father."

"No," Wallingham snapped, pointing at his drunken cousin. "According to Cecil, he is my half-brother. A by-blow and a blackmailer, as it happens. Why in blazes did you never tell me?"

The old dragon's features stiffened until every wrinkle and line seemed etched in stone. The only lively thing was the emerald fire of her eyes. "That low creature is no brother of yours."

"For God's sake, Mother. He could be Father's twin."

"Nonsense. Your father did not have mistresses." She sniffed and turned her green fire upon Jonas. "I expect you to find him, Mr. Hawthorn. You shan't receive a farthing until you do."

The bag of horse leavings groaned again, rolling onto his side. With his hands bound, there was little else he could do.

"Cecil claims this man approached him three months ago." Wallingham flicked a long finger against the sketch. "He demanded payment in exchange for silence. Something about Cecil's recent spate of luck in racing wagers."

"Hmmph. Am I meant to be surprised? Cecil couldn't fall off his horse without cheating."

"Explain, Mother. Explain who he is."

"He is a blackguard and a thief."

Cecil began snoring. Jonas glanced back at the large-chinned sot with disgust.

Wallingham rubbed at his brow, his mouth tightening. "You simply don't want to see it. I know you loved him, Mother, but it is not impossible."

"Yes," she said calmly. "It is."

Jonas watched the marquess's reaction—the sadness, the fury, the reluctance to wound his mother—and felt something he rarely did for nobs like Wallingham: sympathy. The dowager was an exasperating dragon with high-handed ways and a formidable will. But something about her circumstances prickled his nape. He glanced at the trunk. *These are her memories, Jonas. Her memories of him.*

Without thinking, his hand brushed the outline of the box in his lowest pocket.

Another groan from the bag of shite drew his attention. After taking the sketch from Wallingham's hand, he grabbed a fistful of the man's coat, held the drawing in front of his swollen eyes, and demanded, "Tell me where he is."

"Don't rightly know."

Lady Wallingham warned, "Mr. Hawthorn's thirst for vengeance is surpassed only by his savagery. I advise answering his questions. Else, he may leave nothing at all for the hangman."

The man's eyes flew back to Jonas. Widened. Grew fearful.

"He paid me to watch her so she couldn't tell thee more about his plans. That's all. 'Twere a job. I didn't steal nowt."

"What is his name?"

The man shook his head and winced. "Bloody hell. Thy fists're like stone, ye—"

"What is his name?"

"Lynch."

Jonas glanced at both Wallingham and his mother. Neither appeared to recognize the name. He turned his attention back to the bag of shite. "You say you were paid to watch the girl. Do you mean the maid—Elly Allen?"

"Aye. Elly. Sweet one, that. Never gave me a bit of bother."

"Where is she?"

The man shook his head, looking forlorn. "Don't rightly know. She fancied Lynch at first. He has a way with the lasses. But I went out to fetch breakfast, and she disappeared. He were fit to be tied. Set me to watchin' the cave while he searched for her."

"Did he tell you to shoot my wife?"

The man's looked convincingly horrified. "Nay! Don't say she were hit. I fired high above both of ye. Only aimed to drive thee back inside the cave for a time while Lynch found Elly."

Wallingham interjected, "Reaver discovered she has a sister who lives nearby. He's gone to question her. Perhaps she'll know where the girl's gone."

Jonas ran a hand through his hair and braced his hands on his hips. No maid. No thief. No bloody clue. "What business did Lynch have with the Bainbridge family?"

The man closed his eyes and groaned again, complaining about the pain in his head.

Jonas grabbed his coat and shook. "Why did he steal the trunk?"

The man squinted past Jonas's shoulder. "Ask 'im. He's where all this began."

Cecil, who had emerged from his nap slightly less

inebriated, looked positively green. He tried to rise from his chair, but Wallingham held him in place. "Now, now, Cousin. Mustn't leave the party early. Dreadfully rude."

"I already told you, I am the victim. Lynch attempted to extort a fortune from me."

Wallingham glanced at his mother. "Explains all those letters begging an increase in his allowance."

"Mmm," she agreed. "Whereas there remains no explanation for your continued tolerance of this scapegrace. Cecil has done nothing but exhaust his allowance and your supply of cognac for the past decade."

"He was my heir at one time."

"I warned you to cut him off after Bain was born." She waved to the bag of dung moaning about his head. "You failed to heed my advice, and this is the unfortunate result."

Wallingham continued questioning his cousin. Cecil admitted that Lynch had approached him in London the previous year. "I think he was surprised by the resemblance in the beginning," the drunkard said. "I paid him to go away. Thought that would be the end of the matter."

"But it wasn't."

"No. He returned for more. More and more. Eventually, he demanded payment in the form of information." Cecil gestured toward Lady Wallingham. "Wanted to know about her. Grimsgate. Our lineage. One night, he came to my father's old house in Surrey. I was preparing to sell the property, and your father's portrait was down from the attic." Cecil's mouth twisted. "When he saw it, he knew. I hadn't told him, I swear it. He might have suspected, but once he saw the portrait, he knew with certainty. He vowed to find proof that even Lady Wallingham couldn't deny."

Jonas eyed Cecil, who was still half-sotted but lucid. Then, he examined Lady Wallingham. "He tried to blackmail you, didn't he, my lady?" Jonas asked softly.

She glanced at the trunk then raised her chin. "Mr. Lynch

approached me some weeks ago in London. He assumed I would pay rich sums to prevent him from stirring up a bit of gossip. He assumed wrong."

"Because you don't countenance blackmail?"

"Because his assertions are preposterous. My husband did not father any bastards." She clicked her tongue. "Even if he had, do you suppose I give two figs for gossip, Mr. Hawthorn? I could stifle that blackguard's slander in an afternoon and still have time for a beach ramble with Humphrey. Mr. Lynch was never a threat." She gestured to her trunk. "He is a thief. No better—and certainly of no greater importance—than that."

"Then why did you not mention him as a possible culprit?"

"When he appeared at the house on Park Lane, I sent the cur away with his tail between his legs. The matter was settled. He didn't offer his name, and I didn't care to ask it. Until I saw your sketch of Mr. Lynch this morning, I suspected one of my lady's maids to be the culprit. A resentful, ungrateful lot. More than one has stolen from me in the past."

"You should have told me."

"You should have kept me better informed of your progress."

"What do you suppose Lynch hoped to find in your trunk?"

"I've no earthly idea. Evidence of his parentage, I presume. Had he asked, I could have spared him the trouble." She eyed Jonas's coat. "And myself the expense."

Expense was right. She'd offered Jonas the equivalent of a fortune to return one small trunk to her. Again, he traced the lines of the box in his pocket.

The drawing room doors opened. This time, it was Sebastian Reaver. His hair was damp, his expression stern. And beside him, looking bedraggled and wide-eyed was Elly Allen. Several loose feathers dotted her hair.

"Found her hiding in her sister's chicken coop." The giant's twice-broken nose twitched. "Best keep your distance."

The young maid instantly started weeping. Loudly.

"Cease your caterwauling, girl," the dragon snapped.

Miss Allen closed her mouth and hiccupped to a stop.

Jonas approached, nodding his thanks to Reaver and giving the young maid one of his more charming smiles. "Miss Allen. Are you injured? Did Mr. Lynch harm you?"

"N-no, sir. He wouldn't let me leave, but he never hurt me."

Nodding to the bag of shite staring at Miss Allen with a daft grin, he asked, "What about that one?"

"Eddie? Oh, 'ee were a lamb. Kind an' gentle." She sent an equally daft grin back to Eddie. "I wouldn't 'ave left ye, Eddie. It's just that I knew my sister would start to frettin'."

"I forgive thee, Elly." The man began to weep, too. Before long, both pathetic wretches leaked like cracked pots.

"Good God," Jonas muttered, rubbing his eyes. "Miss Allen!"

The girl sniffled to a stop. "Aye, sir?"

"Do you know where Mr. Lynch might be at present?"

Her eyes went wide. She shook her head. "No, sir."

"Did he share his plans with you?"

She blinked. Sniffed. "He talked of Paris a fair bit."

"Paris."

"'Ee promised to take me there once 'er ladyship came round to seein' sense. Said as there'd be many fine slippers. I thought to accompany 'im. But that were before I met Eddie." The maid blinked, her brow crinkling. "You know, I've come to think much of what Mr. Lynch says is a great lot of blather."

Bloody hell. This entire farce had been orchestrated by a blathering schemer who resembled a dead marquess. Eddie and Elly were pathetic fodder, nothing more. Eddie would still pay for wounding Hannah, but it was clear the thickheaded simpleton hadn't intended to harm her.

He spent the following half-hour questioning Eddie, who had worked with Lynch sporadically for years. Lynch was a swindler of the sort Jonas occasionally encountered in his work for Bow Street. He drifted from place to place, seducing gullible women of the servant class into helping him gain information and access to his targets. He likewise seduced vulnerable widows with minor fortunes then left them penniless. He blackmailed men like Cecil Bainbridge, which was no less than men like Cecil Bainbridge deserved. But he'd also blackmailed senile old men after convincing them they'd committed nonexistent crimes.

When he wasn't running such low schemes, Lynch was a petty smuggler loathed by other smugglers for selling their names to save his own neck. This explained his penchant for caves and whisky.

By the time Eddie had finished, Jonas had a clear portrait of the man—he was Bertie Pickens only handsomer.

Jonas glanced to Lady Wallingham. "How much of this did you know?"

She raised a brow. "The better question is: How much of this would I have predicted? The answer is all of it. Should you manage to locate the blackguard, you will understand. He is a low creature. His resemblance to Bainbridge men is but a mockery of their superior character." She sniffed and gestured toward her nephew. "Cecil notwithstanding."

Cecil sat up taller in his chair. "A low creature, indeed. His talk is grandiose, a lot of falderal. But in the matter of his parentage, I fear he has grown impassioned. He believes himself a Bainbridge, Aunt. He believes himself entitled to a share of Wallingham's fortune."

Wallingham frowned at his cousin. "You think he is still nearby, then." At Cecil's nod, Wallingham looked to Jonas. "How do we find him?"

"Revisit his hiding places, perhaps. The caves. Alnwick." Jonas glanced at Reaver, who stood cross-armed and glowering in his usual fashion.

"'Tis a start," Reaver agreed. "Though, we may want to search the castle grounds, as well."

"Aye," Jonas said, following the logic. Lynch had stolen the trunk thinking it would offer a key to the Bainbridge fortune, or at least proof of his parentage. It didn't, of course, but a desperate man accustomed to telling grandiose tales might eventually convince himself of his own rubbish. There was only one reason to remain in Northumberland, only one reason to send Eddie to guard the cave. "He still thinks the trunk is some sort of treasure map."

Reaver grunted his agreement. "He'll come for it again. His accomplices have been captured, and he's being hunted. Desperate men do desperate things."

Voices sounded outside the drawing room. Nash entered looking solemn and far less starchy than usual. He was followed by a trembling, tearful Claudette.

Jonas's heart froze. Ice filled his chest.

"I beg your pardons, my lady, my lords," the butler said. "We have an intruder in the castle."

Nash's voice faded behind the blood pounding in Jonas's ears. All he saw was Claudette, whose fearful gaze found him just before she rushed forward, clutching a white shawl in her hands.

He was shaking his head when she reached him, her eyes beseeching. Distraught. Desperate.

"H-he has a knife, Mr. Hawthorn," she said, plunging him into a nightmare. "I couldn't stop him."

"Where is she?"

"I will show you. But we must hurry." The maid wrung the shawl between her hands. "Please, sir. We must save her."

Chapter Nineteen

"Thieves are the worst sort of vermin. Given the choice,
I should prefer rats. One need not involve a magistrate
in the disposal of rats."

—DOROTHEA BAINBRIDGE, THE MARCHIONESS OF WALLINGHAM,
to Malcolm Charles Bainbridge, the Marquess of Wallingham, in a
letter explaining the need to hire a less verminous lady's maid.

GREAT EVIL DIFFERED FROM COMMON VILLAINY IN WAYS MOST
people were blessed never to learn. Hannah was not so blessed.
She'd known the slithery shape of evil. Felt its vile touch.
Stared into its malevolent eyes while it claimed to love her.

Which was how she knew the man currently holding her in
the tiny, dark cellar was a villain, but merely one of the

common variety.

"What a beauty you are. Come now, tell me your name. I must know."

In the dark, she couldn't see his face any better than he could see hers. All she had was his voice, which was pleasant enough but suffered from forced charm. She found the theatrical tone irritating.

She preferred a voice with a steadier cadence, a lower pitch, hints of Norwich and Dorchester and London. A bit rough and a lot tempting.

The thief sighed. "I've never seen eyes of such an astonishing color." Where he gripped her upper arm, his thumb began to stroke her in circles. "Puts me in mind of a pair of earbobs I once sold to a jeweler in Paris. Lightest jade. Fetched a princely sum."

He hoped to charm her into compliance. From the moment they'd entered the cellar, he hadn't ceased with the overweening compliments, the "casual" mentions of his travels. Apparently, Paris was impressive to other females. He'd mentioned it four times in five minutes.

"Tell me your name, beauty. Tell me, and I shall put the knife away."

In the beginning, she'd had to fight to stay grounded, to force the fear to recede. She'd touched her wedding ring and pictured Jonas. His eyes as he'd spoken his vows. His hands as he'd held her face for a kiss. His mouth as he'd spoken her name. She'd imagined him holding their first babe. Winning his first game of garden chess. Loving her in the moonlight. Visions of him had kept her calm, which helped her see the villain clearly.

The thief wore a disguise, much as Jonas did. He was handsome, as Jonas was. But the two men could not be more dissimilar.

Jonas was good—dangerous but good. His charm was a tool he used in furtherance of honorable goals.

The thief was bad—not evil, but bad. His charm was a lie in furtherance of greed. He used his handsomeness to prey upon those of weak mind.

In the dark, this became impossible not to see.

"My name is Mrs. Hawthorn," she answered, delaying as long as she could.

The blade eased away from her ribs. "Mrs. Hawthorn. Well, it's pleased I am to make your acquaintance, missus. Though, I'd be more pleased if you were a miss." He made an annoying clicking sound with his tongue. "Doubly so if you weren't a Hawthorn."

She didn't bother with a reply. The man obviously recognized Jonas's name. The missing maid must have told him.

"I believe your husband may have stolen my stolen trunk, Mrs. Hawthorn. I'm afraid I must have it back." His hand continued to stroke her upper arm. He made her skin crawl. "I am a Bainbridge, you see. The old dragon simply refuses to admit it."

"Was there something in the trunk that proves your claim?"

"Letters. Nothing said in so many words, of course. But with more time, all will come clear."

Some part of him touched her hair. His chin, perhaps. Or his nose.

He tugged her closer. "My sincere apologies for the necessity of holding you like this. Were there any other way—"

"There are always other ways," she said calmly. "You've chosen the worst one. The wrong one, as you'll soon discover."

The knife returned to its previous position. "Is that what you think?"

"I wouldn't have said it if I did not think it."

His chuckle was condescension. "A beauty with fire. I'm intrigued. Perhaps when I have my fortune, we may come to an ... agreeable arrangement."

She didn't reply. The thought was too revolting to contemplate.

"You've done well choosing this place," he said, his breath washing over her ear. "I could almost imagine you planned for us to spend hours together in dark, intimate quarters." His chin nuzzled her cheek. "Nobody will find us here, hmm? If you were to permit me certain liberties, nobody would be the wiser."

She pictured Jonas. Pressed her moon-and-stars ring into her hand. Breathed.

"I'll not hurt you, beauty. Our circumstances are unfortunate, but you mustn't fear me."

Closing her eyes, she listened to her heart beating, to the hush of the chamber, to the faintest sound of rain. She turned her head until her lips were near his. "Shall I tell you a secret?" she whispered. "I don't."

His hand loosened. His lips lowered.

The door opened.

She tore free.

A wolf prowled into the cellar. In his hand was a pistol. In his eyes, death.

Dangerous. And good.

Hannah ran to him. Slid her arms inside his coat. Plastered her body around his, as close as she could get.

"Everything all right, love?" His voice was calm. Low. A bit rough.

God, how she loved him. "Yes," she answered. "I hoped you would arrive a minute sooner, but this will do."

"I will always come for you."

"I know."

"Shall I kill him?"

She laid her hand over his heart. Laid her ear upon his chest. Listened to the reassuring drum. The cadence was fast. Powerful. "No. He didn't hurt me."

"But you were hurt because of him. That requires punishment."

"Yes."

A pause. "You want me to let the hangman have him, don't you?"

"Yes."

He sighed, his free arm tightening around her waist. "Bloody hell."

Reaver entered, taking half the space inside the cellar. He grasped the thief's wrist and twisted then removed the knife neatly from the man's hand. Stopping only long enough to murmur in his low rumble, "Ye're safe now, Hannah," he hauled the thief through the door.

Minutes later, she was hugging a weepy Claudette in Lady Wallingham's drawing room while Jonas presented the thief to the dowager marchioness like a wolf offering a kill.

Lady Wallingham nodded her approval. "Well done, Mr. Hawthorn. The bounty is yours."

He gave her a bow and a grin.

With her son standing beside her, the dowager leveled the thief with a scathing glare. "You've erred rather badly, Mr. Lynch. Stealing from me? Ordering your man to fire upon Mr. Hawthorn's wife? Taking said wife hostage? Some might draw comparisons to great piles of manure, but as Lord Holstoke would no doubt argue, manure may end in a prosperous garden. Whereas your end shall be far less pleasant."

"I am a Bainbridge," the thief snarled. "I'll prove—"

"You shall be in prison," she snapped, her voice echoing like a queen's command. "Or buried in whatever hole the executioner designates for forgotten refuse."

"I look exactly like him. Your husband. The thirteenth bloody Marquess of Wallingham. I am his son!"

She arched a brow. A small smile curved her mouth. "You are nothing like him. Nothing at all."

"How do you explain it?" the thief demanded, his chest heaving as he pulled against Jonas's grip. "I am owed a portion, you bloody—"

Jonas wrapped an arm across the man's throat. "Keep a civil

tongue, or I will cut it out."

Hannah blinked at her husband's controlled savagery. She wasn't certain how much was real and how much a tactic of intimidation, but it was clear he was still battling his anger.

"Bastards are owed nothing whatever, Mr. Lynch," Lady Wallingham instructed calmly. "Your resemblance to my husband is no more remarkable than the resemblance between milk and pearl. They share a common color, perhaps. But whilst one is rare and prized for its beauty, the other is sold for farthings and may be had of any cow who wanders a field."

Lynch gasped and choked against Jonas's hold until Reaver stepped in to pat his shoulder. "Mightn't wish to kill him just yet, Hawthorn. Easy, now."

Breaths fast and rhythmic, Jonas backed away, allowing Reaver to take over restraining the thief.

Lady Wallingham gestured to the group of footmen waiting to haul Lynch to gaol, and they rushed forward to answer her unspoken command.

As soon as the thief was gone, Lord Wallingham shook his head, frowning down upon his mother's imperious head. "The resemblance is uncanny, Mother. I don't see how you can deny it."

"Oh, I don't deny it."

Appearing flummoxed, his frown deepened. "You don't?"

She glanced up at her son. Patted his hand where it rested upon the back of her chair in a rare maternal gesture. "He is not your brother, Charles." Her gaze moved to Cecil Bainbridge, seated a fair distance away nursing a cup of tea and looking miserable. "He may be Cecil's brother, however. Your uncle's third mistress had similar eyes. He married Cecil's mother shortly after she left him for Lord Muggeridge."

"A cousin, then."

"A bastard," she countered. "But not one of any worth. Had he been, then I should think your infernal generosity warranted. You inherited that trait from your father, along with your chin."

Wallingham looked to the trunk, which sat on the floor beside her feet. He cradled his mother's hand then gently lifted it to his lips. "I am gratified your possessions are back where they belong," he said softly. "Where they have always belonged."

While Hannah marveled at the tender moment between mother and son, Jonas approached. His eyes were stormy, as though the need for violence had gone unquenched. "Perhaps you should lie down, love. Let Claudette take you upstairs."

She shook her head. "I am fine."

"You are not fine; you are injured." His jaw flexed as the storm grew.

"Jonas, you mustn't worry—"

"I do worry. Bloody hell, you were taken. Right under my nose. He held a knife to your ..." He ground his teeth. Silver flashed like lightning. His chest heaved.

Reaching for him helplessly, her fingers barely touched his shirt before he flinched away from her.

His eyes pulled away from her.

Her husband pulled away from her.

He braced his hands on his hips. Stalked to the opposite end of the room and looked out the window rather than at her.

Claudette, small and sweet, offered, "It has been a trying day for us all, mistress."

Hannah swallowed and nodded. He was pulling away. Again. Inside, where she'd fought to give him every part of herself, gray numbness began to rise and swirl.

Distantly, she noticed Wallingham escorting his cousin from the room. Claudette said something about arranging tea. Soon, the room was empty of everyone except Hannah, Jonas, and Lady Wallingham.

Noting how tired the dowager looked, she wandered closer. Glanced down at the trunk. Smelled the faint scent of sandalwood.

"He was left-handed, wasn't he?" she murmured softly.

The white head came up. Ferocious emerald eyes blazed and glossed. A wrinkled mouth tightened. "Yes."

Hannah moved to the adjacent chair and sat. "This is how you remember him."

Silence.

"It is a good way," Hannah said. "Otherwise, how can you bear it?" She took a deep, shuddering breath. Braved a glance at her husband. "I could not bear it."

"You could," the dowager said quietly.

Hannah had never seen her look so creased, so worn. Like the letters she'd hidden away until the ink had faded and the paper had grown thin.

"If you had his child to love, you could bear it." Green eyes dropped to thin, wrinkled hands. "If you gathered friends round you and kept them close, you could bear it." Her eyes came up.

They seized Hannah's heart in a relentless vise.

"But you would never be whole. You would only ever be waiting." Her gaze fell to the trunk. "And, in your weaker moments ... remembering."

Hannah heard the drawing room door open then jolted as it slammed closed. It was Jonas.

Leaving.

On the heels of a fearsome dragon's aching admission, his departure struck with icy devastation. The numbness spread its gray blanket inside her. Even that did not stop the bleeding.

Her hand fluttered to her mouth. Her breaths grew shallow.

"Calm yourself, dear," came a commanding voice from beside her. "Look at me."

She couldn't. He was gone.

"Look here, girl. Now!"

Hannah's eyes flew to the old woman.

"Better. Where did you run off to, hmm?"

A chill settled over her. She had no answer.

"He hasn't left you."

She shook her head. "I don't know how to persuade him, my lady."

"Of what, precisely?"

"To attach."

The old woman sighed. "Attachment takes time, girl. You are asking him to surrender after a mere week of marriage."

"Not surrender. Just ... I want him to let me in." It was the same thing he'd asked of her. And she had done it, but her fear of what might result had been fierce. Perhaps he was battling something equally daunting. "What will it take?"

"For his part, courage. For yours, patience." Lady Wallingham's mouth curved. "He is already yours, my dear. Perhaps you didn't notice that he resisted killing Mr. Lynch in your presence. For a man such as Hawthorn, this is all but an act of worship."

Hannah huffed. "Worship. Don't be silly."

"I am never silly."

"He loves me. I can see it. But I also see his fear, and I do not know how to break through it."

"How did you break through your own fear?"

She thought about it. Remembered all the steps she'd taken, small and large—enrolling in St. Catherine's Academy, meeting Phineas, killing Lady Holstoke, letting Eugenia befriend her, learning to ride. And choosing to love Jonas. Perhaps that most of all.

"Bit by bit," Hannah whispered.

"Quite right. For wild, solitary creatures, love is instinctive. Powerful. That force will keep him with you whilst you build more permanent structures. Count upon it."

Tears flooded Hannah's eyes, turning light into a watery swirl. "H-how can you be sure?"

"Simple, my dear." Lady Wallingham nodded to her trunk. "Dragons need their treasure. Wolves need their moon."

Chapter Twenty

"When will I see you again?
An eternity lives inside each passing hour."

—Dorothea Bainbridge, The Marchioness of Wallingham,
to Malcolm Charles Bainbridge, the Marquess of Wallingham, in a
letter written after too many eternities had passed.

JONAS WALKED A MILE OF BEACH BEFORE HE STOPPED SEEING
Hannah lying dead inside that dusty cellar. Another mile
before he could think of her without a red haze of bloodlust
for the man who had threatened her with a blade. Wounded
her with a bullet. Touched her with trespassing hands.

By the time he stopped and leaned against a wave-
splashed boulder, his rage had dispersed into a lesser fire.

But the pain remained.

You would never be whole, the old dragon had said in a voice that knew. *You would only ever be waiting. And, in your weaker moments, remembering.*

Grunting against the tightness in his chest, he dug into his lowest pocket. Withdrew the box. Ran his fingers over the surface as he watched the sea caress golden sand and dark stones.

He had everything he'd ever wanted. Everything he'd tucked away inside this box.

But what if he lost it? What if he lost her?

Nothing lasted. Even the boulders on the beach would be ground to dust in time. Cliffs would be hollowed out by water and wind.

She could fall ill. She could die and leave him with nothing but the waiting. Biding his time with a box full of paper.

He scraped a hand over his face. She wanted children. She wanted to hold babes like her nephew, tiny and fragile. She wanted him to love them.

What if he lost them, too?

Alone was easier. No complications. He could live in whatever county he wanted without having to ask whether it was better to be close to Holstoke or Dunston. He could wear whatever coat he damn well pleased without wondering if he pleased her. He could be free of fear's weight.

But, then, he'd have to live without her. And who in bloody hell needed a coat with pockets if he had nothing precious to put inside them?

He ran his thumb across the moon and stars. Then, he slipped his dreams back where they belonged and started toward the castle.

Inside, he discovered most of Lady Wallingham's guests had returned from Chatwick. Dunston and Blackmore waylaid him on his way through the grand hall to ask a dozen questions. They were soon joined by Atherbourne,

Tannenbrook, Conrad, and Lacey, who all wanted details about the thief's apprehension.

Jonas answered as briefly as he could, but the men kept at him. He itched to break away. He wanted to find Hannah. He wanted to kiss her sweet mouth and make sure her wound didn't pain her too much.

"And you didn't kill him?" Dunston asked for the fourth time.

Jonas rubbed his forehead. "Bloody hell, Dunston."

"Seems to me you could have done. I doubt the magistrates would give you any trouble. If they did, I could intercede on your behalf." The dapper earl grinned. "The Home Secretary is a friend."

"She asked me not to."

Blackmore hummed his sympathy. "Yes. Women often have different sensibilities about such things. More's the pity."

"Sometimes killing is the best thing," said Colin Lacey. The man who looked like he fell from a painting wore a distinctly uncivilized glare. "The only thing."

Dunston clapped Lacey's shoulder with an approving nod. "I always knew we had more in common than appearances would suggest." His eyes dropped to Lacey's waistcoat, which was plain brown linen. "You may be a glorified country tutor and father of three, but that waistcoat is taking drudgery a bit far, my good man."

Lacey chuckled. "If my life is drudgery, then may every day grow more tedious."

"You make a fair point about killing those who need killing," Dunston said in a darker tone. He looked at Jonas, his eyes hard and purposeful. "Putting down Horatio Syder balanced scales that were long overdue."

Jonas's entire body flushed at once. Sparks of red flew across his vision. Without thinking, he moved in close to Lacey. "You?" he said, his voice an unrecognizable growl. "You killed him?"

Lacey raised his brows in a wary fashion. "I did. Must say, I haven't regretted it a moment since."

"I wish I had done it." The words were pulled out of him, raw and guttural.

But he could see Lacey understood. The other man's eyes held sympathy and savagery and satisfaction in equal measures. "A thousand times over,"

"For a thousand years," Jonas finished. He remembered what Dunston had told him about the man who had killed Syder. "Your wife—she survived."

Lacey smiled. "Yes. She is strong. Like Hannah."

Jonas didn't know what to do with everything inside him. Gratitude to Lacey. Pride in his woman. The need to hold her again. It was too much. He had to grit his teeth against the force of it.

The tension broke when Rutherford joined them. The marquess handed his hat to Nash and approached, coming to stand between Atherbourne and Tannenbrook. "I thought we weren't supposed to discuss Colin's foray into espionage and assassination." He gave Jonas a sardonic smile. "Delicate subject, you know."

Blackmore slanted a disapproving glance at Dunston, who shrugged and replied, "You are the one who saved the boy's skin, Rutherford. Twice. Yet, you're the one who insists I refrain from mentioning it."

Turquoise eyes glinted annoyance. "I believe you just did."

Dunston's grin was unrepentant. "Slip of the tongue."

Jonas was glad to see he wasn't the only one Dunston enjoyed vexing.

Atherbourne chuckled. "Ben always did prefer to be regarded as wicked. Mustn't spoil the illusion."

"As I recall, you relished following my lead on that score, Luc," Rutherford replied. "Alas, our wickedness must now be reserved for quarters in which it is best rewarded. We've daughters to consider, do we not?"

Laughing, Atherbourne clapped Rutherford's shoulder. "Quite right. If your Margaret and my Mary Sophia are to believe us saints, we cannot afford even the illusion of devilishness. I dread the day my girl ventures into the marriage mart."

Tannenbrook frowned at the pair. "Marriage mart? You intend to send your lambs out amongst the wolves, then, do ye?"

Atherbourne shook his head. "This again. I've explained already, man. You've four daughters who, thanks be to God, resemble their mother. The odds of them remaining unmarried forever are—"

"Better they be spinsters than subject to the appetites of wolves and devils."

"I agree with Tannenbrook," said Blackmore.

"You would," said Dunston with a snort. "I predict Emma and her sisters will have different ideas when the time comes."

Lacey chuckled. "And, if I know my brother, they will have him dancing to their tune as easily as Jane does."

Blackmore seemed about to protest but eventually smiled and conceded, "I suspect they will."

As Jonas listened to the men ribbing one another about who indulged his wife's whims most readily, another pang of longing for Hannah struck. He excused himself and went to find his wife.

He found her in the nursery. She sat in a chair by the window, holding her nephew. Westerly light slanted through the glass, painting raven-black hair with watery shadows and gentle whites. Her smile was tender. Her finger wrapped in a tiny fist. And as his chest tightened, she began to hum.

The song was light. Soft as snowfall.

Familiar as his breath.

His legs carried him closer. His hand moved to his pocket. His eyes couldn't leave her.

Her lashes fluttered and lifted. Riveting green focused upon him. "Jonas," she whispered. "Y-you came back."

Heart in his throat, he rasped, "Always, love."

Her eyes filled. She smiled, her lips trembling. Then, cradling the babe, she stood and moved close. "Would you like to hold him?"

Alarmed, he started to shake his head.

"Here now," she murmured. "He won't bite."

"Hannah—"

She transferred the babe into his arms, positioning his hands to support the tiny head. "It is all right. Griffin doesn't mind." She stroked the plump cheek with her finger. Adored the little creature with her eyes. "Isn't that right, my darling? A good meal makes for a happy boy."

Jonas didn't look at the babe. He watched her. No wonder she'd demanded he give her children. She was made to be a mother.

Whereas he had little experience with tiny humans. No siblings, no nieces or nephews. He held his arms as still as possible, hoping not to drop the future Earl of Holstoke on his fragile little head.

"I must speak with you." His voice sounded like frayed rope.

Her eyes came up to his. "I've imagined you holding our sons just like this."

He swallowed.

"Am I silly for wanting them to be as handsome as you?"

"Hannah."

"I love you, Jonas." Her eyes filled and gleamed bright. Tears spilled onto pale cheeks. "Please look at him."

He didn't want to.

"His name is Griffin. He likes bright colors and miniature fruits. He's a curious boy. Clever. He fusses when he's hungry and sleeps when he feels safe. His eyes are like mine."

He shook his head. Fought against her. Against himself.

"Look at him, my love."

Slowly, he gave in. Dropped his gaze. Saw the tiny human with raven hair and Hannah's eyes.

"Griffin," she murmured. "Say his name."

He clenched his jaw. Forced the word to come out. "Griffin."

Her soft palm came up to stroke his cheek. Her other hand stroked Griffin's head. "This is what we'll have one day, Jonas. This is what we must fight for. Our family."

The longer they stood there together, Hannah touching him while he held the babe, the more the tightness in his chest unraveled. Soon, breathing came easier.

She stood on her toes and kissed him, her lips soft and tender against his.

The boy fell asleep in his arms. Hannah showed him how to place Griffin in the cradle then took his hand and led him down to their bedchamber.

Inside, brown velvet and blue silk were washed with gray light. She crossed to the window, tracing droplets with her finger. The rain had started up again.

He shrugged out of his coat and tossed it across the foot of the bed. Running a hand through his hair, he paced as he tried to think of how he might explain. Where he might begin to make her understand. Finally, he came to a stop inches behind her. Looked down upon her graceful hand, her vulnerable nape. And the words fell out of him like rain from the sky.

"I think I died once," he said. "I was on a ship. We were blown to bits. Everyone around me was dead or dying." His throat tightened. "It was hell. Worse than I'd seen before, though God knows, I'd seen enough death by then. My mother. Father. Boys I knew in London. Soldiers in battle. Death, death, death." He sighed. "I always came out alive. Felt like a perverse joke, after a time."

Her head turned until her chin rested on her shoulder. "How did you bear it?"

"Tried to see outside the hell. Find something beautiful wherever I could, as my mother had taught me. That day on the ship before the battle, I sketched the shoreline. But even beauty becomes a taunt when you watch so many men die for nothing." He shook his head. "I was hit toward the end. I don't know if I was dead or dreaming or ... or what, but I had a vision. So bloody vivid, I can still feel the mist on my skin. I was in a garden. Scent of thyme in the air. Willow branches. A house with turrets. And a voice. Soft. Sweet. Humming. I'd never been there, that much I know. But it felt as real to me as anything. It felt like ... home."

She stepped back into him, and he slid his arms across the front of her shoulders and around her waist. "A good dream, then," she said.

"Mmm. It gave me something to want. Something to work toward. Not that particular house or that particular garden, exactly. But land of my own. A place I belonged." He rested his chin upon her head. Gathered her close. "On a soldier's pay, that was a leap. So I left the army. Went back to London. Worked on ships for a time. Became a runner. But the dream never left me. It's what I've saved for. Every bounty. Every spare shilling. All to make a place for myself far from death and suffering. A place no bloody nob could take away. It was my something beautiful."

They fell into silence, holding one another while rain pattered glass. After a while, she whispered, "I am terrified of losing you."

He frowned and held her tighter. "You will never lose me."

"I can feel it, Jonas." Her voice contorted, choked and trembling. Her fingers dug into his forearm. "I can feel how much you want to pull away, and I don't know how to keep you."

He had no answer. No words to explain. What she feared was impossible. What she wanted was already hers.

She turned in his arms. Wrapped herself around him. "I need inside. Just as you needed inside."

His eyes closed. "It is dark in here, love."

"I like dark places."

"You mightn't like this one," he confessed against raven hair. "My love for you is consuming. More than you realize."

"Show me."

"It will frighten you."

"Show me anyway."

He kissed her head. Drew her chin up so he could kiss her mouth. "Very well." He went to the foot of the bed. Dug inside his lowest pocket. Withdrew the box. Offered it to his wife. "Open it."

She ran her fingers over the relief of moon and stars. Traced their lines then looked at her ring. Her lips trembled as she flicked open the small brass latch. Finally, she raised the lid. Setting the box on the bed, she carefully unfolded each of the pages contained inside white satin. Then, she spread them out on brown velvet. Looked at them in watery light. Covered her mouth with shaking fingers.

"Aye, love. It is you. All you." His voice was in shreds, his chest tight and cold as he waited for her to say something. Condemn his obsession. Tell him he was mad.

She didn't. A tear streaked her cheek, but she didn't say anything. Just stared down at his sketches—her in the drawing room at Holstoke House, half-turned and silhouetted against the window. Her sitting at his bedside at Primvale, hair frayed and eyes closed while her hand lay on the bed within an inch of his. Her naked but for moonlight, fingers covering a sensual smile. There were more—ten more, to be precise—and still more to come. He'd redrawn the ones he'd burned and added new ones each day since their wedding.

"You are my something beautiful," he said. "You have been from the first moment I saw you."

Another tear fell. She squeezed her eyes closed.

He felt sick. He'd known he shouldn't tell her. He'd known the damage it could do.

"Did you think I wasn't strong enough?" she asked, her voice trembling. "Did you think I would mistake you for him?"

Yes, he had. Strong though she was, he would do anything to keep from frightening her, reminding her of what she'd endured.

"I am *not* wet paper, Jonas Hawthorn." She swiped a tear away, her eyes beginning to blaze. "And I will *not* let you hide from me."

Suddenly, he found himself gazing down into sheer feminine fire.

She cupped his jaw. Held him tight. Refused to let him look away. "Touch me."

Gently, he clasped her wrists. Tried to pull back.

She wouldn't have it. She snagged his hand and brought it to her breast. "Touch me," she repeated in a growl. "I need no protection from you."

Arousal surged before he stifled it. Controlling his breathing, he moved his hand to her waist, just above the hip that had been grazed by a bullet. "You do."

Her nose flared. Her jaw flexed. "I wore this gown for you. Do you like it?"

His gaze was glued to her breasts, so he vaguely perceived the color. "It's lovely."

"Yes," she snapped. "Do you know what I imagined while I dressed?"

Her nipples were hard. Swollen. Pouting against blush velvet. He licked his lips and willed his fingers to ease their grip on her waist. "What?"

She started gathering up her skirt. Moved into him, forcing him backward until his thighs hit the bed.

He sat, surprised at her ferocity.

Yanking her skirts up to her thighs, she braced her hands on his shoulders and straddled his hips. "I imagined you tearing it from my body," she said. "I imagined your mouth here." She took his hand and brought it between her thighs, pressing his fingers into her wet, silken folds. She moaned and threaded her hand into his hair. "I imagined your teeth on my breasts. Your tongue on my nipples."

He wasn't going to make it. The moment he felt how wet she was, how swollen and sweet and ready, his body flooded with fire. His skin tightened. Flushed. His cock was so hard it threatened to go off like an overheated pistol. Then, she began describing her fantasies. And nothing had ever been so bloody torturous.

Visions of her laid out upon the torn remnants of her gown, writhing for him as he feasted upon her, made him a prisoner of his lust.

"Then, I imagined you inside me," his tormenter continued, her breath hitching, her voice ragged as she rocked her hips against his hand. "Fucking me."

He groaned as the word hit him with a cannon's force. He nearly came, just from seeing rosebud lips form two syllables.

She was his Snow Queen. Pristine. Untouchable.

But that word—ah, God. That word was filthy. And it excited her. He'd noticed it before, when he'd used it, but that had been unintentional. This wasn't.

Helpless to stop himself, needing some small thing to answer his hunger, he slid two fingers deep into her core.

She clenched him hard, rippling a welcome. Mouth open with awed pleasure, she gasped and bit her lip. Gripped his nape. Ground her hips hard against him.

"Take me," she demanded, grasping his other hand and bringing it back to her breast. "Do not stop. Do not be gentle."

The grinding agony of holding back seized his ballocks, demanded he do precisely what she described. He shook his head, his lips helplessly falling upon her throat, his lungs filling helplessly with wet, silken roses and hot, sweet woman.

She unpinned her hair with jerking motions, bringing raven-black curls tumbling down around their faces. "Look at me, Jonas."

He groaned his agony against her skin.

"Look at me, my love."

He did. It hurt to fight through his own resistance. His own need to keep her safe. But as her heat and scent and sheer will battered him, he couldn't help it. He surrendered. Raised his head. Found her eyes. Let her see.

And she held him. Blazing green lifted him. Moved inside. Smiled. "I am here, Jonas." She shook her head as she gestured to the bed where his sketches lay. "Not there. Not in a box." She placed her palm in the center of his chest, her fingertips digging as though she wanted to absorb him. "Here." Her hand clutched his over her breast. "And you are here. I am not broken. Your love makes me stronger. It is nothing like his. I will never mistake that. And I will never let you walk away from me again. No matter what."

"God Almighty." His heart was twisting and pounding and so full he couldn't breathe around it. "I love you, you beautiful, haughty, glorious woman. Christ, how I love you."

Her radiant laugh ended in a long, low moan. Her sheath began to squeeze and demand a deeper penetration. Her sweet brow crinkled in a grimace of desire. She grunted. "Oh, heavens. I'm going to ... you must take me now. Please. Oh, I need you. Hard and strong. Please."

Within seconds, he'd reversed their positions, plopping her onto the bed with a bounce and tearing away his fall as she spread her thighs wide. He tossed her skirts up past her hips, looking his fill for one pounding heartbeat. Two. A third.

"Now, Jonas," she commanded.

But he needed a taste. So he knelt. Gathered her juices on his tongue. Suckled her sweet, swollen bud into his mouth. Savored honey and rosewater.

Her body seized. Her keening cry signaled her climax in a familiar song.

And like music, he played her to draw out the notes, to create a symphony of pleasure. Only then did he grant his woman her wishes.

First, he climbed up between her thighs. Braced his body above hers. Kissed her beautiful lips. Felt her sigh his name. Drew back to meet her extraordinary eyes. Saw love glowing there. New arousal growing there.

He caressed her nipple through blushing velvet. "I hope you packed your thread and needle, love. Your dress will need repair."

She moaned. Arched her back.

He grasped the edge of her bodice and tore. Velvet gave way, revealing stays trimmed in lace. He grasped the corset's edge and forced the fabric down, letting it scrape across her engorged nipples. Then, he set to work.

"I believe you mentioned teeth."

He nibbled. Strummed. Pressured and tormented. Then, he moved to the opposite breast and did the same, using his hand to plump and trap her for pleasuring.

Finally, when he felt her clawing at his shoulders and clutching at his hair, he moved on to her last wish, whispering it in her ear beforehand. "Hard and strong, now, hmm?" He positioned her thighs and took her in one deep thrust that drove another keen from her throat. Sweet, silken fire swallowed him whole. "Hard enough, love?" He gave her what she'd asked, his thrusts drumming as fast as his heart. "Is this strong enough?"

By all rights, she should have protested. He was battering at her like a marauder, clutching her uninjured thigh and forcing it up, pressing it wide so that she could take more and more and more. More of him. More pleasure and friction. More of everything they were together.

But she loved it. Soft little fists clenched his hair. An impassioned mouth suckled his throat. A fiery sheath demanded he take her. Make her his. Give her everything he had.

So, he did. He gave her himself, cupping her cheek and holding her eyes. Telling her to keep him always. To let him have her forever. To take his seed and give him children. To never let go.

And even as she screamed her pleasure and took his own inside her, she held him. Loved him.

Almost as much as he loved her.

Which was all a man could ask for. Moonlight and midnight, roses and rain, passion and strength and a glorious heart, all lying in his arms.

Something beautiful.

Someone precious.

A future better than any dream.

Chapter Twenty-One

"My victories are many, it is true.
But no prize is so precious as your heart."

—Dorothea Bainbridge, The Marchioness of Wallingham,
to Malcolm Charles Bainbridge, the Marquess of Wallingham, in a
letter explaining the difference between triumphs and treasures.

His queen was trapped. He eyed his enemy's position,
absorbing the strategy and predicting the next move. If he
went left, all was lost. If he went right, he'd leave himself open
to attack. Moving back wasn't an option. Any fool could
backtrack. He might as well surrender.

No, the only way ahead was forward. Or perhaps diagonal.

A deep bark sounded from behind the western hedge.

Suddenly, Humphrey bounded across squares of flagstone and lawn, a slobbery boot between his jaws. The dog veered left, knocking over Hannah's knight and two of Jonas's pawns.

"Humphrey!" Hannah cried.

Jonas cursed beneath his breath. If he didn't want to hear her gloating all through luncheon, he needed this victory. He'd won their first two games, and she'd won their last two. This would end the tie.

His wife, he'd discovered, was ridiculously competitive.

Hannah shooed the hound away, but Humphrey took her gestures for playing and instead continued wreaking havoc until the only pieces left standing were Jonas's bishop and Hannah's king. A white pawn rolled past Jonas's boot.

"Jonas! Do something."

He crossed his arms and rubbed his jaw. "What would you have me do, love?"

She frowned at him fiercely. "Stop him!"

"He's already absconded with someone's boot. I've no wish to meet a similar fate." He glanced down. "These are new."

"You did this on purpose."

"Caused the dog to disrupt our game?" He snorted. "I was about to have my third victory. Why would I want to—"

"You, dear husband, were about to lose."

He loved the way her rosebud lips pursed on the word "lose." Grinning, he stepped over a black rook and sauntered toward the woman who held him in thrall. "Is that so?"

"I had you trapped. "

Inching closer, he eyed her pink cheeks and darting tongue. "I had a way out."

"Rubbish and rot. Three more moves, and I'd have had you."

He lowered his head. "You know you can have me anytime you like, don't you, love?"

Her eyes lit. Her breasts swelled on a swift breath. "Distractions are a violation of etiquette."

His grin widened. "Violations of etiquette are my favorite sport."

"Oh, heavens," she sighed. "I do love you so." Her hands settling on his new coat—the one Wallingham had given him as a wedding gift.

"And I you."

"I still say I would have won."

"Of course you do."

"Perhaps we should go to our bedchamber now."

"Luncheon starts soon. We should probably make an appearance."

She looked more disappointed by this than she'd been over the game.

He kissed her and whispered, "Never fear, love. I'll give you all the *victories* you can handle once we're alone."

When they were seated at Lady Wallingham's table, the food was excellent and the company lively, but all Jonas could think about was the gift he planned to present to Hannah later that evening. It had been a week since the incident with Lynch, and the house party was drawing to a close. Most of the guests planned to depart over the following two days. He'd spent the past five talking to everyone from Lady Wallingham to Holstoke and Eugenia about the decisions he faced.

He'd wanted to gather his thoughts and give Hannah everything he could. She deserved a choice in her future. She'd had too few in her past.

He looked at her now, candlelight playing with her raven hair. She leaned close to Eugenia, who said something to make her laugh. She drank lemonade and ate peach tarts while Lord Colin and his wife described her friend Biddy's recent antics at the school. Her brother asked about her chess game with Jonas, and she told the tale of Humphrey's destructive romp. All around the table were people who loved her, friends who supported her, connections she'd built over time.

He glanced to the head of the table, where Lady

Wallingham held court. The old dragon likewise had built a vast fortress of friendships and connections. To be sure, she'd stored away the memories of her husband for when she needed them most. But her son, daughter-in-law, and grandchildren, along with the Huxley family were clearly at the center of her life.

Luncheon ended with a call for battledore and shuttlecock. Jonas instead waylaid his wife and murmured, "I've something to show you, love."

Her eyes flared. Her lashes fluttered. "If it's what I'm anticipating, I do hope you'll do more than show me."

Chuckling, he raised her hand to his lips. Felt the moon and stars brush his jaw. "Will you come for a ride with me?"

She smiled and nodded.

A half-hour later, he was watching his beautiful wife gallop along golden sand while a seaborne breeze played with the feathers in her hat.

She laughed as he fell behind, but she soon slowed until he came even with her. "Jonas! You must keep up!" Her cheeks were flushed, her eyes dancing.

"Come, love. Let's walk while the horses rest."

At her nod, they rode to a grouping of boulders where he helped her down and took her hand. Then, he led her to the farthest boulder, a flat, broad stone where they could rest and talk. Where he could show her their future.

"Do you remember when I told you about the house in my vision?"

She nodded. "Turrets, yes?"

He took his moon-and-stars box from his pocket and opened the lid. "It lived in my mind for a long time. Years and years." He spoke as he started unfolding the sketches, smoothing them out and anchoring them on the flat stone surface with smaller rocks from the beach. "But always, that house was merely a representation. A symbol, in a sense."

She smiled. "Of home."

"Aye." He held her eyes so she'd see the truth of his words. "But home for me is you. And wherever we live together is just a place. Could be anywhere, really. A grand castle by the sea or a cave named after a dead saint. So long as you're contented, I'll be the happiest man alive."

She looked down. Her fingers came up to her lips. "What ... I don't understand."

He pointed to the first sketch, which illustrated a small manor house with a tidy garden and a large oak. "This is a fine house in Suffolk, near Dunston and Wallingham. The land is good, particularly for livestock. Sheep and such. It would put us inland, but there'd be ample room for riding. Wallingham has promised us two horses to begin our own stables."

Her eyes roamed across to the second illustration, a depiction of a beach very much like the one they were on. On the cliffs above lay another house, this one made of sandstone. It had a steep roof and dormers. It had a long drive that circled a fountain.

He leaned over and tapped it with his finger. "This one is here in Northumberland, south of Alnwick. The garden wants expanding, but Lord and Lady Rutherford tell me the land is excellent for wheat. And it's near the sea. I know how you love the sea."

"Oh, Jonas."

"Holstoke has offered to help us with the gardens. He's already suggested a few improvements you'll no doubt enjoy. An orchard. A pond."

He pointed to the third sketch, a half-timbered, large-scaled cottage with a thatched roof and rosebushes clustered around the entrance. "This is in Dorsetshire. It belongs to the Martin-Mace family, and according to Eugenia, it has all the charm of a cottage with all the elegance of a manor. It is but a few hundred yards from the Channel and less than an hour's ride from Primvale. Holstoke assures me our crops would flourish and the rents are excellent due to its proximity to Weymouth."

Her fingers trembled as she moved close and tucked into him. She reached for the fourth illustration, lifting it from the rock.

He watched her, his chest tight with love and hope.

A tear tracked down her cheek. "Wh—where is this one?"

"Now, there's a funny story, love." He leaned back against the rock and gathered her against him, looking down upon the illustration she held. "It seems this house once belonged to Lady Wallingham's family before her marriage. Her family fell upon some difficulty, and her father was forced to sell the property to Malcolm Charles Bainbridge. Earl Bainbridge was his title then. Lord Bainbridge planned to use it for hunting and as a residence for his mistresses. He was a young man, not yet married. But Lady Wallingham—Lady Dorothea Penworth, at the time—was outraged that her ancestral home might be so defiled. She took up a campaign of correspondence with him, bent on dissuading him from his course."

Hannah smiled beneath her fingers and shook her head. "I can only imagine he felt besieged."

"Hmm. Their first meeting was months later when she and her sister, Lady Margaret, traveled to London for their first season. I gather things went poorly. She accused him of turning her home into a brothel."

"Oh, dear."

"Dorothea thought him 'handsome and silent as a decorative vase, and approximately as useful.' But he was heir to a marquisate, and she had a profound determination to regain her home. So, in her usual fashion, she devised a plan."

Hannah grinned. "She would marry him."

"Aye."

"That is what all the letters were. She was trying to seduce him with her cleverness."

"It appears so."

She traced the lines of the illustration with her finger. "They fell in love."

"I expect the process was a bit more complicated, but yes, that was the result. They were utterly devoted to one another. According to Wallingham, their marriage was fraught with trials—lost babes, difficulties in producing an heir, her interventions in matters political—but nothing could pry them apart."

"She was so certain he never took mistresses." Hannah looked up at him. Stroked his cheek. "He must have loved her very much."

He brushed the illustration with his knuckle, his fingers stroking his wife's. "This was their home together for the first few years of their marriage. When he became the thirteenth Marquess of Wallingham, they moved to Grimsgate. But they kept this place. Lady Wallingham said if she could have fit it into her trunk, it would be there beside her slippers and sandalwood soap."

A tear coursed down her cheek as she regarded the illustration. "Did you draw this from her description?"

"I didn't draw it, love. She sent it to me with her letter soliciting my services. Offered the property as a bounty for locating her trunk and the man who stole it."

"Oh, Jonas. How can it be?"

"I don't know. But it surely brought me galloping here without delay."

She traced the twin turrets marking the front of the manor, the weeping willow tree beside a small pond. "This is your house."

"No, love. It is hers. It shall only be ours if you wish to make it so."

"Where is it?"

"Somersetshire. A half-day's ride from Lord and Lady Colin, several hours from Primvale. It is inland. No sea, I'm afraid. But excellent land. Woodlands. Vast acreage. Fruitful." He paused, gauging her expression. "Lady Wallingham gave me a choice—either the property or an equivalent sum to purchase another. So, you see, love, we may live wherever we'd like." He laid a kiss upon her palm. "Wherever you would be happiest, for your happiness is mine."

More tears spilled onto her cheeks. She ran her thumb across his lips. Glowed her love up at him through extraordinary eyes. "And yours is mine, Jonas Bartholomew Hawthorn." She turned in his arms. Reached for the box with the moon and stars. Folded the fourth illustration and placed it reverently upon white satin. Then, she slid the box into his lowest pocket, slipped her arms around his waist, and smiled up at him with heart-melting tenderness. "Your dreams are mine. Your heart is mine. Your house is mine." She stood on her toes and beckoned a kiss.

He couldn't resist her, his moonlight and rosebuds, midnight and rain. His everything beautiful.

"You are mine," she whispered. "Always."

Epilogue

"Come along, Humphrey. Let us ramble through the garden together and remember how beautiful everything is while it blooms."

—THE DOWAGER MARCHIONESS OF WALLINGHAM to her boon companion, Humphrey, on a lovely September morning.

HIS DREAM WAS FRAGRANCED WITH THYME. SQUARES OF THE herb cushioned his boots, sending up a green, spicy scent to tease and delight.

It was lit with September-rich sunshine streaming through soft morning mist.

It was dappled with laughter—childish and sweet. A boy's shouts to a new pup. A girl's squeals of half-fright, half-excitement.

It was accompanied by humming. Snowfall in summer. Soft and warm.

It was painted in green. Draping willow branches caressed the surface of a pond. High hedges formed a backdrop for white roses and ivy-laden urns.

It was shared by the woman who cradled his third babe. The strongest, most beautiful woman he'd ever known.

The pup darted between the willow branches, his brown, pendulous ears flopping. A black-haired girl wearing a red-ribboned hat giggled and chased after him. A gray-eyed boy with a roguish grin tempted the pup with a bone.

"Lady Wallingham intends to spend the week with us," said his wife. "Phineas and Eugenia will be bringing her with them tomorrow."

"Griffin, too?"

She smiled, a twinkle of affection in her eyes, then glanced toward the squares of their oversized chessboard, visible from where they sat in the southeast corner of the garden. "All their children, but yes, you and Griffin may play a rematch after your previous stalemate."

"He's a worthy opponent, given he's not yet old enough to sprout whiskers."

"Hmm. With Dunston and Maureen's brood visiting, as well, we shall have a very full house, indeed, my darling."

He stroked the plump cheek of his youngest daughter. Leaned down and kissed the raven-black hair that gleamed in the golden light. Raised up and kissed his something beautiful. "It's just as it should be, love. Everything is just as it should be."

The End

Author's Note

Yes, this is the final book in the Rescued from Ruin series. And while I'm sad to say a bittersweet goodbye to Lady Wallingham and all the couples she helped shepherd to their happily-ever-afters, I'm thrilled to begin a new chapter with a brand-new series ... featuring some familiar faces.

As the brother to five spirited sisters, John Huxley, Viscount Huxley, knows females. He's charmed more than a few into his bed. But this English lord with a bad case of wanderlust has never met anyone like the Scottish lass he encounters on a sojourn in the Highlands. Will she tempt him to put on a kilt and grow some strong Scottish roots? Or will his heart always be longing for the next shore?

Don't miss their passionate story in:

THE MAKING OF A HIGHLANDER

NOW AVAILABLE!

And if you've traveled the road to ruin with me from beginning to end, I just want to say how much it means to me that you've made these stories and these characters part of your life in some small way. Thank you will never be enough.

Wishing you all the best,

Elisa

More from Elisa Braden

*Be first to hear about new releases, price specials,
and more—sign up for Elisa's free email newsletter at
www.elisabraden.com so you don't miss a thing!*

Midnight in Scotland Series
*In the enchanting new Midnight in Scotland series,
the unlikeliest matches generate the greatest heat.
All it takes is a spark of Highland magic.*

THE MAKING OF A HIGHLANDER (BOOK ONE)

Handsome adventurer John Huxley is locked in a land dispute in the Scottish Highlands with one way out: Win the Highland Games. When the local hoyden Mad Annie Tulloch offers to train him in exchange for "Lady Lessons," he agrees. But teaching the fiery, foulmouthed, breeches-wearing lass how to land a lord seems impossible—especially when he starts dreaming of winning her for himself.

THE TAMING OF A HIGHLANDER (BOOK TWO)

Wrongfully imprisoned and tortured, Broderick MacPherson lives for one purpose—punishing the man responsible. When a wayward lass witnesses his revenge, he risks returning to the prison that nearly killed him. Kate Huxley has no wish to testify against a man who's already suffered too much. But the only remedy is to become his wife. And she can't possibly marry such a surly, damaged man...can she?

Rescued from Ruin Series
Discover the scandalous predicaments, emotional redemptions, and gripping love stories (with a dash of Lady Wallingham) in the scorching series that started it all!

EVER YOURS, ANNABELLE (PREQUEL)
As a girl, Annabelle Huxley chased Robert Conrad with reckless abandon, and he always rescued her when she pushed too far—until the accident that cost him everything. Seven years later, Robert discovers the girl with the habit of chasing trouble is now a siren he can't resist. But when a scandalous secret threatens her life, how far will he go to rescue her one last time?

THE MADNESS OF VISCOUNT ATHERBOURNE (BOOK ONE)
Victoria Lacey's life is perfect—perfectly boring. Agree to marry a lord who has yet to inspire a single, solitary tingle? It's all in a day's work for the oh-so-proper sister of the Duke of Blackmore. Surely no one suspects her secret longing for head-spinning passion. Except a dark stranger, on a terrace, at a ball where she should not be kissing a man she has just met. Especially one bent on revenge.

THE TRUTH ABOUT CADS AND DUKES (BOOK TWO)
Painfully shy Jane Huxley is in a most precarious position, thanks to dissolute charmer Colin Lacey's deceitful wager. Now, his brother, the icy Duke of Blackmore, must make it right, even if it means marrying her himself. Will their union end in frostbite? Perhaps. But after lingering glances and devastating kisses, Jane begins to suspect the truth: Her duke may not be as cold as he appears.

Desperately Seeking a Scoundrel (Book Three)
Where Lord Colin Lacey goes, trouble follows. Tortured and hunted by a brutal criminal, he is rescued from death's door by the stubborn, fetching Sarah Battersby. In return, she asks one small favor: Pretend to be her fiancé. Temporarily, of course. With danger nipping his heels, he knows it is wrong to want her, wrong to agree to her terms. But when has Colin Lacey ever done the sensible thing?

The Devil Is a Marquess (Book Four)
A walking scandal surviving on wits, whisky, and wicked skills in the bedchamber, Benedict Chatham must marry a fortune or risk ruin. Tall, redheaded disaster Charlotte Lancaster possesses such a fortune. The price? One year of fidelity and sobriety. Forced to end his libertine ways, Chatham proves he is more than the scandalous charmer she married, but will it be enough to keep his unwanted wife?

When a Girl Loves an Earl (Book Five)
Miss Viola Darling always gets what she wants, and what she wants most is to marry Lord Tannenbrook. James knows how determined the tiny beauty can be—she mangled his cravat at a perfectly respectable dinner before he escaped. But he has no desire to marry, less desire to be pursued, and will certainly not kiss her kissable lips until they are both breathless, no matter how tempted he may be.

Twelve Nights as His Mistress (Novella - Book Six)
Charles Bainbridge, Lord Wallingham, spent two years wooing Julia Willoughby, yet she insists they are a dreadful match destined for misery. Now, rather than lose her, he makes a final offer: Spend twelve nights in his bed, and if she can deny they are perfect for each other, he will let her go. But not before tempting tidy, sensible Julia to trade predictability for the sweet chaos of true love.

CONFESSIONS OF A DANGEROUS LORD (BOOK SEVEN)
Known for flashy waistcoats and rapier wit, Henry Thorpe, the Earl of Dunston, is deadlier than he appears. For years, his sole focus has been hunting a ruthless killer through London's dark underworld. Then Maureen Huxley came along. To keep her safe, he must keep her at arm's length. But as she contemplates marrying another man, Henry's caught in the crossfire between his mission and his heart.

ANYTHING BUT A GENTLEMAN (BOOK EIGHT)
Augusta Widmore must force her sister's ne'er-do-well betrothed to the altar, or her sister will bear the consequences. She needs leverage only one man can provide—Sebastian Reaver. When she invades his office demanding a fortune in markers, he exacts a price a spinster will never pay—become the notorious club owner's mistress. And when she calls his bluff, a fiery battle for surrender begins.

A MARRIAGE MADE IN SCANDAL (BOOK NINE)
As the most feared lord in London, the Earl of Holstoke is having a devil of a time landing a wife. When a series of vicious murders brings suspicion to his door, only one woman is bold enough to defend him—Eugenia Huxley. Her offer to be his alibi risks scandal, and marriage is the remedy. But as a poisonous enemy coils closer, Holstoke finds his love for her might be the greatest danger of all.

A KISS FROM A ROGUE (BOOK TEN)
A cruel past left Hannah Gray with one simple longing—a normal life with a safe, normal husband. Finding one would be easy if she weren't distracted by wolf-in-rogue's-clothing Jonas Hawthorn. He's tried to forget the haughty Miss Gray. But once he tastes the heat and longing hidden beneath her icy mask, the only mystery this Bow Street man burns to solve is how a rogue might make Hannah his own.

About the Author

Reading romance novels came easily to Elisa Braden. Writing them? That took a little longer. After graduating with degrees in creative writing and history, Elisa spent entirely too many years in "real" jobs writing T-shirt copy ... and other people's resumes ... and articles about giftware displays. But that was before she woke up and started dreaming about the very *unreal* job of being a romance novelist. Better late than never.

Elisa lives in the gorgeous Pacific Northwest, where you're constitutionally required to like the colors green and gray. Good thing she does. Other items on the "like" list include cute dogs, strong coffee, and epic movies. Of course, her favorite thing of all is hearing from readers who love her characters as much as she does. If you're one of those, get in touch on Facebook and Twitter or visit **www.elisabraden.com**.